THE KUIPER BELT DECEPTION

DONALD F. AVERILL

Printed in the United States of America.

INK START MEDIA
265 Eastchester Dr Ste 133 #102
High Point NC 27262

THE KUIPER BELT DECEPTION

DONALD F. AVERILL

CHAPTER 1
TRAINING CAMP

"That trajectory is too complicated, cadet Nelson. Try it without Saturn; Jupiter should give the velocity boost we need." Kuiper belt trainee, Virginia Nelson, a pretty brunette with short hair and dimples stood confidently at the main display console waiting for her team's results. She had only taken a few breaths before the new solution appeared on the viewer. A supercomputer had calculated the results for her multibody analysis, but the mission time and the ship velocity were not quite what she had expected. She felt a bit discouraged. Maybe Sunul was right, too many orbital maneuvers were causing her trajectory to be over complicated. She had included too many gravitational forces and orbital corrections to solve the class exercise most efficiently.

Gina, the name she preferred, instead of Virginia, eliminated Saturn's position and mass from the equations and said, "Reset—Run." She looked at Sunul as a chorus of cheers erupted from the other trainees. His advice was right-on. She was a little irritated with Sunul and somewhat envious of his seemingly intuitive knowledge of the steps used to solve manned vehicle and orbital calculations. She had yet to ask him who his brain implant (BI) was from, or whether he inherited his superior intellect from his birth parents. She backed away from the orbital display screen, making room for the next of the sixteen contestants, and slowly drifted to the gray wall, next to nearly six-foot Sunul, who was leaning against the mock command ship bulkhead.

She whispered, "Want to go out after this class?"

"You're asking me out?" Sunul replied. He had been watching Gina with great interest, wondering how to get her attention. He had discovered she was Doctor Nelson, a medical doctor. Most of the trainees were PhD's. Sunul possessed two doctorates, in physics and mathematics. Gina had noticed his furtive glances but didn't want to encourage him too soon. She wanted him to know she wasn't a pushover.

"No, idiot. Do you want to go outside the complex and get some fresh air? Being alone in the desert is almost like being cooped up in here. After three weeks, I haven't even begun to get used to it. I'd like to bake in the sun for a while—get some vitamin D."

"After that blonde finishes her simulation—then we'll go." Sunul Burke wanted to get a rise out of Gina, or VN, as he called her the majority of the time, and he thought he would try the blonde routine on her. It seemed to be working. She turned away, shaking her head, and began walking toward the outdoor hatchway.

"Well, I'm going outside for fifteen minutes."

Sunul tipped his five-eleven frame forward from the wall and took several quick steps to catch up with Gina. She had activated the exit panel and the seal released with a swooshing sound. Sunul could feel the warm dry air rushing into the air-conditioned enclosure as the doorway swung open just far enough to allow an adult human body passage. The complex was hidden within sheer rock that rose over two-hundred feet above the desert floor. Sandstone and volcanic rock debris had accumulated around the megalithic structure for tens of thousands of years. About fifty feet above the desert sand, there was a narrow path, no more than two feet wide, flush against the rock wall, which extended part way around the towering, eons-old, skyscraper of barren stone. The debris at the base reached out seventy feet or more to the almost flat, nondescript, surrounding desert.

Camouflaged to blend with the rocks, the door exterior surface was difficult to detect unless one was closely inspecting the rock wall. The interconnected cylindrical rooms on earth replicated the system the astronauts would occupy on 5K23m in a couple of years, if all the preparations were completed satisfactorily.

The designation 5K23m was for a one-kilometer diameter moon of Kuiper Body Object (KBO) 5,023, a nearly spherical icy-mass of diameter 261 kilometers. The tiny moon, mostly frozen gases, but denser than its parent body, contained a significant amount of iron, a minute quantity of other heavy metals, and orbited KBO5023 in ten point nine two days. It was to be the astronauts' home for approximately forty-three years, travelling at one-tenth light speed (c) to Alpha Centauri. The five relatively new nuclear-electronic-railgun engines had a limiting velocity of 0.225c, limited by the mass of 5K23m. The calculations were, of course, only approximations.

"So, you didn't wait for the blonde's dance at the console? She's always trying to get the attention of the men. I will admit she has a sexy body. I don't know about her intellect though.

"Nope. She's a mechanical engineer/HVAC specialist; we would never be paired up. Besides, she's too slow entering data. She'd miss orbital adjustments and end up heading the ship for the galactic center. I don't mind her gyrations though. She's beautiful, and that stimulates my hormones, however, I'm sticking with the body I know most about." He scanned Gina's figure from head to toe.

Gina turned away and commented, "That must be your own. You don't know anything about my body."

Sunul smiled, "You don't know anything about my imagination, VN."

Gina pointed to the desert floor and started climbing down the rocky slope to the yellowish sand below. Sunul followed, picking his way through an obstacle course of large rocks sprinkled with smaller pieces of debris, occasionally jumping from boulder to boulder. Gina sat down in the shade of a large boulder at ground level, removed her boots, and dug her feet into the warm light-yellow rock powder. She leaned back and pushed the fingers of her left hand into the warm silt. She brushed some strands of hair from her eyes, looked up at Sunul and inquired, "Whose BI did you get?"

"I don't think I should tell you, unless you promise to tell me yours," he smiled. "It's kind of personal, the thing I might only tell my physician or psychiatrist."

"Well, I'll find out eventually—if I'm chosen to go on the mission with you. I'll be your doctor."

"Don't forget, you'll also be my wife. Okay, I'll tell you. My BI was the last fraction of Stephen Hawking's brain."

Gina sucked in her breath, pulled her feet from the sand, and shook her head. "My God! No wonder you are so good at everything celestial."

"Your turn. Who was it?"

She said slowly, "Carson."

Sunul laughed loudly, "Johnny Carson? The comedian? No wonder you're so funny!"

"No, you dimwit!" She threw a handful of sand at Sunul. "Dr. Ben Carson, the pediatric brain surgeon that ran for President in 2016."

"That's very impressive. I thought his segments would have been used up long ago."

"Apparently not. He was my first choice. There was no delay in the surgery. I only wore that protective head cap for two days."

"Same here. Have you noticed any post-operative differences in your thinking?" Sunul was curious about VN's medical knowledge, his hadn't changed. He still had to work hard to retain medical procedures, but he noticed a dramatic increase in his ability to solve orbital problems. He could now see the solutions to problems in three dimensions, whereas before surgery, he had to do the mathematics and physics on paper and submit data to a computer to verify his calculations. Difficult mathematical calculations were now as easy as middle school plane geometry and trigonometry.

"Uh-huh. I used to work at remembering medical terms, diagnostic procedures, and the names of drugs. Now those things just pop into my head like magic. I surprise myself every day."

"You surprise me every day, Gina. I think I'm bonding to you."

"Just don't get too serious too soon. I'm not stuck on you—yet." She smiled and tossed another handful of sand at Sunul with her right hand.

Sunul noticed the sand moving a few inches from VN's left hand. He was in the sun, so he squinted to see into the shade.

"Don't move, Gina! There's a scorpion next to your left hand."

Gina glanced down where her left hand was half-covered in sand and froze. The arachnid was light-brown and as long as her index finger; a dangerous bark scorpion, its stinger arched above its body. "Can you cover it with something so it can't sting me?"

Sunul removed his cadet shirt as rapidly as he could. As he moved behind the scorpion, he scooped a couple of handfuls of sand into his shirt and swung the makeshift club at the scorpion's segmented body, crushing it into the sand where it had been hiding.

Gina sighed and jumped to her feet. "Thank you! That little shit could have ruined my career. It's the most venomous scorpion in the United States."

Sunul, shirtless, standing in the sun, looked like an Olympic gymnast; hairless chest and highly developed arms and shoulders, "You're welcome. I thought those creatures were nocturnal."

"They are. I must have interrupted its daylight snooze by digging into the sand where it's shady."

Gina put her right hand behind Sunul's neck and pulled him to her. She gave him a kiss he would remember for a long time. She had wondered what it would be like to kiss him. He was certainly above average in the looks department and his physique was that of a physical fitness trainer. She imagined doing exercises with him—naked.

Sunul had expected his first kiss with VN would come after a casual date to the movie module. They had every Academy Award winning picture, since the awards began in 1929, as well as every color film ever produced. When he knew the kiss was coming, he reached for Gina's hips and could feel the curves of her waist. He drew her body closer and the kiss continued until she stepped back and whispered, "I think that's enough for today, Mister Burke." Her grayish-blue eyes looked into Sunul's piercing black eyes, her thoughts of making love tempered with a little regret, but the courtship protocol, devised by senior space pioneers, had to be followed, or risk expulsion from the program. Gina didn't know when she was being observed, as there were cameras hidden throughout the complex. She desperately wanted to be one of the first earthlings to travel to the stars. She couldn't afford any mistakes.

Recalling the protocols, Sunul stepped away from Gina, but he wished the code of conduct didn't exist. It was difficult to be spontaneous with cameras watching every move.

Gina pointed across the yellowish desert sand at two black spots emerging from a cloud of dust, apparently gliding across the desert floor. "What's that?"

Sunul climbed the incline about six feet and looked where Gina pointed. "Looks like two gasoholics coming towards us, riding turn-of-the-century dirt bikes. I wonder where they got their fuel. They're burning up the sand—maybe running from someone; probably the Air Force Police." He had gotten higher off the ground to avoid the mirage caused by the refraction of light through the hot and cool surface layers of air hovering above the sand. He would have to climb higher to get an even better view.

"Do you think they can see us?"

"I doubt it, but maybe we should go back inside anyway. I need to get a clean shirt."

"Don't ask me to do your laundry. Those days are over. Modern women frown on that."

"I wouldn't think of it, but would you give me a back rub?"

"Funny, Sunul. You almost made me laugh. I know we're to avoid contact with outsiders, but it might be fun to talk to someone new. We don't have to tell them anything about the complex." Gina glanced at Sunul for support.

"Yeah. Okay, let's see who they are and what they're doing out here. We can always call a desert patrol unit."

The two cadets watched the distant riders converge on the large, fluted, stalagmitic rock formation that concealed the training complex. Sunul stepped over to his shirt and cautiously lifted the material to see if the scorpion was dead. The body of the poisonous arthropod had been crushed, leaving a wet spot on his rumpled shirt. He removed the sand and, using the shirt like a napkin, scooped up the dead scorpion and folded it up in his shirt. He was thinking he might use the scorpion's body to some advantage if the travelers were hostile.

VN was still watching the riders. They were a few hundred yards away and approaching fast. She could hear the high frequency whine of the gasoline engines which had no longer been made after 2040. All modern vehicles except those for farming and air travel between continents had solar-powered, electric motors, and the only use of hydrocarbons was for toys, decorations, and building materials. Wood products were now extensively used as in previous decades prior to hydrocarbons.

The two motorcycles, each with a single rider, slowed and coasted toward the cadets stopping about ten feet away. The riders dismounted, removed their headgear and goggles, and spit in the sand.

Gina whispered to Sunul, "They look like they're from the movie Mad Max."

"Uh-huh." Sunul was watching for any hostile actions, but the men didn't seem to have any weapons, but their appearance would probably unnerve most civilians. Sunul noticed both men had lunar detention numbers tattooed on their arms and necks. Both had shaved heads.

The closer man, heavyset and about five-inches shorter than the other, snickered, "You're kinda far from school, ain't ya? Where's yore ride? Yore school bus leave ya out here?"

"We parked our air scooters about a kilometer from here. We felt like walking in the sand," Sunul lied. "You're driving polluters. What are you gentlemen doing out here?"

The taller man laughed and slapped his buddy on the back. "Gentlemen! Hah! That's a good one, Puff."

Puff smiled, "Best I heared all day, Slip. Now, we're gentlemen. We come out here to see where the astronauts train for goin' to Centauri. Ain't that right, Slip?"

"Yep, but you young birds sure ain't astronauts. You take a day off from classes at Roswell? You playin' hooky?"

Gina decided to join the conversation. "Like he said, we're out for a walk in the sand. We go to school in Las Cruces—New Mexico State. We're on a field trip."

"Now, yore sure a pretty thing, ain't ya? How about leavin' your lab pardner here and we'll go have some fun? Take off that uniform and cool down over there in the shade. We won't do nuthin' but look." Puff loosened his belt, reached into his dirty right trouser pocket, and pulled out a switchblade.

Sunul stepped up to confront him and said, "I'd like to beat the shit out of you ass-holes, but I recently had brain surgery and I'm not allowed to fight." Another lie, but fighting was another violation of protocol. Sunul couldn't risk expulsion after all the sacrifices he had made to get into the program.

When it looked like Sunul was going to have trouble, Gina squeezed the two buttons on her collar, a standard request for immediate assistance. In a couple of seconds, a computerized male voice could be heard, "Travelers, you are under arrest. Please drop your weapon in the sand. This is your only warning. You have five seconds to comply."

"Hah! I'll cut this little boy to bits in five seconds. How about that!?"

Slip yelled to Puff, "Lookit yore hand, Puff!"

There was a small red area expanding on the knife in Puff's left hand. He suddenly yelled, "Goddamn!" and dropped the switchblade.

The computer voice had given Sunul directions over his earpiece. Sunul picked up the warm knife, walked over to the two bikes and stabbed the gas tanks twice, once on top and once on the bottom, twisting the blade to make large holes.

"Hey! That's all the gas we got, you little shit!" Slip rushed to his bike and tried to cover the bottom hole in his tank with his fingers, but the gas continued to leak from the punctured container and dripped into the sand.

Sunul said, "I'd advise you to step away from your bike." Sunul joined Gina and they stepped back to the rocks, about twenty yards from the men and their bikes. He whispered into Gina's ear, "The gasoline might explode, get down and turn toward the rocks."

There was a short laser burst from above them and the gasoline in the sand burst into flames which ignited the rubber tires and the seats. Puff and Slip stepped back and watched as their bikes were consumed by fire, black smoke rising into the air. Before the smoke had cleared, there was a prolonged laser burst, perhaps twenty seconds in duration. The engines melted, the liquid metal puddling beneath what remained of their motorcycles.

Puff looked at the two cadets, "Son of a bitch! How can we get back to civilization? We're fifty miles from nowhere. You gonna give us a ride?"

"Nope, those guys will." Gina pointed at the incoming light-blue air-patrol vehicle. "They'll take you to a temporary location, until you are returned to the lunar facility: your final destination—right where you belong."

CHAPTER 2
SOME OTHER CADETS

Monel Trask and Jar'l Mason had grown up in Detroit, the manufacturing center for nearly all solar-powered vehicles since the Trump era. The only exception was for large trucks, which were assembled in Dallas, Texas. The only ebony Americans in the program, they were sure to be selected for the final crew headed to Alpha Centauri. They had passed the psychological testing without any negative scores, an exceptional accomplishment.

Monel and Jar'l had ascended the rock wall tower which housed the training complex and had begun rappelling from the apex, when they saw the Air-Police vehicle arrive over one hundred feet below. By the time the descent was complete, the police vehicle had been loaded. Two prisoners were on their way to Las Cruces, where the southwestern holding facility for criminals was located. Once sentenced, the guilty were taken to either California or Florida to begin their journey to the far side of the moon.

The two climbers waited by the hatchway for Gina and Sunul to work their way up the incline from the desert below. As they waited, they removed their climbing gear, and recoiled the long ropes.

"Hey, Sunul, what was that all about?"

"Not much, actually. Two gasoholics were attempting to get some sexual favors from Gina. The robotic sentry guard detected their intent and melted their gas engines. Gina called air patrol to come pick up the subhuman freaks. They'll do a lot more time at the lunar detention facility. Maybe they'll learn, but I doubt it. We'll be off earth by the time they get released."

Jar'l questioned, "You think Gina and you are going to Centauri?"

"I'm pretty confident. We're tops in our respective fields, and we like each other." Sunul looked at Gina and they both smiled.

"That's the way we feel, too." Monel grinned and put her arm around Jar'l's waist. Monel and Jar'l had become engaged just prior to their acceptance into the interstellar training program.

Jar'l waved toward the sun and suggested, "Let's go inside. It's going to be 112 degrees today at four o'clock. It must be over 100 now and we could all get too much sun."

"It won't be long before we'll only have artificial sunlight—for forty years. I wonder how we'll feel about the sun then." Monel raised her eyebrows, took a deep breath, and followed Jar'l through the hatch.

Sunul guided Gina through the opening and said, "Monel made a good point. We should make use of a good thing while we can." Gina reached to the side and tapped the gray close and red lock panels.

She wiped her forehead with her shirt sleeve and uttered, "I do prefer the air-conditioned atmosphere of the complex. Sunul, you need to get a clean shirt. I don't like the way the other women are looking at your muscles."

Sunul smiled and replied, "I don't mind. The looks don't hurt." He started to sit in the nearest chair, but then straightened up and walked quickly toward his quarters. About ten feet down the hall, he stopped and keyed in his personal code on the wall panel. The door slid sideways and he stepped into his room, tapped the door frame to shut the entryway, and sat on his bed. Isolated from the others, he opened his lockbox, a small safe located in the wall above his pillow. He withdrew a small rectangular notebook about half-an-inch thick.

He stated, "Personnel notes."

"Crew member, please." The voice belonged to the secretary at mission headquarters in Pasadena, California. Sunul smiled, the lady had a slight hesitancy when she said words beginning with m. He thought it was because of a stutter she had as a child.

"Virginia Nelson."

"Observation, please."

"I think she's the one. She knocks me out—just the woman I've been looking for."

"Anything else?"

"Yes. What are the specialties of Jar'l and Monel?"

"Jar'l: Nuclear Propulsion and Communications; reverse for Monel."

"Thank you, Data One. Please update master file. End."

"Yes, Lieutenant Burke. Files updated. Out."

Sunul slipped into a clean shirt, replaced his personal data book in the concealed safe, and said, "Lock data." A two-tone sound was heard and Sunul went back to the master console.

He sat beside Jar'l and asked, "Who's the cadet with glasses—at the console?"

"Name's Brinar Wicks. He's a specialist in resource conservation and waste management. He likes the blonde bombshell, Brea Foster, but I don't think it's mutual. She likes more muscles. With your physique, you'd better watch out. He'll have to start working out if he wants to hook up with her."

Of the sixteen cadets on site, Sunul knew the names of only six, including himself. He would have to ask Data One to review all the candidates. He needed to know all their names and intellectual strengths. He wasn't sure, but without instructors, the cadets might have to choose the crew members of Operation Far Ice.

When plans for the mission were initiated, those in charge selected individuals that were self-learners. Other than computers and extensive data libraries, the cadets were on their own. Sixteen cadets were selected from a group of thirty-two potential astronauts.

Prior to travelling to the complex from the NASA Propulsion Laboratory, each cadet was given intelligence and psychological examinations and had to have a minimal adjusted IQ of 140. The adjustment was accomplished by a surgical implantation of brain segments from world-renowned experts in various fields deemed important to the success of the mission. The only assistance given the cadets was computers, various specific libraries, and a protocol manual. The cadets had to rely on common sense. Four married couples would make the journey to Alpha Centauri, the closest star to the sun.

A two-tone signal sounded indicating assembly. When the sixteen cushioned chairs were occupied, a message appeared on the main console screen. IN ONE WEEK, YOU WILL VOTE FOR A MISSION COMMANDER. HE OR SHE WILL BEGIN MAKING DECISIONS FOR YOUR TRAINING, CHOOSE WISELY, YOUR LIFE AND SUCCESS ARE AT STAKE. OUT. The message displayed for ten seconds, then faded to a transparent screen.

Gina poked Sunul and said, "I'm voting for you, partner. You'll take me where no woman has gone before." She laughed and squeezed his arm.

"Well, I'm voting for you. You're a doctor—you keep me in stitches." He looked at her and winked.

"Funny, Sunul. No, please don't vote for me. As a doctor, I don't want to be in charge of the ship as well as the crew. That's too much responsibility."

"All right, I understand. Let's go over the cadets' records together tonight after classes and dinner."

A single, high-pitched tone sounded, and a new message appeared on the screen: IN THREE MINUTES, A PROGRAM CONCERNING

THE NUCLEAR PROPULSION DRIVES WILL INSTRUCT YOU ON THEIR OPERATION AND MAINTENANCE SCHEDULE. REMAIN SEATED. THE PROGRAM'S DURATION IS 33 MINUTES.

Sunul glanced over at Jar'l, "You'd better pay attention to this program. Someone out there knows about you and Monel." Jar'l frowned at first and then gave Sunul the finger. Sunul laughed and sat back to enjoy the propulsion unit instructional presentation.

Two lab techs, both working at Hanford, one male and one female, wearing yellow jump suits with radiation danger signs on their backs, appeared, standing at a model of a propulsion unit. The female opened a compartment on the side of the model, a cylindrical structure about ten feet in diameter and eighteen feet long. As soon as the access door was removed, the technician stepped back and a robot, designated NT-1, took over and reached into the structure. The male technician operated the remote-controlled android.

As the robot inspected the various parts of the engine, a simulation appeared on the large console screen, with pointers indicating the salient parts of the unit that were accessible from that particular compartment. What Sunul found most interesting about the engine was the amount of thrust regulated by introducing higher atomic weight matter into the nuclear chamber. As the atomic weight of the fuel increased, there was a nearly instantaneous increase in velocity of the ship. Sunul had a question to ask Jar'l.

The video presentation continued for another thirty minutes, but Sunul's question was not answered in the lecture program. As Sunul thought about it, he conjured up a simple answer, but he didn't know if his approach was a realistic application in the vacuum of outer space. He posed the question and answer to Gina. She replied, "That sounds reasonable, but why not ask Jar'l? That's his area of expertise."

Sunul smiled and replied, "Say, that's a good idea."

Gina slugged him in the stomach and said, "You already thought of that, didn't you?"

"It might have crossed my mind."

"Did I hear you mention my name?" Jar'l was moving down the row of chairs toward Sunul. Jar'l had a question for him and wanted to ask it before something else popped into his mind to swamp his neurons, causing momentary forgetfulness.

"If we need to make mid-course maneuvers, how much thrust would be necessary from the four satellite engines?" Jar'l expected an immediate answer after witnessing Sunul's earlier advice to Gina, which had impressed all the other cadets.

Before he could answer Jar'l's question, Sunul needed to know some details about the engine designs. "Is there a gimbal on the main engine?"

"Yes, there's a ten-degree limit from the central axis in any direction."

"You asked about thrust. Unless there is a radical course alteration, we don't have to worry about thrust."

Sunul than asked, "What about the gimbals on satellite engines?"

"They're all the same. All five engines are identical in design, but the four outboard power plants are rated at one-fourth the main engine."

"What's the distance of each satellite engine from the main power axis?"

Jar'l answered immediately, "Two hundred fifty meters."

Sunul dropped his pencil without using it. "As I said, we have plenty of freedom for course adjustments without sacrificing velocity. Now I have a question for you."

"Shoot." Jar'l dropped into the seat beside Sunul and took a deep breath, expecting a difficult question about the nuclear engines, but Sunul surprised him. "How is mass transferred to the engines from the inside of our traveling moon?"

Jar'l relaxed and said, "There is a robot laser cutting tool that transfers ice and rock to a large hopper which feeds the engines automatically. Each engine has a feedback system. When fuel gets low, an auger is activated and fills the hopper for the engine requiring fuel. It's automatic. There is a crude mass sorter so we can select the amount of thrust we want, but it only allows a fifteen percent variation."

"And if it fails?"

"That engine is placed into an idle mode and waits for new fuel. According to the specs, only minor servicing is required during a ten-year period."

Sunul nodded and followed with, "If the service robot can't fix the problem, what takes place?"

"I have to go out and fix the problem myself. We have a number of extra-vehicular suits available. Meet me tomorrow in the Service Module at 1300 hours and we'll suit up. I'll show you one of the mock-up engines and the mass-transfer equipment."

Sunul said, "It's a date," smiled and shook hands with Jar'l. "No more fingers, okay?"

Jar'l said, "Sorry about that, I thought you were trying to get a rise out of me."

"No. It was a just a good-natured comment about your special training."

CHAPTER 3
THE FOOD SUPPLY

Triel Arbon was the first of the biology/botany experts that Sunul and Gina met, Twitchel Ames was the second. The two young women were sitting apart from the other crew members eating dinner in the cafeteria. They had met in graduate school at Lincoln, Nebraska, where they were enrolled in the extra-terrestrial agricultural group, or ETAG.

They were having an animated conversation. Purple haired Triel was waving her fork in the air, metal bracelets clanging together, at Twitchel, adorned with orange hair and a silver ring hanging from her septum, concealing part of her upper lip.

Sunul and Gina moved from the dining area to the adjacent entertainment center to play a game of chess. After a few minutes, Gina was losing. While Sunul was contemplating his next move, Gina watched the two women, wondering why they had decided to mask their true looks with such garish makeup and ornamentation.

Sunul announced, "Checkmate!"

Gina laughed and replied, "It's about time. You could have done that two moves ago." She reversed the preceding two moves and showed Sunul the move he had overlooked.

"Remind me to be more alert next time. You're a better player than I thought."

"Next time I'll get you—I have to use my knights better. Let's see if those two dressed for Halloween want to play bridge. Maybe we can get them talking and find out if they're really serious about space travel."

Sunul directed his voice across the room. He asked the young women if they would like to play duplicate bridge. Triel and Twitchel agreed and they all moved to a larger, computerized game table. Gina entered instructions for the main computer to keep score. They sat at the games table, each player wearing polarized glasses, to prevent observations of the cards on another player's table screen, and Gina said, "Deal."

Gina had received a message on her private com-module the night before, requesting she talk to the two women about their seeming disinterest in associating with the other potential crew members, especially the male members. The Command staff was certain the two women were not lesbians. Gina had mentioned the staff's concern to Sunul, and they planned to involve the women in conversation.

After the first hand, Sunul directed a question to Twitchel, "Is that nose ring made of magnetic material?"

"No. It's platinum. Why?"

"Well, the modules on 5K23m have magnetic flooring. If you're walking around for years with magnetic material hanging from your nose, your nose will gradually lengthen toward the floor."

Twitchel replied, "Bull shit! You must have a problem with my type of jewelry."

"No, I don't mind at all. I just think it makes you look like a cow. Why do you think those available men aren't over here talking with you two? Did you ever think it might be the way you look? I hope you realize that, within a year, if you aren't married to one of the cadets with training similar to yours, you won't be going to 5K23m. Perhaps you really don't want to go."

Gina added, "But that isn't the only reason we wanted to talk to you. We have some questions about the food supply on the ship taking us to the Kuiper belt and the growth chambers in 5K23m."

Twitchel and Triel looked at each other and shrugged their shoulders. Triel said, "We'll have enough prepackaged food for about two months at 0.01 c, or 1,860 miles per second to the Kuiper belt. The trip out is expected to be a twenty-four-day excursion. There will be a one-year food supply on 5K23m. Those figures are assuming a crew of eight: four females and four males. After leaving for Alpha Centauri we will begin growing our own food. Actually, seeds will be planted by the advance group. They'll be there three months ahead of us."

Twitchel continued, "All organic waste material, water, and carbon dioxide will be recycled through the growth chambers. We will recover oxygen from rock that is used for propulsion purposes. Liquefied methane will be burned to create more water for drinking and bathing and more carbon dioxide for food crops—."

Triel quickly added, "and a little weed." Both women laughed.

Gina snapped back, "I hope you're joking. If anyone is discovered with drugs, other than prescriptions, the individual will be ejected from 5K23m into space. That activity will not be tolerated as it puts the entire crew at risk."

Twitchel crossed her arms over her chest, leaned back in her chair, focused on Sunul and said, "So who are you guys to give advice and read us the riot act?"

"The command staff sends us memos each night. We are half the medical staff at the earth training site. Lois Keiten and Hiren Drumond are the others. They might contact you if our words are ignored. You have eighteen hours to react favorably, or you will be dismissed and replaced. Once you are off-site, your BI will be destroyed by a virus and you will resume your previous life."

Gina asked, "Is your septum perforated? If so, I can remove the ring and close the opening in your septum for you. It will be painless."

Twitchel stood up, turned and walked away from the games table.

Triel said, "Well, I guess we're finished with the bridge game. Sorry about that. Save the game and maybe we can continue it at a later time."

Sunul replied, "Think about what you want out of this experience. I hope you make a good decision—something you won't regret."

The next morning's atmosphere was different than it had been the last few days, more like a gathering for a backyard barbeque than waiting for the hangman to appear at the gallows. There seemed to be an unusual buzz of conversation in the mess hall. Sunul joined Gina and they selected breakfast from the auto-dispensers. They were cognizant of the positive change of mood in the room. Sunul noticed a redhead talking to two male cadets. Someone had told a joke and all three cadets were laughing.

Sunul asked, "Who's the redhead, Gina?"

"That, my dear, is the new Triel, courtesy of last night's talk."

"Where's Twitchel?"

Gina was head counting and, in a few seconds, said, "I think she's gone, I only counted fifteen cadets. I'll ask Triel what she knows." Gina finished her eggs and toast, swallowed her vitamin C tablet and took her last sip of hot green tea. She wiped her mouth and walked over to Triel and her two companions.

"You look very nice, Triel. What happened to your friend, Twitchel?"

"Thanks, Gina. Twitchel left early this morning. She refused to give up her individuality and elected to resign from the program, since that was a provision of her contract. She said she didn't want to lose to me in the competition for the position on the crew, and she knew she would. If she couldn't go to 5K23m, she wanted to return home and forget about it."

"Was she going to Albuquerque to have the procedure performed?"

"That's what she thought would happen. After a few days, she'll be going back to Lincoln to work on her doctorate."

"How do you feel about her decision?"

"She'll be fine, but I'll miss her company." Triel looked at the two men, smiled, and said, "I'm making new friends, though. I'm having a good time."

Three sonorous notes, reminiscent of an oriental gong, sounded throughout the complex, announcing the arrival of an outsider. Everyone's eyes scanned the four hallways connecting the centrally located dining hall with the rest of the complex. In about five seconds a young woman appeared, dressed in a blue jumpsuit, her auburn hair cropped close to her ears, almost a bowl-cut. Clutching a small, yellow backpack slung over her left shoulder, she waved self-consciously like a young girl riding a New Year's parade float, and said, "Hi! I'm Ora Hensley. I'm the new biologist/botanist. I just arrived from Las Cruces."

Gina walked over to her and asked, "Have you eaten? We're just finishing breakfast."

"Yes, thanks. I ate on the shuttle as we came across the desert. God, this place is really hidden in no man's land. Have you gotten used to the isolation?"

"Well, we've been pretty busy learning about all the systems in the complex. You'll have to use your private com-module after hours to catch up with the rest of us. You'd better get friendly with the two men that share your academic background. As soon as you get a companion, the isolation of the complex will dissolve away."

Sunul joined the two women and said, "We'll show you your quarters, Ora. Glad you are on board. I believe you are going to fit in nicely."

As Sunul, Gina, and Ora made their way through the dining area to the bunks, Vincent Wynon's eyes followed every move Ora made. She held her head high and walked with confidence. Her good looks couldn't be missed. The minute he saw her, he believed in love at first sight. Vince stood and began walking toward the bunk area. He looked back at Hugh and said, smiling, "I think I see my wife."

Hugh watched Vince disappear down the hallway, but he wasn't distracted in the least from his conversation with Triel, who was sharing interests in ancestors with botanist/biologist Patel.

Triel questioned, "Patel is a common name in India, but you don't look like you're from India. What's your story?" Triel placed her elbows on the table with her head cradled in her hands waiting for a reply.

"My great grandfather was a dentist in Oregon. His son married a woman from Canada, and then things really got mixed up. Native Americans, Eastern Europeans, some Irish and English got mixed in the genetic soup, but I think most of my intellect, and my middle name, came from my great grandfather. My last name is Churchill, but I use my middle name as my last. I like it better and it honors my great grandfather."

Triel commented, "My name is not as complicated or as rich in as many cultures as yours. My ancestors were English or Welch, with a little Scandinavian mixed in. After arriving in the United States in the middle 1800s, everyone in my family tree came from Tennessee and Washington State. I've never traced my DNA back to see if I have any famous relatives. Maybe I'll do that on the trip to the stars. I imagine we'll all have plenty of time to kill."

CHAPTER 4
TESTS

Vince stood a few paces down the hall from Ora's quarters listening and watching Gina and Sunul brief the new cadet with her accommodations. When Gina and Sunul left, Sunul gave Vince a shoulder tap, grinned, and said, "She's all yours."

Ora was humming as she put her clothes into the small closet area. She sensed someone was watching her, and without turning around, she said, "Come in and get acquainted. We'll have to join the others in a couple of minutes."

"I'm Vince Wynon. We might be paired for the trip to Alpha Centauri. Do you believe in love at first sight?"

"I've heard that line before. It didn't work. The guy was all muscle and nothing between the ears." Ora finished putting away her belongings and took a look at Vince. "What's was your IQ before the BI was done?"

"134."

"After?"

"148. I won't ask you yours. Your numbers would probably embarrass me, plus my eyes tell me you've got a head start as a ten."

Ora planted her feet directly in front of Vince, put her hands on her hips, and said, "You sure know how to add mass to a black hole, don't you?" She motioned with her right hand for him to back into the hall.

"We need to join the others. When I arrived, I got an inkling we are in for a challenge today."

Vince moved back, giving Ora a little space to enter the hallway. She touched the keypad on the wall, locking her room and motioned Vince to go ahead, but Vince said, "You take the lead—I like to watch the way you walk." She wasn't amused and strutted down the passage toward the others.

As the cadets assembled in the main conference room, a loud warning signal and a robotic voice came over the loudspeakers, "The carbon dioxide scrubbing system has failed. You have approximately six hours to remedy the problem. Outer doors and ventilation systems have been locked and shut down. You are on your own. Good luck."

Ira Conway, the other orbital navigator/physician and co-captain of the team of cadets, was standing in front of the main computer console. He motioned for the other captain, Sunul, to join him. Sunul wasn't sure of Conway's intentions, but he stood beside Ira and they faced the crew.

Ira looked around at all the cadets and voiced his concern, "What do we know about carbon dioxide? How do we trap it out of our atmosphere? Can it be removed by the plants in the growth chambers? Sunul will enter the info on the display so we can come up with a solution to this problem."

Ora volunteered important information, "The botany-center can only remove the CO_2 from eight people, and we have sixteen. That won't work unless half of us hold our breath for six hours. Good luck with that."

Vince added, "We could bubble the air through sodium hydroxide or calcium oxide solutions, but we don't possess enough of either chemical to make it useful. The robo-chem synthesizer can't make quantities of those chemicals fast enough."

"How about freezing it out with liquid nitrogen?" Hugh Patel's suggestion was followed with several emphatic replies of "Yes!" Hugh stated, "We'll have to disconnect a compressor from one of the refrigerated food vending units so we can liquefy air, then feed the liquid nitrogen through the condenser coils and clean off the dry ice periodically. Let's get busy and get this problem out of the way!"

Kaethe Artiste raised her hand. Sunul called on her and she asked, "How are we going to dispose of the dry ice?"

"Good question." Sunul looked at Jar'l for an answer.

Jar'l spoke confidently, "We'll feed it into the nuclear power generator through the waste disposal system."

Sunul entered the plan into the main console and in less than a minute a message appeared on the display screen. "You have solved the problem. Good job. You may now go back to your regular duties; the normal CO_2 removal system has been reset. You will be challenged again one week from today."

Every week for over three months, challenges were conducted, and solved admirably, even though each task was more demanding than the last. The final test was entirely theoretical: there was not enough mass remaining on the interior of 5K23m to slow the moon to a stable orbit around Alpha Centauri. Without mass to feed the nuclear rockets, there wasn't going to be enough thrust to oppose the kinetic energy of the moon to slow it for capture by Alpha Centauri.

Everyone had completed breakfast and at 0900, the sixteen cadets had assembled to view the main console screen, which showed the position of the earth, sun, 5K23m, and Alpha Centauri. The starship, 5K23m, was about ninety percent of the distance from the sun to its destination.

Sunul whispered to Gina, "Alpha Centauri is a multiple star system, there are three members: Alpha Centauri A, Alpha Centauri B and Proxima Centauri. The moon can be slowed by multiple close approaches to the three bodies."

Gina poked Sunul with her elbow and motioned for Sunul to take the console position and show how to solve the problem.

Sunul said, "Okay, I've got it. No sweat." He went to the console, entered a command, and the Alpha Centauri system was magnified to show the three components. The other cadets, except for Conway, who began nodding his head, just stared at the triadic configuration with great interest. Conway knew what Sunul was going to propose, but he had thought of it too late. At that moment, Conway realized he would not be going to Alpha Centauri.

Sunul advanced the positions of the stars forty-three years, the length of the journey, and began steering the starship toward the most massive, and brightest, of the three stars, Alpha Centauri A. The class of cadets watched as Sunul guided their moon ship into the star's gravitational field and followed the little moon's swing around the brightest of the three stars toward the second, slightly less massive companion star, Alpha Centauri B. The moon was now moving at less than half the original velocity, and entered into a highly elliptical orbit around Alpha Centauri B.

One of the cadets yelled, "Bravo!" and the others applauded. From the data that appeared on the screen, they knew that Alpha Centauri B possessed two earth-like planets, one of which was in the habitable zone, a possible home for the star travelers. Triel asked, "What about the third star?" No information about planets for Alpha Centauri C, Proxima Centauri, was listed.

Sunul replied, "It's a red dwarf and too far from Alpha Centauri AB to be of any use for this situation. No one knows if it has any planets. We might be the first to find out. Its mass is only about one-eighth the mass of the sun."

The large screen's message was erased like an old slate blackboard and then a new message appeared: CONGRATULATIONS. YOUR TRAINING HAS BEEN COMPLETED AHEAD OF SCHEDULE. THE 5K23 MOON WILL BE READY FOR OCCUPANCY IN LESS THAN ONE MONTH. YOU WILL BE TRANSPORTED TO THE CAPE FOR FURTHER INSTRUCTIONS. BE READY FOR TRAVEL AT 1200 HOURS.

Lively conversations broke out among the cadets, astonished that they were moving on to new assignments so soon, about nine months ahead of their original schedule.

Sunul sat down beside Gina and asked, "Do you think we will have time to get married?"

"Well, maybe I'm old-fashioned, but I haven't gotten a proposal yet, so I guess I won't be getting married—even if I have the time." She glanced at Sunul, gave a trace of a smile, and looked away at some of the other couples.

Sunul realized he had assumed Gina would marry him, but he had never asked her. He reached out and took her hands in his and said, "Virginia Nelson, I love you. Will you be my wife?"

"How romantic, Sunul. We're in small room full of people trapped inside a rock and we have no idea where we're going: to the edge of the solar system and then to the nearest star, to a small colony on Mars, or somewhere else we don't even know about yet. I would be taking an awfully big chance if I married you."

"All right. You don't have to answer me now. I'll buy an engagement ring and wait for a more romantic setting, but please don't say no. Just think about it, if you say no, neither of us will be going to the Centauri system. I thought you would want to go on the adventure with me."

Gina stood up, still holding onto Sunul's hands. She pulled her hands away, placed them on Sunul's shoulders, smiled, and said, "Yes, I will marry you." Sunul stood, wrapped his arms around Gina, lifted her off her feet, and kissed her.

"Sunul."

"Yes?"

Gina laughed, "Put me down—please."

Sunul said, "You just love to give me a hard time." He kissed her again, but this time on the tip of her nose as he lowered her to the deck.

The first week back at the Cape was spent getting things in order. First on the list was fitting suits for space travel, followed by complete physical exams. Eight weddings were performed, three on one hectic day, and celebrations started in the early afternoon extended into the wee hours of the next morning. The following week, on Wednesday, the eight couples met for their assignments: the alpha group would be going to 5K23m for operation Far Ice. The beta group was to relieve the astronauts stationed on Mars for the last two years, operation Exchange. There, mining and growing crops were the chief activities underway in a controlled atmosphere inside a gigantic plastic hemisphere.

The beta group would begin important investigations before terraforming Mars could begin several years in the future. Planned by the International Space Agency (ISA), the transforming of Mars was to be initiated within nine years and would take about fifteen years before a breathable atmosphere would exist. Plants releasing oxygen to the atmosphere would only supply a small percentage of the O2 necessary, so laser ablation of silicates would supply the bulk of the gas and the remaining highly pure silicon would be shipped to the earth's moon for solar panel construction by penal colony inmates.

The alpha group had to learn to use the stasis chambers, which would put them in a nearly suspended animation state to slow their aging. The chambers would be programmed so the occupants would be awakened every two years for a twenty-two-month period, after which they would reenter the chambers. Compliance was not optional.

Four crewmembers would be monitoring the progress of the little moon while the rest of the crew were in stasis, though, at the outset, all eight crewmen would be monitoring the progress of the ship for the first six months. The ages of the crew would be approximately twenty years less than if they were functioning normally for the entire trip. However, the recovery time following emergence from stasis after each hibernation would be greater than the last cycle's recovery period. Mental recovery was rather rapid, but musculoskeletal atrophy was a much larger problem following the extended periods of dormancy.

CHAPTER 5
JOURNEY TO 5K23M

It was sunny, but windy, not unusual weather close to the ocean in Florida. A few high clouds drifted across the light-blue sky at the Cape as Sunul and Gina walked toward the mission assembly room to find whether they were going to the nearest star or to Mars. Sunul was hoping to be on the first star trip, but Gina wasn't quite so sure. At twenty-three years of age, there were many things on good old earth she hadn't had time to see. She was resigned to looking at pictures of the giant gorge in northern Arizona. She regretted not being able to take time to visit the Grand Canyon when she was close to the scenic wonder during the training in New Mexico.

All eight couples had been forced to forego honeymoons, investing almost all their time studying for their upcoming flights. Gina and Sunul entered the building and saw Jar'l and Monel ahead of them being admitted to the assembly hall. The two security guards, a male and female dressed alike in bright blue uniforms, were verifying identities with a retinal scanner, which sent signals to the computer inside the room. When the sixteen cadets had taken seats, the doors banged shut.

Mission Director, Dr. Bernard C. Kirkwood, dressed in a light blue suit and white shirt, open at the collar, with an Einstein hairdo, approached the lectern. The audience grew silent. The noise from the air conditioning system was the only thing that could be heard in the room. Kirkwood pointed a remote at the ceiling and a large holographic display appeared in the space over the lecturer's desk. The names of the alpha group appeared in yellow and the names of the beta group appeared in red.

The list for Kuiper 5K23m was:

Sunul and Gina Burke; captain and mission doctor, respectively,

Jar'l and Monel Mason; nuclear propulsion and communications,

Hugh and Triel Patel; biology and botany, and

Rob and Leanne Griswalt; electronics and mechanical engineering.

Excitement enveloped the entire room, including the Mission Director. His big smile began to fade as he said, "Beta group, please move to Briefing Room 200. I will give you further instructions. You will be transported to Edwards Air Force Base this evening, so say your goodbyes to alpha group right now."

Hugs and handshakes took place as members of the two groups congratulated each other. When the Mars' group had left the assembly hall, the door slammed shut. Everyone heard the loud clicking of the locks and the air conditioning fans stopped. Gina looked around at the concrete walls, scanning to see if she could detect some evidence of mechanical or electrical failure.

Some murmuring spread through the small audience. Gina whispered to Sunul, "What's all the secrecy about? Why the locked doors?"

Sunul shook his head and said, "I don't know. Maybe they're afraid we'll change our minds and run for the exits."

Jar'l was beside Sunul and commented, "Maybe they're afraid we'll all have to use the bathroom at the same time." He laughed nervously.

The cadets sat fidgeting, a little uneasy with the situation, until a side door opened. An Air Force officer took position in front of the group.

Jar'l whispered to Sunul, "He's Air Force—four stars—General. What the hell is going on?"

"You got me. Must be something big, though. Why would a General be talking to us? We're not military."

"I'm General Clark Ohland. I have something to share with you, but first, I need you to turn in your pocket re-trans devices." He pointed the remote and a barely audible click was heard. The display showed a seating chart of the assembly room with red dots blinking on five of the chair positions. "I see that four women and one man possess a device. You must give it to my adjutant before we proceed."

A uniformed assistant came into the room from a side door and gave a sheet of paper to each member of the alpha group. It was a further description of each member's academic background. The short memo advised the list of academic specialties was not exclusive, the crew had at least some advanced training in every science offered at universities. In addition to the memos the assistant carried a small box into which the collected transceivers and earpieces were placed, and the red dots disappeared from the display. When the dots were all extinguished, the general activated the display screen a second time. The display filled with numbers. "Do you recognize these?"

Jar'l answered, "The first row is pi, but without the decimal."

Sunul added, "The second row is e, the base of natural logarithms, also without the decimal."

Gina said, "The next two lines just repeat the first two."

General Ohland commented, "That is correct. Does anyone recognize the next two numbers? Our scientists are not sure what they mean, but the second number is exactly half the first.

Sunul offered, "I think so. The first one appears to be the distance, in their light years, to our sun, and the second is half that distance." Sunul's interest was piqued. "Where did these numbers come from, Sir?"

"Exactly the question I wanted, cadet. The display shows a radio transmission that we received from Alpha Centauri two years ago on the large radio receiver array in Chile."

Sunul commented, "It's difficult to say which of the two stars has the habitable planet, but I'd guess it would be Alpha Centauri A. It's more massive than the sun, and brighter. The Goldilocks region would be farther from their sun and their year longer than ours; that would explain why their light year numbers are smaller than ours. But that is just my guess. I'm also guessing that the second number means they want to meet us half-way. That would cut the travel time in half for representatives to make contact."

Monel whispered, "A woman must have decided to do that." She grinned and sat back in her chair.

Jar'l whispered, "Undoubtedly a relative of yours."

Gina covered her mouth so she wouldn't laugh out loud.

Jar'l said, under his breath, "I'm not sure I want to shake hands with a lizard, even a female one."

Monel reacted with an elbow in Jar'l's ribs and said, "Hush!" Then she raised her hand and asked, "Will we need any defensive weapons, Sir?"

General Ohland thought for a moment, scratched his grayish hair above his right ear, and responded, "We don't know their level of technology. If it is much greater than ours, they will probably know if we have weapons. It is our position that we do not carry any weapons. However, there is certainly a level of danger."

Rob Griswalt, the electronics and mechanical engineer, snickered and whispered, "We could use spit wads or shoot paper clips with rubber bands. He's not a general, he's a typical politician; probably a democrat. He might think of fighting, but he won't give the troops any weapons. I think he just told us that we are expendable."

Gina frowned, glanced at Rob, and said, "You really think that?"

Leanne Griswalt whispered back to Gina, "He's just venting. He's tired of not being able to start the journey."

The general cleared his throat and said, "I know you are all anxious to get underway, but this mission is being carried out with extreme secrecy. That is why we took your cell phones. While you have been here, my men have removed all communication devices from your quarters. You must not divulge anything about this mission. If anything is leaked, you will be substituted by your training partners from the beta group possessing your same expertise. I trust that you will accept this responsibility."

He looked around his small audience and asked, "Any questions?" It seemed like a minute of silence passed, but it was probably only a few seconds before he said, "If not, you are excused. Please report to the propulsion center in Building 9, Room 7." As the cadets stood, he said, "Oh, have a successful journey. We are counting on you. I hope to see you again. However, we on earth may all be considerably older. I might have retired, so you will be in touch with my replacement." He picked up his briefcase, turned, and walked out of the room.

The alpha group heard the lock on the main door click and all eyes watched the door swing open. The sentry stepped into the room and said, "Please follow me. There is a bus outside to take you to Building 9. Do not converse with anyone in the hallway."

As soon as the group was on the bus, the sentry boarded and signaled the driver. It took about five minutes before they reached Building 9. Most of the talking was between partners, going over the meeting that had just concluded. They were all trying to digest the information just presented by General Ohland and the secrecy involved in the mission. They realized what would happen if word reached the media that a message had been received from a nonhuman civilization and a group of young astronauts was on its way to contact aliens for the first time in history. Wall Street investors would panic, lawlessness would break out, and military forces would have to be mobilized to control rioting. Fear would run rampant.

The bus slowed to a stop in the asphalt parking lot near the back door of Building 9. The sentry stepped to the ground, waited for the alpha group to disembark, and then led them into the building. They descended a stairway to Room 7 in the basement, but when the door opened, a large elevator big enough for at least two dozen people, was waiting for the group. As soon as they had entered onto the moveable platform, an expressionless female dressed in a long white lab coat, her bun of black hair covered with a net, entered a code on a numerical keypad and the elevator began a slow smooth descent.

Rob was watching the woman at the control board. He glanced at Sunul, raised his eyebrows and gave a thumbs up. Rob was, as usual, enjoying everything mechanical he had never seen or experienced before.

When the elevator stopped, a side panel slid open, revealing a large laboratory with about twenty technicians. Some were busy at benches analyzing various types of data with computers, others were conducting experiments. The mission director was talking to one of the technicians, but excused himself when he saw the cadets, and approached the alpha team. "Follow me, cadets."

He escorted the group around the lab, showing them electrolytic cells, fuel cells, and a robotic system that would operate in the vacuum of outer space, primarily tending to the disposal of waste products from the astronaut's living quarters and nuclear reactor waste. The nuclear reactors ran the powerful rockets that propelled the moon through space and provided energy to sustain the life support systems. The robot resembled a squatty human being, with arms and legs that could be extended, and an elliptical head containing both a microscope and a telescope. It could be reprogrammed from within the living quarters using radio signals.

Following the laboratory tour, the bus took the group members to their base living quarters, a four-unit apartment complex, isolated from other base units. All their belongings had been moved from their previous location and there were no communication devices on the premises. They had TV reception and could request music and movies. Food was available in the apartments, but anything extra had to be requested from the base kitchen. There were keypads in the units so they could submit requests.

Gina was the first to enter their new quarters, Sunul was outside talking to Jar'l. She went into the bathroom and when she came back into the living room, she was laughing. Sunul was on his back testing the comfort of the bed. He sat up and asked, smiling, "What's so funny, VB?" He almost said VN, out of habit, but Gina's initials were now VB.

"These," she answered. Gina tossed a handful of prophylactics on the bed, ran over to the door and locked it, then jumped on the bed beside Sunul. "I believe they don't want any pregnancies until after we've been in space for a while. I wonder, has there ever been a child conceived in space?"

"I'm not aware of any. When do you get your anti-pregnancy injection?"

"Not until the day we leave earth, but it's only good for one year. I'll have to give every woman another shot in a year. You can administer mine."

Sunul picked up one of the little packages and turned it over and over, looking at it closely. "Are there any directions?"

Gina started laughing, kicked off her shoes, and began stripping off her uniform.

CHAPTER 6
CARGO SHIP

A half-day of visits to laboratories began early the next morning. Alpha group went to the suit-fitting area in Building 9 and spent the entire morning working with the space suit teams to make sure the suits for extravehicular activities (EVA) were fitting appropriately. After testing the suits for leaks underwater, the group ate a special lunch; meals similar to those they would have available on the cargo ship that would transport them from the moon to Kuiper 5K23m. Once on the small moon of ice, they would have a large menu of prepackaged meals to choose from, and after the first crops were harvested from the in-moon garden, fresh fruit and vegetables would be available.

Following their lunch experience, a message was received for the team to be ready for launch in forty-eight hours. The afternoon was spent getting all their personal things in order. Each member of the group prepared a will that gave instructions for disbursement of any and all possessions and funds. None of the group had any remaining family members, most having grown up in foster homes, so any items of value were to be donated to charities. The four couples were given one day off and escorted to a private beach, isolated from onlookers or other human contact, except for custodial assistants possessing high-level clearances.

Swimming, soaking up sunlight, and joking around wasted most of the next day. As the fledgling astronauts sat around a bonfire in the evening, they talked about things they were going to miss when off-world. Among the activities mentioned, driving a car occurred most often, then shopping. Attending sports events and barbequed hamburgers with beer were a consensus of the men. Going to a movie, sitting in the back necking, and drinking milkshakes were also mentioned more than once. As the moon rose and the bonfire dimmed, the group climbed into the bus and were driven to their quarters for their last night on earth.

The next morning, the crew was presented with new flight suits. They had thirty minutes to prepare for boarding the low-orbital craft that would ferry them to the nearest of the four international space stations maintained in geosynchronous orbits.

Gina was ready in less than ten minutes and was sitting on the bed watching Sunul shave. She was thinking about unpredictable events that might cause the flight to be cancelled:

Too much wind, overcast skies, thunderstorms, electronic or computer failures. *Why am I thinking about these things at this late date? Am I afraid?*

A dream had caused her last night on earth to be full of unrest. She had been alone, floating in space, tumbling end-over-end, with no way to stop her rotation. She had awakened at three in the morning, drenched in perspiration, and couldn't go back to sleep, even after changing to dry bedclothes. Sunul was sound asleep. Nothing seemed to disrupt his slumber. She was a bit irritated with him for sleeping when she was suffering from a stupid nightmare. When she analyzed how she felt, blaming Sunul, she was embarrassed. The dream wouldn't be mentioned. Such a trivial thing. She and Sunul would be going into space later in the day. She hoped the dream was not a foreboding of a disastrous event.

"Let's go. Are you ready?" Sunul was standing beside the door with his hand on the wall pad ready to open the door. Gina glanced at Sunul and stood up. She had gone back to sleep following her nightmare. For a moment she almost asked, "Where are we going?" But then she came out of her trance-like state, suddenly awaked, like a plane coming out of a cloud into sunshine and blue sky. She rubbed her eyes, "I'm ready."

Sunul tapped on the lock pad and stepped out into the sunlight with Gina. She looked at him apprehensively and gave a weak smile. Sunul put his arm around her waist and said, "What's wrong?"

"I didn't sleep very well."

"Don't worry. You'll have plenty of time to catch up while we're going to the moon. There isn't much for us to do, everything is handled by computers. You're not worried, are you?"

"Not really, we have a highly competent crew. I was thinking about what I would have told my parents, if they were still around."

"I have some thoughts about that, too. Let's talk on the way to the low orbital flight. We'd better join the others; the bus is waiting."

Neither Gina nor Sunul had eaten breakfast, and as they sat on the bus rolling toward the runway for the low orbital plane, ten miles distant, Sunul's stomach began to growl. Gina laughed and placed her hand on Sunul's noisy belly. "Don't let anything escape on the bus."

"Don't worry, I'll apply a rocket assist as we get on the plane."

She laughed, "Okay, but let me get in front of you. Oh, I've thought of what I would tell my parents."

"Me too. I would just say I'm going on a trip for the government and I might not be back for a long time, but I'll be thinking of them. What would you have said?"

Gina hesitated, thinking of what Sunul had mentioned. "I would tell them I was going on a long honeymoon, but I also had to carry out some research for my employer. I might be gone for a number of years. Don't worry about me, I'm with my husband and some very good friends."

"Would that be the first time they heard of your marriage?"

"Oh, no, I would have invited them to the wedding. They would have been impressed with all the military men in their dress uniforms," she laughed, thinking of the wedding that had actually taken place: four weddings in the astro-base chapel, conducted by the on-base minister, in a fifteen-minute period. A cleaning lady and a cook were witnesses. There would have been too many opportunities for information to leak out if regular weddings had been conducted.

It took about fifteen minutes to arrive at the runway. The crew had never ridden in the low orbital flight (LOF) vehicle before, but it was common knowledge that the ride would be short and smooth. The fuselage of the vehicle was parted so the passenger section could be inserted into the airframe, becoming an integral part of the plane's body. The eight passengers watched as workers swarmed over the vehicle like bees caring for their queen.

After their compartment was locked into place, the plane was twelve feet longer. Sunul and his crew were seated in softly cushioned seats and belted in, only for precautions, according to the LOF crew. As preparations were being completed, they heard multiple times that the ride would be uneventful. Five minutes later, the eight astronauts could feel the plane roll down the runway, then climb at a steep angle.

The captain's voice could be heard calling out the altitude every ten thousand feet above the earth's surface. At 80,000 feet, Sunul and his crew were forced into the cushioned seats, as the acceleration from rockets boosted them to an altitude of eighty miles.

The com system came to life with the captain's voice, "The tail assembly will now be jettisoned. It will be replaced by the propulsion system that will take us to Geo-syn-1 and Lunar Base. You will hear some banging around as robots are completing the transfer. Don't worry, we've done this a thousand times with no accidents."

Gina looked at Sunul and asked, "Were you aware of this procedure?"

Sunul shook his head, "It's new to me. I have a feeling we are in for some more surprises. The space agency has kept out of the news for some time, even though the budget has doubled each of the last three years."

He grinned and followed with, "I checked out the agency's budget about a month ago. I suspect the alien contact has been known for more than two years."

Gina's frown showed her annoyance with the information the agency had presented to the crew. "So, you think they lied to us?"

Sunul grinned. "No. You know the government never lies to its citizens."

Gina and the others all laughed. Anyone in the cabin could hear everything said by any crew member, unless it was whispered.

There were several large bangs and jolts to the cabin as the ship was being converted. After the eight-hour trip to the moon, the crew would transfer to a larger, much more complex ship for the journey to the Kuiper belt. In the new ship, the four couples would take over control, assisted by computers. Following the twenty-three-day trip, the final transfer would take place at Kuiper 5K23m, when the crew would leave the solar system behind and accelerate toward Alpha Centauri in their spherical, ice- and rock-encased vehicle. Immune to small body collisions, the little moon would take them on a trajectory half-way to Alpha Centauri to contact our nearest known alien neighbors.

One last noise resounded throughout the passenger unit, followed by several seconds of complete silence before the captain announced, "Everyone must be seated with belts in the lock position. There will be a rapid acceleration. When the green light comes on, you may move about."

The seats rotated ninety degrees and locked into position. Gina was reminded of a rollercoaster when the restraint was engaged to keep her from falling out while careening, sometimes inverted, through twisting sharp turns. She looked at Sunul and raised her eyebrows. He shrugged his shoulders and said, "I suggest that we all relax and enjoy the ride."

For about a minute, they felt their bodies being pushed into the cushioned seats. There was no noise, only a slight vibration associated with the acceleration of the ship as it moved away from the earth, increasing in velocity to six-thousand miles per hour. The video screen on the forward wall flashed green for about ten seconds and then a spectacular view of the earth appeared, the ocean and continents clearly defined.

The screen then went blank for a second before the geostationary station became visible, growing in size as they approached. Docking maneuvers were performed and after five minutes, a new voice came over the com system. "I am Commander Hellman. I will ferry you to the moon."

The ship decoupled from the station, and after a few maneuvers, the screen showed Earth, a blue and white sphere, gradually diminishing in size as cloud formations slowly drifted across the circular image toward the terminator. Watching the image for about ten minutes, at least one astronaut wondered if she would ever again set foot on the small planet she called home.

"Do you think we'll ever come back, Sunul?" Gina asked, misty-eyed, as she grasped his arm. Everyone was listening to her words.

"I hope so. We'll all be about seventy years old, but with all the low gravity, you ladies don't need to worry about anything sagging." The other men laughed, but the women booed and hissed, and then joined in the laughter.

Gina replied, "Well, if we don't sag, I'll look around for a younger man when we get back. I'll be ready to have some babies." The other three women laughed and applauded.

CHAPTER 7
WAITING TO LEAVE THE MOON

Arrival at the moon was uneventful but transfer to the ship bound for the Kuiper belt was delayed. The four couples were instructed to remain secured while the trans-lunar ship was touching down in Grimaldi crater. In the moon's shadow, they were protected from high-energy radiation from a solar storm. Since their craft for the trip to 5K23m was still being prepared, they would be forced to stay at the station for twenty-four hours.

Twelve hours earlier the beta group had departed for Mars in a much smaller vehicle than the ferry carrying the alpha group destined for the Kuiper belt. The primary differences in the two vehicles were the main engines and the amounts of fuel carried. The beta group's engine was a traditional chemical fueled rocket; while the alpha group's engine power came from a nuclear reactor in addition to four liquid fueled rockets used at liftoff. The ferry from Earth going to the edge of the solar system had to be refitted at the Grimaldi site.

The astronauts were aware of the orientation of the ship when landing, and the entire crew could feel the craft being tipped, what they envisioned, to ninety degrees. Several minutes of vibrations followed the change in orientation.

Sunul spoke to the others, "I'm not sure what all the jostling was for. I guess we'll find out before long." A huge thump occurred which shook the entire ship.

Gina reacted, "I'm glad they told us to stay strapped in. That last jolt would have knocked me over."

Monel asked, "Does anyone know what is going on out there?"

Jar'l glanced at Sunul, but he was no help. Sunul just raised his hands and shook his head. He felt as if he were blindfolded, being taken on a student prank trip in a car trunk. After the first few jolts, he had become disoriented and had lost his sense of direction.

A voice from the com link broke the relative silence. "You will be able to leave the ship now. There will be a slight difference in atmospheric pressure in the cavern compared to that in the ship. And remember, the gravity of the moon is only one-sixth that on the earth, so be careful moving around until you get used to the difference. Try not to bang into each other or knock over equipment. Look for things to steady yourself while you adjust to the low gravity and follow the blue lane to your temporary quarters."

Monel and Gina looked at Sunul as Jar'l commented, "I think we're inside the moon, maybe at the edge of the crater."

Sunul replied, "I think you're right. But don't worry, they wouldn't let us exit into a vacuum."

There was a slight pressure difference when the hatch was released, and a hiss was audible. Triel and Leanne had been talking and both women gasped when they heard the hiss, ready to fill their lungs with air before stepping out of the craft. The two women latched onto their husbands thinking added stability would be gained with four feet touching the surface rather than two. They were correct.

There was little privacy in the over-night quarters, except when using the toilet, but the accommodations were warm, well-lit, had an entertainment center and cooking facilities. No one had eaten during the trip from earth, so prepared meals were consumed as they investigated their new quarters. The microwaved dinners allowed for quick cleanup. There was a stringent rule: no garbage was to be left on the moon. All plastic-ware was dropped into an incinerator.

Hugh and Triel sat down and began playing Robot War on the entertainment center's three-dimensional holographic screen while Monel and Leanne watched. Rob's eyes were scanning the interior of the quarters and he noticed a small com panel next to the door that led to the spacecraft assembly area where their craft had been repositioned after landing in the crater. He moved to the green and red checkerboard panel and pressed it.

A synthetic feminine voice, sounding somewhat robotic, answered, "May I help you?"

"Yes. Would it be possible to tour the assembly area outside our living quarters?"

"That is admissible. Please do not interfere with the personnel as they work."

Rob looked at Sunul and Jar'l and tipped his head toward the door, indicating he was going to investigate the construction bay. Sunul and Jar'l stood and began moving toward the door.

"Hey, wait for me!" Gina jumped to her feet, but leapt two-feet off the floor, forgetting the moon's gravity was only one-sixth of the earth's force of attraction. She landed off balance and might have fallen, but Sunul and Jar'l kept her from tumbling. "Oh! I forgot about using too much force on the moon. Thank you." She grabbed Sunul's hand and steadied herself, her look of concern turning into a smile as she clutched a handful of Sunul's shirt.

The ship they had arrived in had been dismantled, but the passenger compartment containing view ports was being merged in the center of another unit three times as large, in the shape of a historical merry-go-round. Jar'l was standing beside Sunul and commented, "I wonder where the engine is?"

Sunul pointed to the other side of the zeppelin-sized cavern in the moon, beyond the structure in front of them. "Could those four spherical things be engines or fuel tanks?"

Jar'l replied, "Jesus, Sunul, I think you're right. Those eight-meter diameter soccer balls are engines, or part of the engine, but how do they attach to the craft? I don't see any way to attach them to the spacecraft."

"Do you think part of the ship is outside?" asked Gina.

Jar'l snapped his fingers and answered, "I think you're right, Gina."

"Good thinking, Gina. I should have thought of that." Sunul grinned. "But I can't think of everything. Since we all have about the same IQ, we should all get credit for things we come up with as a group, don't you think? No individuals, it's a team effort." He raised his eyebrows and smiled. Sunul moved over to one of the spheres and asked Jar'l, "Can you tell us how these things work?"

He pressed on one of the pentagonal shaped segments, marked MC-1A. It popped open revealing a connector that had to be an attachment position for mating to the spacecraft.

The cavity was isolated from the sphere's internal mechanism but held a metal bar. A hook from the ship probably secured the sphere to its side with a latch. Adjacent to the MC-1 segment was a hexagonal shaped section labeled EC-1A. Sunul couldn't detect how to open it, even though he pressed on different portions of the hexagon. He noticed a neighboring section labeled EC-2A, but he couldn't reach high enough to find if there was a pressure point that would open the segment. "Well, I guess I'll have to wait to see how these panels are opened."

Jar'l suggested, "Maybe they're open electronically, the EC designation might mean electronic connection, and the MC could stand for mechanical connection."

"Way to go, Jar'l. You're not as dumb as I thought." Gina laughed and tried to give Jar'l a punch in the stomach, which he backed away from as he saw it coming. He caught her fist in his hand before it could land. He smiled and said, "Gina, haven't you heard of a high five?"

"Sure, but I thought I'd change it up and give you a low five—in the gut. I like to give out surprises."

Sunul smiled and agreed, "She's right about that. She surprises me all the time; she's a crazy woman occasionally. That makes living with her a lot of fun."

Two technicians approached the sphere where the astronauts were talking. Sunul was going to take a chance and ask some questions about the spheres, but he didn't want to interrupt their work. Jar'l asked the first question, "Can you tell me if these spheres are engines or fuel tanks?"

The taller of the techs, both dressed in white jump suits, answered, "They're a little of both. Inside the shell liquid fuel circulates around a nuclear reactor, centered in each sphere. You'll have to activate the reactor once you're off the moon. You'll be catapulted off the surface, liquid fueled rockets will get you free of the moon's gravity and then the nuclear power will take over to provide thrust to the Kuiper belt. That's all I can tell you; we don't have time to go into details."

He looked at his buddy and said, "Let's get on with it, Stan, we've got eight of these babies to move to the other assembly area. These four balls go outside first. Step away, please." He motioned with his right hand for Gina, Sunul, and Jar'l to step away from the area, painted in blue and white squares, toward the living quarters. "You can watch from over there, if you like."

As the four astronauts moved away from the spheres, they heard a whirring sound from above their heads and a low frequency slapping sound along the floor. Two cables dropped slowly from the ceiling, seeming to dance in the space above the engines. The technicians grabbed the hooks on the ends of the cables, touched the first sphere's segments marked with MC, and secured the hooks to the bars inside.

A low clearance truck, like that used in underground mining, equipped with tracks rather than wheels, was plodding across the floor toward the sphere. It was being controlled by a remote, similar to an old-time TV remote from the early 2000s. Modern TV was controlled by voice commands, the old-fashioned remotes were now junk. One of the techs hoisted the sphere and the other tech moved the truck underneath. The sphere was lowered onto the truck's padded concave top and the cables were released.

"Why do they use a remote-control system instead of voice commands, Sunul?" Gina thought she had asked a reasonable question, but she had overlooked one fact; voice commands could not be used on the surface of the moon because there was no atmosphere for propagation of sound. Speaking instructions from a space suit would add another, more complex problem for the engineers to solve.

Sunul answered quickly, "No atmosphere outside, dear."

Gina grinned and replied, "I should have thought of that, but you guys have to contribute. We are a team, you know."

Rob spoke up, "I've seen enough. I'm going back to see how Leanne is doing with her game. Let me know if you find anything exciting." Rob turned and bounded back to the astronaut's temporary quarters.

Sunul put his arm around Gina's neck, like a headlock, and hugged her to his shoulder. "See, Jar'l, she keeps me on my toes all the time and, unfortunately, she remembers everything I say."

"Hey, look!" Gina twisted away from Sunul and moved to get a better look at the vehicle carrying the sphere. It had stopped and suddenly dropped out of sight, almost without a sound.

They jogged to the location where the truck and sphere had vanished, but the floor showed no visual indication of an interface, the floor was continuous. Jar'l and Sunul knelt and ran their hands over the floor, detecting a slight seam, apparently where the floor was sealed to become airtight.

"I'm amazed at the advances in this facility. I had no idea these things existed. What do you think, Sunul?" Jar'l was shaking his head in partial disbelief at what was taking place.

Sunul answered, "I'm just as amazed as you are. I think I'll go back in the lounge area and see if there are some instruction manuals, but I'm getting the idea that things are going to be self-explanatory on the spacecraft."

Gina commented, "I'm just trying to imagine what our ship will look like. Let's go inside and see what we can find out. We can't get much from the techs—they're too busy and probably instructed to ignore us. I'm wondering what's below us."

Inside the lounge area, the other astronauts were still playing computer games, but Rob Griswalt was reading a brochure. Sunul sat beside him and asked, "May I ask what you're eyes are glued to?"

"Sure, it's about new electronics, but it's about two years out-of-date. I've seen all this stuff already. What did you guys see out there?"

"Some big prolate spheroids, apparently engines and fuel tanks. Not too interesting, except when a truck carrying one of them vanished in front of our eyes, well, in front of Gina's eyes. Jar'l and I weren't watching too closely. We think there is something going on below us. Have you heard any banging around?"

"Nope, but I've been reading, and those jokers have been yukking it up about their games. I couldn't have heard anything unless it was a moonquake."

"Okay, thanks. I'll ask our service computer some questions."

Sunul bounded across the room in three steps, grabbed a wall handle, and pressed the black and white checked panel.

"May I help you?"

"Yes. Are there any brochures or travel manuals available for trips to the Kuiper belt?"

Sunul was answered with laughing, three voices in all, and one louder than the rest. Were there two other women listening in the background? He began to question whether the voice on the com unit was robotic. "What's your name?"

"I don't have a name, I'm a computer."

"Computers don't laugh—and I heard other laughter in the background. What's your name?"

"Arlene, if you must know."

"Where are you from, Arlene?"

"From? You mean where was I programmed?"

Sunul smiled, still thinking the voice came from a living being. "Well, yes."

"The Jet Propulsion Laboratory, 2078. I was commissioned April 11."

Sunul was getting tired of the lack of success, so he asked his most important question, "Is there an illustration of the ship that will take us to the Kuiper belt?"

The voice hesitated far a couple of seconds and replied, "Game 131: Interstellar Voyage."

"Thank you, Arlene."

"You are very welcome, Commander Burke."

Sunul stood in front of the panel for a moment, frowning and thinking. "How would the computer know my name? Damn! The computer must have voice, and probably facial recognition, but on the moon? How many more advances are in store for us?" Sunul wouldn't have been surprised on earth, but sophisticated computer systems were unexpected in an outpost on the moon.

He walked to the computer games table and said, "How would you guys like to see a three-dimensional view of our spacecraft? We're going to be in it for more than three weeks."

Leanne Griswalt slid her chair back from the games table, stood up, and motioned for Sunul to sit down. "Show us, Sunul. We just completed our game."

As everyone gathered around the games table, Sunul said, "Arlene: play game 131."

CHAPTER 8
PROGRESS TOWARD
THE KUIPER BELT

Leaving the moon was nothing like exiting from earth. A cluster of five reusable solid fuel rockets lifted the ship clear of the moon's surface and broke away explosively from the bottom of the spacecraft. Little change in acceleration could be felt by the eight astronauts as the liquid fuel/nuclear rockets took over and continued increasing the velocity of the craft as it left the moon and earth behind.

The crew had been confined on the moon for over sixty hours; more than twice the wait time they had been told to expect before launch toward Kuiper 5K23m. Now they were sitting at various consoles monitoring acceleration, velocity, distance, fuel consumption, and direction. Though Alpha Centauri is below the ecliptic, the plane of the earth's orbit, Kuiper 5K23 was slightly above the ecliptic at fifty-eight astronomical units (au) from the sun. About eighteen au beyond Pluto and having a period of slightly more than 380 years, Kuiper 5K23 orbited the sun inclined at twenty-five degrees to the plane of the solar system. During the trip from earth to their destination, 5K23 would move less than one-tenth of a degree across the background of stars; an arc length of about 3.9 million miles.

The second day speeding away from the moon, Sunul positioned himself in front of the main console and ordered, "Show current positions of the outer planets with regard to Kuiper 5K23." When the holographic image of the planets appeared in the air above the console, Sunul studied their positions for a minute and declared, "I want to deviate our course. Does anyone object?"

Jar'l quizzed, "What kind of shortcut are you talking about?"

Monel whispered into Jar'l's ear, "Don't you think he knows what he's doing?"

"Look, Monel, no one is infallible. If a mistake is made out here, we might not be able to recover."

Sunul heard the concern and explained, "It's not a shortcut. If we follow a direct course, we will use most of our fuel to slow down and we might not be able to land on 5K23m. The Space Agency has calculated the amount of fuel and we will have little left over—only one chance at landing. They must have figured our expertise and the use of computers should make the landing a sure thing. Our little moon home is moving very slowly; only about 5,300 miles per hour. Now, compare that with our present speed. You have probably noticed how rapidly the earth and moon receded from us. Our present speed is approaching sixty million miles per hour and in a day we will begin coasting for a week. When we get about halfway to 5K23, we start putting on the brakes; using up fuel to slow us down during the remainder of the trip. However, if we make a close approach to Neptune, even though it isn't on our direct route, we will save about twenty percent of our fuel. We might need every drop to land on our moon-ship. Think about it and let me know what you want to do."

Gina added, "The close approach to Neptune will slow us by nearly thirty percent."

Triel asked, "How will the Neptune approach affect the length of our trip?"

Sunul responded, "Good question. I figure it will make our trip three days longer; maybe as much as eighty hours longer, since we will be moving more slowly for a longer period of time."

Hugh added, "But we'll have a lot more fuel for maneuvering. Right?"

"That's correct."

Hugh said, "Okay, I'm in. What about the rest of you?"

There were no dissenting votes, the close approach to Neptune would be programmed into the system so the current course could be altered immediately; fifteen degrees from the direct route to 5K23m.

Sunul asked Jar'l, "Do you anticipate any problems with the change in trajectory?"

Jar'l replied, "No, but it's a good idea to do the course change now rather than wait until we get much closer to 5K23m; less fuel will be required, and the angle is a lot smaller if we deviate now. I'm wondering why the Agency didn't anticipate this long ago."

Sunul shrugged his shoulders and smiled, "They probably didn't know if the program would get funded by Congress. When the alien message was received and the mission was funded, the procedure was just pieced together. With the turnover of personnel at the agency, the original planners might have moved on to other positions. We are probably starting the mission with plans that are several year's old—never upgraded to the present positions of the planets and the Kuiper objects."

Rob Griswalt commented, "I don't think they forgot anything in the electronics area. There are enough parts in the tech lab to rebuild every piece of equipment at least three times. I hope all the equipment on board gets transferred to our moon-ship home."

Jar'l said, "You'll have to make sure of that, Griz. Don't depend on the robots to get everything right. We don't want to come up short of any electronic parts during our twenty-year journey. There are limitations to our on-site fabrication of printed circuits."

"Okay. If the transfer robots don't do a perfect job, Leanne and I will make sure everything's transferred."

Sunul and Gina were busy at the consoles, making changes to the course by altering the engine thrust vectors and making some minor changes to fuel consumption. The rest of the crew resumed their normal duties. After a few minutes of reprogramming the engines, Sunul announced, "Get ready for some changes in acceleration. You shouldn't feel much of a change—maybe a slight jolt."

Gina watched Sunul. Using his fingers, he counted down from three, and they pressed their initiate keys simultaneously on zero. Nothing happened.

Jar'l commented, "I didn't feel anything. Did any of you notice a change?"

Sunul was sitting still, frozen in place. He suddenly leaned back in his chair and said, "Computer, follow instructions to change trajectory."

"Such changes are not permitted. The Agency does not allow alterations of trajectory made from the consoles." The robotic voice was monotonic, without the tiniest hint of emotion.

Sunul motioned to Jar'l and Rob to join him in the galley. To avoid being overheard, Sunul put a meal pouch in the microwave and activated the magnetron. The exhaust fan prevented any conversation from being detected. Jar'l and Rob moved closer to Sunul when he said, "Any ideas?"

"Looks like we'll have to hack into the main computer." Jar'l looked at Rob, who contributed, "Yeah, we can force a computer shut-down, but it will reboot to the original program. We'll have to overload the system so it will shut down long enough for us to get a subroutine added to the master. If we can repeatedly force a shut-down, maybe it will ask for help. Then we can access the system code. That's the only thing I can think of."

Sunul stated, "Okay. That's what we'll have to do. At least we can give it a try. Let's spread the word. Gina and I will have the code ready. We'll only need a couple of seconds."

Jar'l said, "I'll have everyone compute an endless sum or pi to 100,000 decimal places."

Sunul suggested, "Have someone calculate the positions of all the moons of Jupiter for, the next century, that'll require some computer power. Okay? Let's do it."

As the three men separated, the oven chirped. The meal was ready to eat. They ignored the sound and went back to their consoles. It took about five minutes to get everyone ready for the computer overload. Sunul and Gina were functioning as one person but operating two consoles. They believed they could accomplish their task in slightly less than three seconds because Sunul had minimized the subroutine to five lines of code, only seventy-eight characters.

Gina stood up and got everyone's attention. She counted down; three, two, one, and made a fist. All the astronauts reacted nearly simultaneously. In about five seconds, the computer shut down, but only momentarily, and then returned to normal. Sunul and Gina didn't have enough time to insert the new code.

A message, in flashing red capital letters, appeared on Sunul's console screen. DO NOT ATTEMPT TO ALTER CENTRAL PROCESSOR CODE. CHANGING CODE WILL ENDANGER YOUR LIVES AND THE MISSION.

Jar'l was entering an audible communication message into his out-file. He copied the file to all on board so everyone could follow what he was doing. The message was directed to the Command Center at the Cape. It asked for permission to change course, over-riding the computer's anti-tampering provision. He told Sunul to continue the message, explaining the change in trajectory and accompanying savings of fuel for maneuvering in the Kuiper Belt. Sunul explained, recorded his proposal, and sent the message. The radio broadcast would take about an hour to reach earth, and not knowing when a response would be received, the crew relaxed and continued their normal activities, hoping for a positive response.

The lack of alternating light and darkness experienced on earth caused a variety of effects; the couples responded with erratic sleeping and waking episodes. Gina and Sunul had retained their normal routine, but not the others. Gina decided to set up a schedule of eight-hour equipment monitoring shifts so someone was always cognizant of the ship's functions; no more than six crew members were allowed sleep at any one time. The crew was not going to rely on computer warnings.

When the positive message from earth was received, the Masons and Patels were sleeping. It had been four hours twenty-three minutes since Sunul had sent the request. Terminals 1, 3, and 7 had to be used simultaneously to circumvent the protective firewall of the main computer. Hexadecimal c7e9 had to be entered at all three stations within a one second interval. Sunul, Rob, and Leanne sat at the consoles and Gina provided the countdown. Entry into the computer was successful and Sunul entered the new subroutine for the trajectory change. This procedure was only permitted once. Earth would have to be contacted for any further code alterations. The computer replied, in flashing red capitals: WARNING: NO FURTHER ALTERATIONS OF CODE ARE ALLOWED.

The trajectory changed within seconds; two of the engines increasing in thrust and two decreasing in power output. Sunul, who was standing, could feel the change taking place. A slight vibration occurred, but he held firmly onto his station island to keep from being gently jostled across the cabin. The maneuver was over in ten seconds, the low frequency vibrations disappeared, and the four engines resumed their previous monotonous tone that propagated throughout the spacecraft.

Within an hour, the computer consoles began to flash a message. The robotic female voice duplicated: THE PREDETERMINED MAXIMUM VELOCITY HAS BEEN ATTAINED. THE ENGINES WILL BE SHUT DOWN UNTIL NEEDED FOR COURSE CORRECTION NEAR THE ORBIT OF NEPTUNE. COMMANDER BURKE IS IN CHARGE OF TERMINAL 1. ENGINE RESTART COMMANDS MUST ORIGINATE FROM TERMINAL 1. HAVE A NICE DAY.

Gina reacted, "Have a nice day! She makes me want to puke! I'd like to slap the programmer that tried to add a personality to the main computer."

Laughing, Leanne added, "That programmer probably worked in sales to earn credits for computer courses."

On the twelfth day, the ship crossed the orbit of greenish Uranus, but the third biggest giant planet wasn't visible from the viewing ports. A computer inquiry indicated the planet was far from the ship's trajectory but should be observable with the four-inch camera scopes. No one showed much interest in seeing the giant, however. Thousands of pictures taken from satellites were available in the library, but the crew was looking forward to the encounter with Neptune, still almost six days away, when the planet's gravitational field would slow the ship.

CHAPTER 9

ENCOUNTER WITH NEPTUNE

Sunul had worked on the close approach details for two days prior to arriving at Neptune. He had Jar'l and Gina run various simulations and had made his final preparations about twelve hours before he had to relieve the computer of engine control. Since making the course correction, the engines had been shut down and the ship was coasting at nearly constant velocity only slowing slightly from the attraction of the sun.

One of the simulations executed by Jar'l had ended in disaster; the craft entered the atmosphere and burned up. Sunul and Jar'l checked the data and found that one datum had been a mistake; it was in error by only one percent, but that slight mistake had catastrophic consequences. Sunul decided Gina would monitor all data entries so no errors were possible. The close approach to Neptune had to be perfect, there was no room for error; if too close to the planet, the ship would penetrate into the gases, and with no ablative shields, there would be a fireball; if too far from Neptune, they would have to recover by consuming more precious fuel. The procedure would have been a wasted effort.

As the time for the maneuver approached, everyone was in a heightened state of anxiety. Although they had faith in Sunul, there was always a possibility for an unexpected negative outcome. As Sunul took over the engines and adjusted the ship's trajectory, Jar'l asked, "Did you take into account the position of Triton?"

Sunul smiled, and replied, "Triton is going to help us put on the brakes and will enable us to change direction toward 5K23m without using any fuel. Watch how this works." The engines were in sleep mode, but in ten minutes, they were ready to bring to full power if needed. Sunul guided the ship close to Neptune, between the planet and its moon, Triton, in an S shaped trajectory. As the craft left Triton behind, Sunul rotated the ship nearly 180 degrees so the engines were facing the Kuiper belt. Then he applied full power to further slow the ship.

"What's our velocity, Jar'l?" Sunul asked, as he watched the simulator showing the ship and 5K23's estimated position barely changing but starting to converge. It would take another six to eight days before they would be close enough to 5K23 to see it without telescopic aid. Slowing down had added a significant amount of time to their original planned rendezvous with 5K23m; almost three days.

"We're at forty-three percent of our previous velocity, Sunul. Your maneuver saved us nearly forty-nine percent of our fuel—well done!"

The crew broke into applause and Gina kissed Sunul on the cheek, not wanting to disturb his concentration at the controls, otherwise she would have punched him on the shoulder. Sunul didn't even look away from the controls, but he reached up with his hand and wiped his face where Gina had left her pink lip gloss and saliva smear.

Sunul asked, "Monel, can you detect any signal from the beacon yet?"

Monel replied, "I haven't checked since we slowed down. I thought being around Neptune might interfere with the homing signal. Just a minute, I'll monitor that frequency."

She talked with Jar'l for a moment, sat down at her console, entered the frequency, and watched the display for about ten seconds. "Nothing yet, Sunul, but the homing transmitter left by the engineers is very low power, only five to ten watts. I'll update you every twelve hours, unless you think I should check more often."

"That's fine. As soon as you get the signal, track it on the main display screen, updating every hour. I don't want to waste fuel jockeying around out here. Hopefully, our little moon will be isolated and easy to see once we're about a day out."

Six days passed without detecting a signal from 5K23m. Station keeping was becoming a bore, but games, music, and movies helped lessen the monotonous existence of the four couples travelling together in a vehicle, little bigger than a rural school bus from the 1980s. On the seventh day, a signal was received from the beacon, however, at first it was a bit confusing to Monel; there were two signals, one strong and another weak. The weaker arrived at a slight delay to the more prominent radio pulse.

Jar'l suggested, "I think we're getting an echo. The stronger signal is being reflected off another body. If so, the weaker signal will go away when the two bodies distance themselves from each other so their spatial orientation changes with regard to us. The echoes are just an artifact."

Monel put the tone on audio and turned up the volume. The beacon tone was loud and clear, but the weaker signal was nearly inaudible—just what Jar'l had suggested seemed to be occurring. The next beacon signal was isolated with no echo. Monel performed a simulation of 5K23 with 5K23m and illustrated the condition for the formation of the echo. The echo was coming from a reflection of the beacon from the surface of Kuiper 5K23, the much larger of the two bodies. She expected the same phenomenon to occur in about five and one-half days. Therefore, they would not experience the echo again; they would be inside the moon and have silenced the beacon.

Fourteen-hours later, the master display began showing the ship's distance from their new home, Kuiper 5K23m, steadily decreasing. Jar'l activated the ship's radar and began monitoring the positions of five bodies in the near vicinity. Monel began working with Jar'l, superimposing the beacon's signal with that of the ship's radar.

Sunul was watching the 3D display and began making estimates of the extent of slowing and velocities necessary for the ship to meet with 5K23m. A flashing red warning signal suddenly scrolled across the display: LOSS OF FUEL PRESSURE; ENGINE 3. A loud staccato siren sounded, followed by the computer voice and flashing display: FUEL TANK #3 HAS RUPTURED. SHOULD THE REMAINING FUEL BE TRANSFERRED TO THE UNDAMAGED CONTAINERS?

Sunul reacted in less than a second. "Arlene! Please transfer fuel from tank three to tanks one, two, and four—immediately."

"Yes, Commander Burke." Five-minutes elapsed before the computer voice stated, "There has been an eight point three percent loss of fuel from tank number three. The remaining fuel has been transferred. Tanks one, two, and four are at fifty-seven point two percent capacity. Tank three needs to be repaired as soon as possible. Engine three has been shut down."

Sunul smiled and announced to the crew, "We won't need engine three to rendezvous with 5K23m. I can probably get us there with two engines, so don't worry. Rob and Leanne, I want you to figure out how to transfer the remaining fuel to the starship, and if it's not too difficult, I'd like to move our present engines to our new ship. It might take all of us to do it, so be ready to work. Gina will set up shifts; we will have to work in EVA suits."

Triel asked, "Why are we going to all the trouble to salvage our present engines, Sunul? Aren't they too small to be of use?"

Sunul replied, smiling, "The engines on the starship are new technology and I don't have complete confidence that there won't be some failures. I'd like to have some backups—just in case. From the diagrams of the interior of the moon, we should have plenty of storage space."

Hugh joined his wife in questioning the need for the smaller engines, "What if the access doors are too small for the engines and fuel tanks?"

Rob sided with Sunul and said, "We've got some laser cutting tools. We can trim just about anything to fit. If need be, we can open a new hole on the surface of the moon and slide things in, melt the ices on the walls and let them refreeze to close the holes. I've never done it, but I'm confident it can be done. Just call me Mr. Ingenuity."

Leanne agreed, "If it can be done, we can do it."

Rob replied, "I stand corrected—I should have said Mr. and Mrs. Ingenuity."

Leanne reached out and pinched Rob's butt.

"My profound apologies, my dear." He bowed and stuck out his tongue.

As the laughter subsided, Sunul motioned to Gina to come closer so they could talk in confidence. "What did you make of the Patels' comments? Don't you think my reasoning is sound?"

"Sunul, you have to remember they're biologists. They haven't dealt with physics and mechanics like we have. I don't think they were out-of-line questioning your motives. But, now that you've drawn my attention to that pair, I'll keep an eye open for any strange behavior. I'll ask Jar'l and Monel to observe them, too."

Sunul replied, "Let's be careful, we don't want to alienate them; they're responsible for our food supply." Sunul glanced around, saw that everyone was busy at their consoles, and then announced, "Fasten your seat belts, everyone. I'm going to slow us again and make a few maneuvers as we get closer to the starship. We're coming up on it pretty fast. If you're interested, you can watch our position on the big display as we converge with our new home."

Rob commented to Sunul, before Sunul was involved with the mating maneuvers, "We could probably tether the motors and fuel tanks to the outside of the moon if they can't be moved inside with ease."

Sunul replied, "Good idea. We'll go over all the options when we begin transferring equipment to the moon. We'll need to see what the place looks like before we do anything drastic."

"Sure. We'll talk about it later. I'll let you get us there first."

Sunul began concentrating on the images from the ship's video cameras which were automatically being focused on the object broadcasting the homing signal. When the ship edged within 100 meters of the moon, Sunul was startled; intense light emanating from the ship illuminated the surface of the moon where the airlock was located. The computer voice began announcing the distance to the moon's surface.

When Sunul had piloted the ship to within ten meters of the airlock, explosive charges on the ship directed tether cables to the surface and winches drew the two bodies together. It was all automatic, Sunul didn't have to use the thrusters he had practiced with on the simulated landings. Once the tethers were engaged, he sat back, relaxed, turned off the thruster controls, and enjoyed the short ride. He felt like he had taken part in a video game being played mostly by computers.

The ship shuddered momentarily when it came in contact with the moon. The computer voice announced:

"PLEASE REMAIN SEATED UNTIL THE JETWAY HAS BEEN LOCKED INTO POSITION AND IS PRESSURIZED. YOU HAVE REACHED YOUR DESTINATION, KUIPER 5K23M. WE HOPE YOU ENJOYED THE TRIP. HAVE A NICE DAY."

Hugh Patel said, "Nice going, Sunul. You did a masterful job of guiding the ship to its berth."

Sunul responded, "Do I detect a little sarcasm, Mr. Patel?"

Hugh laughed, "Just a little. I do believe you were as surprised as the rest of us at the automated landing procedure. I saw you flinch when those charges went off."

"You got that right. The engineers did more than was necessary. I wonder how many more surprises we're going to encounter." Sunul turned off engine control and released his seatbelt. He smiled at Gina and said, "Let's go inside and see what awaits us. I hope there aren't any frozen aliens that have thawed out while waiting for us. Remember to observe all warning signs; if someone accidently destroys the atmospheric pressure, we're all dead."

CHAPTER 10
DISOBEYING INSTRUCTIONS

Triel was the first to get to the exit panel. She was empty handed, but the others had taken their time and collected some of their belongings. Triel punched the red exit-bar and air swooshed out of the ship for a second as the pressures between the ship and the Jetway equilibrated. The door swung ajar and she squeezed through the opening, then pulled the hatchway into the fully open position. She wanted to be the first of the crew to start exploring the new facility, so she took a few steps into the complex.

"Hey, Triel, get some of your things and start transferring!" Hugh yelled after her, but she didn't want to stop investigating. She passed through the command center and the galley without much of a glance, but when she found the living quarters, she surveyed the station schematic in the hallway and picked the rooms with easiest access to all the facilities.

"Triel! Where the hell are you?" Triel heard Hugh call and she yelled back, "I'm in here."

She was on the bed closest to the bathroom, scanning the entire room, amazed at the plush surroundings. Hugh entered the large room, arms full of items from the ship. "Where do you want this stuff, babes?"

Triel smiled and replied, "Just drop it anywhere. We'll put things away later. We've got lots of space for everything. This place is like a ritzy hotel in Las Vegas. Wait till you see the bathroom." She watched a large bag of clothes slowly drop to the bed, like seeing a movie playing in slow motion.

"Well, you'd better help me get the rest of our things. We have to wait in line to go back into our taxi ship. There's only so much room with everyone bringing baggage into the complex. We don't have two-way streets, you know."

"Oh, all right. Go ahead, I'll be right behind you." She rolled off the edge of the bed and put her feet on the floor. When she began walking, it was almost as if she was on the surface of the earth. The magnetic flooring interacting with the soles of her shoes simulated normal gravity. She hadn't noticed the interaction when she first stepped through the hatch into the new environment; she had been so intent on investigating, little else had registered.

The entire crew made about four trips transferring personal items, including their EVA suits, and Triel was making her last entry into the taxi. She unlocked her personal locker and emptied it into a small bag, then headed toward the Jetway. As she entered, she heard the ship's computer voice announce: "YOU HAVE SIXTY SECONDS TO VACATE THE SHIP. THE ATMOSPHERIC PRESSURE WILL DROP AND THE SHIP WILL BE JETTISONED FROM 5K23M. THIS IS YOUR NEXT TO LAST ONLY WARNING."

"Oh, shit! Sunul is going to be pissed!" She scurried into the moon's compartments and yelled at Sunul, "Sunul, the ship is going to be jettisoned! You only have about forty seconds!"

Sunul came running, carrying his EVA equipment, which he hadn't had time to put in his personal locker. He dashed through the Jetway and into the ship, stopping at the main computer console. The screen was scrolling a flashing red warning message and the ship computer stated: "IN THIRTY SECONDS, THIS SHIP WILL BE DISCARDED INTO THE KUIPER BELT FIELD AS A DERELICT." A countdown ensued, and as Sunul was twisting his headgear into place, he began to hear small banging sounds, almost like rifle fire; one, two, three, four. He felt the thumps, and then he experienced the ship beginning to drift. There was one last abrupt noise and the ship began to move faster.

The computer was still functioning, so he checked the cabin pressure; it was rapidly dropping toward zero. The last bang he had heard must have been the interior gas being released to the vacuum outside the ship. That would have acted as a thruster and propelled the ship away from Kuiper 5K23m. He looked around but knew he was alone. Sunul wondered how long it would take for him to freeze, the temperature inside the ship was going to drop precipitously to nearly absolute zero. He had to act quickly if he was going to save the engines, the fuel, and himself.

Fortunately, the engineers had not considered anyone would remain on the derelict craft, so they had not shut down the computer system. It would run until the battery power was depleted. Sunul sat at the main console and accessed the engine control program, then the video cameras so he could observe 5K23m. He shut down all the other keyboards and displays to conserve battery life. The moon was moving ahead of the ship, so he would have to apply enough thrust to come alongside the icy moon and figure a way to dock. The original docking cables had been disabled.

He felt like he was on a freeway moving at sixty miles per hour and the moon was in the fast lane moving at sixty-five or more mph, but he was drifting farther away radially as well as falling behind. He checked the video display of the surface of the moon in the vicinity of the docking area and noticed a blinking light. Was someone trying to signal him or just let him know where the docking area was? He hoped Gina was at the other end of that twinkling beam. She would know how to communicate using Morse code.

When Gina heard the airlock slam shut and seal, followed by four small explosions, she knew what had occurred. Sunul was back on the ship, trying to get control to maneuver into position to reattach to the moon, but the original explosive barbs on cables were no longer available. She grabbed a high intensity diode lamp and moved to the nearest observation porthole. She turned toward the Griswalts and yelled, "Rob, is there a cargo door that we can open?"

"Just a minute, let me check." Rob brought up a schematic of the complex on a display, and, using his finger, traced across the diagram to the mechanical operations center. Yes, there was a large rectangular door that he estimated to be large enough to hold the leading twenty feet of the ship Sunul was trying to dock manually for the first time.

Rob answered Gina, "Yes. There's a large access door about thirty-yards from here—but there's no atmosphere. I'll suit up and get to the mechanical bay. Tell him to stick his nose in there and I'll attach a cable to him. Tell him to be gentle." Rob laughed and moved down the corridor to get into his EVA suit. As Rob moved down the long passageway to the mechanical bay, he yelled back at Gina, "Tell Sunul I'll flood the bay with light from laser torches. He'll be able to see the opening without using any ship lights. I should have it ready in about ten minutes."

Gina began signaling Sunul that they were ready to help him dock the ship back on the moon. She asked if he had enough oxygen and he answered back with yes. He said he was starting to get cold, but he would wait to use the heater in the suit until absolutely necessary. Gina told him she could see the ship approaching, but he should not try to dock as before, instead use the large bay about 100 feet away. The opening would be large enough to house the front end of the ship. Rob would set cables to lock onto it.

Gina had been concentrating on the console and figured out how to use the radio to talk with Sunul. She flashed him a message to turn on his com channel.

"Gina, did I get your message right? Rob's going to light up the mechanical bay so I can see where to dock?"

"That's correct." She looked at her watch and said, "The bay should light up about now. Rob said to be gentle. Oh, Sunul, keep your suit on. There's no pressure in the bay."

"Right. There it is! I see it, but it looks too small from here. I'll try to stick the ship in as slowly as possible. I hope he can tie a cable onto me. He might have to puncture the skin of the ship and insert a hook of some sort. As soon as I get close to the opening, I'm killing the engines and drifting in. I don't want Rob to get injured by the ship hitting too hard."

"Don't worry, Sunul. Rob's a clever guy. Be careful."

"Right. Oh, I just thought of something. The cables that held us in place while we used the Jetway might be dangerous when I hit. Their inertia might whip them around. Warn Rob to watch out for flailing tentacles."

Rob's eyes were locked on the ship as it slowly approached. Everything seemed to be in slow motion, but he knew the moon was moving several thousand miles per hour, the ship not quite as fast as it came toward the cargo bay. Two of the arresting cables could be seen as the ship came closer to the moon. When the separation of the two masses was around ten meters, the ship nearly filled the bay opening. Rob anticipated the arresting cables whipping about when the ship collided with the moon, so, at the last second, he moved behind a large support beam for protection.

There was a massive vibration when the ship hit and two of the cables snaked through the vacuum, lashing about like the tail of a blind dragon, trying to kill its hunter. He waited a few seconds and grabbed one of the ship's cables, quickly tied a cable attached to the bay wall to it and pulled the cables as tightly as possible. Then he went for the other cable and followed the same procedure. If the ship was going to get away, it would have to extract most of the moon base with it.

"Rob, be careful of the cables attached to the ship!" Gina's voice came over the com unit in Rob's EVA suit.

Rob commented, "Now she tells me."

"Sorry, Rob, but I just figured out how to talk to you in your suit. Sunul asked me how to get him from the ship back to the moon's quarters—any ideas?"

"Yeah, give me a minute to look around."

Rob checked the supply cabinets and found a laser cutting torch, as well as an old oxy-acetylene torch that was a relic from the past. He passed up the gas system, preferring the much easier to handle laser. He radioed back to Gina, but Sunul heard Rob. The suit-to-suit com system was now functioning.

Gina announced, "I think you should be able to talk to each other now, gentlemen."

"Thanks, Gina. Sunul, I've got a laser cutting torch. I'm going to cut through the wall of the ship. Don't come forward until I tell you to."

"Roger, Rob. I'll be waiting. Do it quickly, I'm starting to feel a little cold. My battery-operated suit warmer must not be working properly."

Rob began to cut a hole about a meter in diameter, but as he punctured the ship wall, a self-sealing material began to ooze from the hole, resealing the puncture. "We've got a problem, Sunul, the PeneSeal membrane won't allow me to cut through the wall of the ship. Can you remove a piece of the membrane?"

"I'll try. Where are you trying to get through it? Knock on the ship's skin and I'll locate where you're trying to cut through."

"Right. Here goes." Rob began striking the outside of the ship with the composite handle of the laser torch.

Inside, Sunul realized that without an atmosphere, he wasn't going to hear the rapping, so he touched his headgear to the inside wall of the ship, listened, and then moved in the direction that increased the noise level. He had to move behind a wall that separated the pressurized living quarters from the ship's reinforcing structure. He kept talking to Rob as he made progress toward the rapping noise.

"How far are you from the nose of the ship, Rob?"

"It looks like four meters, Sunul. Can you tell where you are?"

"Yes. The construction crew left markings on the structures. It looks like I'm about two meters shy of your tapping, but further progress is impossible; the passageway is too narrow."

"Okay. Locate a seam on the PeneSeal membrane, slice through it, and put something in the opening to keep the membrane from resealing. Once you get about a foot of it separated, you'll be able to pull it out of the way. The membrane can't seal such a large gap; it only works for small tears and punctures."

"I have to back out, find something to keep the membrane from resealing and return. You can stop the noise. I know where to remove the PeneSeal." Sunul went to the nearest living area and searched through the storage compartments but found nothing. The storage cells were all empty. He skipped Gina's and his room and went to the medical area, figuring the rest of the crew had stripped everything useful from their quarters.

He opened every compartment of the medical room but found nothing. Gina had done a masterful job of cleaning. He stood back, wiggling his fingers to keep blood circulating in his hands, and suddenly remembered. There was a blanket below the pull-out patient table. He hoped that Gina hadn't noticed it. She hadn't had to do much medical work during the trip between the moons.

Sunul pushed the table into the wall and released the catch on the compartment door below. The door swung open and there it was—the blanket that would save his life. He jerked it out and made his way back to the spot where Rob was going to cut through the ship's skin. As he returned, he had to laugh at the mess he had made of the rooms he had searched. He withdrew the utility knife from his waist pack and began cutting, stuffing the blanket into the gouge as he sliced the membrane open. When he had cut a triangle about two feet on each side, he stood and pulled the blanket back, exposing the metallic wall of the ship.

"Rob, I've done it. Start cutting, my ass is freezing."

"Okay. Step back—when the laser cuts through, it doesn't stop for EVA suits."

Sunul did as he was told. He watched the metal melt in a curved track as Rob cut a hole big enough for Sunul to crawl through. It took nearly ten minutes before the opening was large enough, but as soon as the somewhat circular hole was completed, Rob stuck his head in the ship and reached for Sunul, who was hardly able to move. As soon as Sunul had cleared the ship, Rob carried him to the mechanical bay access door and entered the pressure equalization chamber. Rob latched the door and hit the ATMOSPHERE-IN wall panel pad. When the atmospheric pressure had reached seventy percent, Rob removed his and Sunul's head gear.

"How are you doing, Sunul?"

He grinned, "Am I still at the South Pole?"

"We should be nearing the tropics. Let's get your suit off so you can warm up faster."

"Tell Gina to get in here; she'll warm me up fast."

Rob picked up his EVA suit and talked into the microphone. "Gina, bring us something warm to drink. What would you like, Sunul? Milk?"

"Are you kidding? I need something more festive. I'm celebrating being rescued and saving four good engines and the remaining fuel."

"Did you hear that, Gina?"

"Sure did. I'll be there in a couple of minutes."

CHAPTER 11
SALVAGING ENGINES AND FUEL

Gina was waiting inside the airlock to the cargo/mechanical bay. Rob and Sunul were running in place and swinging their arms trying to warm up. Sunul seemed to be the colder of the two men; Gina handed him a container and a plastic spoon. His hands were shaking so badly he could barely grip the spoon, so Gina took it from him and they sat down together. When she opened the container, steam bellowed out. Sunul looked inside, took a sniff, frowned, and said, "Chili beans?"

"Uh-huh. These are going to warm your insides and get you producing methane," she laughed. She held out the other container and a spoon to Rob. He sat down with them and said, "I like chili beans, bring 'em on."

"No beans for you, Rob. You get chicken noodle soup."

"What? Chicken noodle soup? Why not chili beans?"

"Your medical profile indicates soup, any variety. I chose chicken noodle." She smiled, "Just like your grammy made. Remember, I'm your physician. Be happy it's not clam chowder, you're allergic to clams."

A half-hour later Sunul and Rob were back at their stations checking out every detail of the moon complex. The computer system was made of eight co-processors sending and receiving data from and to all sections of the system. The central processor could respond to audible instructions from anywhere within the complex, but not with the EVA suits. Gina had discovered how to communicate with each of the EVA suits specifically or as a group. An EVA suit was selected by voice commands to the main CPU. She instructed each of the crew how to talk from their suit to any other, or to the entire group.

Hugh and Triel were immersed in work in the growing chambers, which had to be monitored every day. The plants had to be harvested once a week. Hydroponic gardens had been developed following the 2053 revolt of the garden workers' union. Everyone on planet earth could now grow their own food with almost no assistance from professional growers. For those people living in extreme environments, each continent possessed a linkup to call for assistance. Each hotline was an automated center for the retrieval of information pertinent to at least ninety-nine percent of all questions. When the computer failed an agronomist was available for consultation 24/7.

Sunul repaired his EVA suit, labeled SB1, with Rob's assistance so he wouldn't have to rely on using his backup suit, SB2. Although the suits were identical, Sunul preferred the one he had used in training. He had used his initials and added the numbers 1 and 2. Gina suggested the labels were due to Sunul's interest in barred spiral galaxies. Sunul ignored her whimsical notion, he used the numbers one and two, rather than a and b. She thought he had ignored her joking because of his episode of near freezing. However, he was thinking of how to salvage the engines and fuel from the recently abandoned spaceshuttle.

"Hey, Rob, come here for a moment. I need some info about the fuel tanks on our vacated spacecraft."

Rob left Leanne working at one of the consoles and with a partial frown, approached Sunul. He was wondering what Sunul had in mind after their extreme cold experience. He was beginning to doubt the need to recover the engines and fuel from the moon-to-moon taxi, although there was some wisdom in the plan. He didn't want to admit it.

"What can I do for you, Sunul?"

"How are the fuel tanks uncoupled from the ship? How difficult is it going to be to recover the fuel, or is it even necessary?"

"There are couplings inside the ship for fuel flow. The fuel is kept from freezing by heat from the nuclear engines centered in each spheroid. Engine controls and fuel flow valves can be accessed from wall panels. They're pressure sensitive—easy to remove. We don't have any replacement fuel if we bleed off what we have."

"What happens when the fuel flow coupling is released? Does the fuel escape?"

Rob thought for a second and replied, "Not a problem. By now, with the engines shut down, the fuel should be frozen solid."

Sunul responded, "Damn, I hoped we could pump the fuel out and store it while we recover the spheroids."

"We don't need to do that. We can detach the three working spheroids from the ship and store them in the cargo hold. We'll recover the damaged tank, cut it up and use it for fuel."

"What about the engine in the center of the tank?"

"I'll set up a remote actuator and have it pull out the spider control rods. The reactor will go critical and boom! Or we can build a time delayed device to pull the rods. We can push the reactor away from us, let it drift away and then blow it."

"All right, I guess you know what we need to do. How do we get the working spheroids off the old ship and into the cargo hold?" Sunul was concerned about the amount of work that would necessitate using the EVA suits. Working outside the complex was always dangerous.

"In the EVA suits, it will take some time, even with two of us working. We can attach a cable, release a tank, and pull it into the cargo bay by hand. The gravity is so small here, we could muscle the tank into the bay." Rob had just suggested the course of action that Sunul agreed was the best approach, maybe the only practical procedure.

"Can we restart the engines?"

Rob scratched his head and said, "I don't think that will be a problem. I can restart them manually but running them from the control panel in the complex might not be so easy, but I'll figure it out. I have to make some screw eyes for the tips of the tanks. We'll also attach a cable to the coupling where the spheroids are attached to the ship. Two cables will give us more control over the tanks."

"How long will it take to make what you need?"

"Give me an hour. I'll alert you when I'm ready."

It took nearly four eight-hour work shifts to disengage the fuel tanks and their fuel, now solidified, from the nuclear propulsion units and tow them into the cargo bay. The empty tank was the easiest to handle, but they developed the technique so the remaining tanks, though partially filled with fuel, were handled without incident. Rob commented several times that the designers and engineers hadn't made the units to be dismantled with ease. After the fuel tanks were secured in the cargo bay, Rob and Sunul sat in the galley drinking coffee, discussing the problem with the engines; two and a half days had passed since they had begun work on the tanks.

Rob held a pen and sketched the nose of a rocket module. Sunul asked, "Is there a release on the inside of the ship like the tanks had?"

Rob stopped drawing and looked at Sunul. "Yeah, two of them. They're much bulkier than the tank connecters. But we can't get at them until the engine is released. The engine will float away before we can attach a cable to it. So, we'll cut a hole in the front of the engine cover and insert a screw eye. The PeneSeal will form a bond to the screw eye and we can attach our cable. Then we'll release the coupling and pull in the engine.

Sunul smiled and said, "Good idea, Rob. Have you got four screw eyes?"

"Hell no, I'll have to make them. It'll only take another hour. I just have to program the small equipment assembler." He held the pen up to Sunul and continued, "They only need to be about this big."

Sunul stood up, gave Rob a pat on the back and said, "Good man. Let me know when you've got them made. As soon as we salvage the engines, I want to eject the rest of that ship from our moon. Then we'll set course for Alpha Centauri."

Three and a half hours later, the first engine was secured in the cargo bay and the second one was being pulled through the opening in front of the ship that was jutting halfway out of the cargo area into space. Rob and Sunul alternated the EVA work attaching the screw eye and cable to the engine fairing and releasing the connectors from inside the ship. Rob was initially fearful they would lack the amount of cable necessary to tow the engines and secure them, but he found a large spool of cable the engineers had unintentionally left behind.

It had been marked *RETURN TO EARTH* in large red letters. With their oxygen levels running low, they returned to the warmth and safety of the moon complex.

Jar'l had just gotten up and was sitting at the galley table eating when Rob and Sunul joined him.

"How's the salvage business?"

"We're halfway there," Rob replied, as he grinned and stretched his arms and legs. His arms were tired, but his legs were somewhat stiff from lack of use. Nearly all control of motion in the nearly weightless environment was being accomplished by use of hands and arms. The EVA suits did not allow for unrestricted movement; pushing and pulling occasionally caused some muscle strain.

Jar'l acknowledged with a nod and squeezed some hot coffee between his lips. He swallowed hard and said, "I got a message from earth, they want us to leave orbit for Alpha Centauri in twenty-eight hours. Will you be finished with the engine recovery and be able to jettison the ship by then?"

Sunul glanced at Rob and answered, "Yeah, we've got enough time to finish. I'll be glad to push that hulk out into space. What's left won't be of any use to anyone—unless they want some cushioned seats."

The two salvagers ate high-protein meals and drank eight ounces of water before continuing the operations in the cargo bay. After completing the recovery of the third engine, Rob and Sunul took a break, removed their EVA suits, and visited the restroom. They had missed scheduled sleep times by four hours, so they both took a four-hour nap before they went back to work.

They worked quickly so they could resume their normal sleep-work cycle. When the last engine was secured in the cargo hold, Rob released all but one of the cables holding the ship in place.

While Rob was releasing the ship's constraints, Sunul arranged two cables as tethers for Rob and himself. They tethered themselves to the cargo hold, released the last cable holding the ship to the moon, leaned against the ship and gave a powerful shove to the nose of the stripped spacecraft.

They stepped back from the opening of the cargo hold and watched the degraded ship drift away, gradually falling behind the moon, and slowly turning end-over-end. When the cargo hold hatch was closed, they would probably never see their old ship again. They checked the cables restraining the engines and fuel tanks, moved to the air lock, and extinguished the laser lights.

Back in the main control suite, Gina put down her e-book module, looked at Sunul, and asked, "All finished?"

"Yes, ma'am. We're both glad that's finished. It was a lot more work than I had anticipated, but after the first unit was stored, the others were salvaged much easier; we developed an efficient routine."

"We've got about twelve hours before we begin the last stage of our journey, are you going to try to get some rest?"

Sunul slumped into his console position and read the latest messages from earth.

"Gina! It says we're going to be put to sleep for twenty minutes when the rockets fire to put us on course to Alpha Centauri. What the hell is that about?"

"I received a similar message, but with an explanation. The engineers think there is a finite probability the engines won't fire in the proper sequence and the moon might start an erratic spin cycle. They think we might become alarmed and try to do something that might make the situation worse, so we're all going to be put asleep until the moon's trajectory is stable."

Sunul thought about it for a minute and replied, "I don't like it. I'm more than a little suspicious of those twits back on earth. There's no way we could be spinning out of control. The engines aren't powerful enough to cause erratic rotation of our little moon. They might be able to cause some rotation once we're out of the gravitational attraction of Kuiper 5K23, but nothing to worry about. I don't want to be anesthetized. Do you know what the agent is?"

Gina smiled and said, "Uh-huh, nitrous oxide—laughing gas. It's what dentists used before the law changed in the 2060's."

"How do I avoid it?"

Gina laughed, "You could hold your breath for twenty minutes."

"Look, I'm not joking. How do I avoid going to sleep? Can I breathe oxygen?"

Gina thought for a few seconds before replying. "Sure. I can give you a nasal cannula and one of our portable oxygen cylinders. You can put the cylinder under your seat where it will be out of the way. You will be breathing mostly oxygen, but a little nitrous oxide will get into your system. It won't be enough to anesthetize you though."

"Okay. That's what I want to do. I don't want to lose control of my mental faculties. I want to experience everything firsthand. Let's set it up so no one else will know about it. I don't want to use up all our bottled oxygen too quickly, we might need some for other reasons. The amount we get from plant growth is generated slowly."

When other crewmembers were either out of the command stations eating, gaming, or in bed, Sunul and Gina fabricated Sunul's oxygen breathing apparatus. Several hours later, when the cabins were flooded with nitrous oxide, Sunul quickly attached the nasal cannula and turned the oxygen to a preset level. He relaxed and watched as the rockets were scheduled to fire. He didn't feel anything. As far as he could tell, nothing happened.

A minute passed, then two, and then he saw Hugh Patel, wearing a breathing apparatus, moving to the main command console, sit, and insert a memory module into the main computer memory-access receptacle.

CHAPTER 12
CAUGHT IN THE ACT

Before Sunul could retrieve the portable oxygen cylinder from beneath him in order to move around the control room, Hugh had entered an access code and the main computer had down-loaded the contents of the memory module. REMOVE MODULE appeared on the screen in flashing red letters.

Sunul carried his oxygen supply with him, came from behind Hugh, and said, "What the hell are you doing?"

Hugh was startled, not expecting anyone to be observing, much less, questioning his actions. He gasped, dropped the module, and turned toward the voice. "Damn, Sunul, you scared the crap out of me. You aren't supposed to be awake."

"Neither are you. I'll ask you again, what are you doing?"

"When we were on earth's moon, I was given a small package and instructed to down-load its contents into the main computer. They said to do it when everyone was anesthetized. Someone put this breather in my clothing case. That's all I know. I just followed orders."

"Didn't you ask what the module contained?"

"There wasn't anyone to ask. The instructions were on my private com unit. They told me not to tell Triel or anyone else."

"Hmm. I wonder what secrets you downloaded. Now I'm really

suspicious. Aren't you wondering what files were in that module?"

"Yeah, but I don't think I would know what they were if I saw them."

"Well, let's take a look." Sunul reached out and Hugh put the module in his hand after picking it up from the floor. Hugh stood up and moved away from the console so Sunul could take his place. Sunul inserted the module and scanned it to investigate the code. It was blank; any information it had contained had been erased. "So, someone didn't want us to see what was done to the computer, but why?" He scratched his head and exhaled. A message appeared on the console screen; ANESTHESIA IS BEING EXHAUSTED. Sunul glanced at Hugh and said, "Everyone will be awake in a few minutes. We'll tell them what transpired."

Sunul tried, without success, to determine what code had been downloaded. He wanted to find what part of the main program had been altered, or what had been added, especially if it would affect control of the moon's propulsion system. Jar'l would be the next crew member with whom to discuss potentially malicious code. Sunul's salient thought was: "What if the instructions Hugh had received were not from the International Space Agency?" He looked for a copy of the original programs, but even the back-up systems had been altered. He sat, frustrated, turning a small plastic disk over and over from finger to finger, waiting for Jar'l to recover from the nitrous oxide-induced slumber. His check with the medical index indicated the recovery time from the nitrous oxide should be about thirty minutes.

As Sunul sat thinking about the attempt to anesthetize the crew, save one member, he realized there had been no sudden acceleration or other effect, nothing that would require the crew to be secured to their seats, since the nitrous oxide had flooded the ship. Had the moon actually left its orbit around 5K23 and headed toward Alpha Centauri?

He asked the computer, "Please provide telescopic images of Neptune from cameras EQ-1 and EQ-3." Sunul had reasoned if the moon were on course for Alpha Centauri, the equatorial cameras, separated by one-hundred-eighty degrees, should be able to focus on Neptune, about twenty-eight astronomical units behind them. He waited about five minutes for the cameras to find their target, record images, and relay them to the main viewing screen. As the images appeared, Sunul was joined by Jar'l, still a little groggy, but able to communicate clearly.

Sunul removed his oxygen supply cannula, shut off the flow of gas, and said, "Have a seat, Jar'l. I've got something to discuss with you."

"What's going on? Didn't you go under with the rest of us?"

"Nope. Hugh and I stayed alert. He downloaded some data into the computer—something he was instructed to do when we were on earth's moon. It was supposed to be done secretly, but I caught him. He was just a pawn, he didn't know what was contained in the memory module, but whatever it was, I can't determine whether it was good or bad."

"You think it would be something to sabotage our voyage?"

"I hope not. We could be stuck out here with no way to return if we haven't started toward Alpha Centauri."

"You think we're not on our way?"

"Except for the surreptitious data transfer to the computer, there was no reason for the anesthesia. I was wide awake and felt no changes in vibration, no jostling about requiring constraints—nothing to necessitate the use of nitrous oxide."

"Now you've got my attention. What can we do to investigate?"

"I just took some telescopic shots of Neptune from equatorial cameras one and three. I want to see if there is any parallax; there should be a slight difference in the backgrounds of the two pictures." Sunul glanced at the display and the two camera images had appeared. He overlaid the two images and asked the computer, "Computer. Display any differences in the two images." The screen turned dark. "Computer. Display image differences, please."

"TASK COMPLETED. IS IT NOT WHAT YOU DESIRED?"

"Yes. I just failed to consider these results. Thank you." Sunul glanced at Jar'l and commented, "Either only one camera is functioning, and copying the data, or the picture is one from computer memory, duplicated as shots from both cameras. We should be seeing a slight doubling of the background stars near the edge of Neptune, and we have nothing. How do you explain these results?"

"Your analysis is as good as or better than mine. Since we'll have no luck trying to investigate the computer, we could slide out one of the wormholes and take a look at the camera; at least we could tell if it's functioning."

Sunul laughed, "Wormholes?"

"Yeah. That's what those small access tunnels are called. Whoever named them must have been reading some sci-fi books, but we can get to the cameras and the engines through them."

"Good. Another thing I want to investigate is an engine. I don't think any of our ice moon engines are operational. What appears to us on the display panels is artificial—I believe it's being produced by the computer to simulate engine thrust."

"You think we're still in orbit around 5K23?"

"That's correct."

"Hmm. That would mean the material that's being fed to the engines is just piling up on the surface; it's too cold to be evaporating. When do you want to take a trip out there?"

"The sooner, the better. What have you planned for the next couple of hours?"

Jar'l thought for a second and replied, "I need to check the main reactor; I'm sure it's working, or we would lose power and atmosphere, but I check it once a day. It'll take about fifteen minutes, then we'll have to suit up."

"Okay. While you're busy, I'll check our EVA suits. Will we need extra oxygen?"

"I don't think so. There's a battery-operated magnetic-rail system we ride the seven-tenths kilometer to the sites. It takes about two minutes to get there. We'll join two dollies together; they're more stable that way." Jar'l started toward the reactor access door but suddenly stopped, completed an about-face, and said, "On second thought, Sunul, maybe you should include an extra oxygen cylinder for each of us. I don't expect any problems, but the way things are going, we'd better not take any chances." Jar'l waved to Monel as he entered the access door to the main reactor. She was talking animatedly with Triel and Gina. The women looked unhappy, especially Triel.

Sunul was in his EVA suit waiting for Jar'l next to the hatch leading to the mechanical compartment where the salvaged engines and fuels tanks were stored. He hadn't attached his headgear yet; it was easier for crewmen to use the buddy system to ensure a proper seal. When Jar'l joined him, Sunul asked, "Have you gone out to one of the engines or cameras before?" He received a short answer, "Nope."

After they assisted each other attaching and sealing headgears, they entered the airlock. Jar'l pressed the red evacuate panel and they waited, watching the digital pressure indicator drop to zero. Jar'l led the way to one of the two arrays of three hatchways imprinted with either equatorial or polar marks. The other set of three hatchways was on the opposite wall. The hatches were about a meter in diameter, big enough so that a crewman, wearing an EVA suit, could move unencumbered on a six-foot-long dolly, but with little extra room for carrying anything but small tools or replacement equipment parts.

Jar'l popped the hatch to camera EQ-1, which also led to engine E1. As the door swung open Jar'l motioned for Sunul to enter the opening. Sunul bent to go in head-first, but Jar'l stopped him and motioned to enter feet-first. Sunul grabbed a horizontal bar above the hatch and inserted his legs into the wormhole and wiggled his way onto the dolly. As soon as Sunul was in place, Jar'l pushed Sunul's dolly forward, inserted a second dolly into the tunnel, latched the two transport devices together, climbed in, and got comfortable. They began to move, slowly at first, but their speed increased, much like a sled or toboggan moving downhill in snow, until the inside walls were flashing by. LED bulbs, mounted along the ceiling, blinked as they passed through the wormhole.

Suddenly, the motion began to decrease as the dolly decelerated, and the two men came to a stop, as if they had been on an elevator. A light came on illuminating the bottom of a twenty-foot-high cylinder, five-meters in diameter. There was a large open tunnel, marked E1 with red LEDs, which led to the right. On the wall, opposite the tunnel, an arrow outlined in blue LEDs, labeled EQ-1, pointed straight up.

Sunul pointed at the tunnel, "You check the engine, and I'll climb up to the telescopic camera." The camera-telescope combination was mounted on the top of a triangular spire that extended about three meters above the surface of the moon. Sunul extended his right hand, grabbed the rung slightly above his head and pulled. Twenty-four hand-over-hand motions put him adjacent to the automated telescope. It looked as if it were pointed back toward the position of Neptune, but he had to be sure that it was functioning properly.

"Gina, please point camera EQ-1 toward Alpha Centauri. Tell me when the reorientation is complete." Sunul watched the telescope-camera assemblage, expecting to see it rotate 180 degrees, but nothing happened.

"Okay, Sunul. The computer says the operation has been performed."

"Thanks, Gina. We should be back in about ten minutes."

"See you then."

Sunul reversed his hands on the rungs and descended to the bottom of the cylinder.

Jar'l was waiting for him. "Sunul, the fuel for the engine is just being dumped on the outside surface. There is no reactor core—there's no internal engine at all, just the outer shell."

"Okay. Let's return to the complex. The camera is not working either. The images we saw were computer generated. We need to gather the crew and figure out what we're going to do."

"Any ideas?" Jar'l quizzed.

"Uh-huh, but they're going to require some difficult work. We'd better discuss our findings with the others first—before I tell you my plan."

"Come on, buddy, give me a hint."

Sunul laughed, "Don't get excited, you'll use up all your oxygen."

When the two men arrived at the cargo hold, Jar'l climbed down from the wormhole first, removed his dolly from the tunnel and pulled Sunul's dolly to the opening. As he waited for Sunul to get to his feet, he surveyed the contents of the cargo hold. He suddenly had an aha moment. He was sure he had figured out what Sunul wanted to do. He would wait and see what Sunul was going to say to the rest of the crew, although keeping it to himself was not going to be easy.

They entered the airlock and waited for it to fill with a breathable atmosphere. As the pressure rose to seventy-five percent of normal, they removed their headgear and began divesting themselves of their EVA suits. As they walked down the hallway to the main control room, Sunul turned to Jar'l and asked, "Why have you been so quiet? You usually talk my leg off when we return from an EVA mission."

Jar'l replied, "I've been thinking of what you're going to say to the crew. I think I know your plan. It will take some inventiveness to do it, though."

Sunul commented, "I was thinking you might figure it out when we passed through the cargo area."

CHAPTER 13
THE PLAN

Jar'l spoke to the crew first, explaining what he had found at the E1 engine site. When he said there was no engine at all, just the outer housing, Leanne questioned, "So that confirms that we're still in orbit around 5K23?"

"Exactly. Sunul has more to tell you."

Sunul explained what he had discovered about the telescopic camera. Hugh and Triel stood up simultaneously, the outrage showing on their faces.

Triel looked around at everyone and asked, "What can we do to get out of this mess? We seem to be stuck on this moon and for how long? Will someone come to rescue us? I hope to heaven we're not going to be stuck here for twenty years!"

Hugh asked, "What plan did the space agency have, anyway? Are we just going to be sacrificed to see how long we can survive in space? Have you contacted the agency, Sunul?"

"No. Jar'l and I just discovered the information we relayed to you. I have an idea though. Let me tell you what I would like to do. If it works, it will surprise the hell out of the agency; they sure won't expect what we can do." He grinned and said, "We'll give earth another large space station."

There were some frowns and smiles that rippled through the crew.

They had confidence in Sunul. Whatever plan he had; it was bound to work. They all sat back and listened attentively as he started to advance his ideas.

"Okay. I haven't done any calculations yet, so I don't know how effective this will be, but you all know our little moon is mostly composed of ices that on earth would normally be gases. Our earth buddies didn't expect us to have a way to return, but we have four engines that Hugh and I salvaged from our old ship. The core of each engine emits a reasonable amount of thermal energy, enough to turn our surroundings to gases. Those gases can be directed out the exhausts of the fake engines, giving us enough thrust to break free from 5K23. The only problem is either moving the engines from the cargo hold to the fake engine sites or making some sort of conduit to transport the gases."

Several hands went up, so he stopped to answer the questions. Triel was the closest, so he called on her.

"Why don't we use the four salvaged engines to move the moon?"

"They're only able to use the fuel we brought with us. If that fuel is used up, we'll have no way to move toward the sun, or only at an exceedingly slow velocity. It might take us years to get back to earth."

Leanne asked, "How long will it take to escape from 5K23 the way you described, years?"

"I'm not sure but let me tell you what I think is a better option. I only related plan B, now let me give you plan A." He smiled as if he was going to tell them a secret.

The other hands dropped, and the room became quiet again as they waited to hear about plan A.

Gina had to say something. "I hope this one sounds better, Sunul."

Sunul laughed. "Shush! I think this plan is far superior, and it might be more entertaining."

"Entertaining? How will it be entertaining to us?"

"Not us, dear, those back on earth." The entire crew was smiling now.

"First of all, Rob and Leanne are going to make us some hair dryers. Second, we'll start subliming the ices covering the outside of our living quarters. When our complex is no longer covered with solids, we're going to back off the moon, fire up our salvaged engines and head back to earth. My rough calculations indicate our travel time will be about six months, but right now, that's just a guess."

Jar'l grinned and asked, "When will the earthlings see us, Commander?"

"Hah! Good question! Spoken like a true alien, Jar'l." Everyone laughed and applauded. Sunul smiled, realizing everyone was on board with plan A."

"Due to the size of the complex, I believe astronomers will detect us at about five astronomical units from the sun, or roughly, when we have progressed to Jupiter's orbit. Since our mission was secret, the space agency will have an interesting time explaining us to the public and to the military. The public will think we are aliens!"

Monel asked, "So we're going to maintain radio silence?"

Sunul thought for a moment and replied, "Well, if earth communicates with anyone, tell them everything is functioning normally, and you are enjoying the trip. If you reply to any message, just act normally; we don't want to divulge our plan."

Triel said, "What if they let the military believe we are aliens and they try to shoot us down?"

Sunul looked at Jar'l and asked, "Can we transmit directly to the military, Jar'l? Not just text, but pictorial data?"

"Sure, we can change our broadcast frequency to correspond with any of the United States Air Force communication network frequencies. I was going to say that I would post them on the computer, but the computer might not accept the data. There's no telling what the agency has anticipated. I'll post a list of important frequencies from my personal com-module."

"So, if the agency threatens to exterminate us, we can send our pictures, and bio-data to the military. That will keep them from doing anything drastic, unless, of course, the commander-in-chief orders them to get rid of us."

Gina was concerned and commented, "Do you really think President Peele would order us destroyed?"

Sunul answered, "Who knows? She's only the second woman president of the United States and she probably won't do anything rash, but remember, the last one was unpredictable, and almost got us into war with China and Russia simultaneously."

"Yes, but that was nearly thirty years ago. Things have changed."

Rob laughed, "Does anything ever change in DC?"

Rob and Leanne joined Gina and Sunul. Rob began to quiz Sunul about the hair dryers. "What do you have in mind to melt the ices around the complex?"

"I don't really care how you do it, Rob. We need to warm the ice, which is primarily methane, by about ninety degrees Celsius. It will melt and we can drain it off from the complex in a warmed tube of some sort. If you can get the temperature up another twenty degrees, the methane will be a gas. We can exhaust it to the surface where it will condense as methane snow, or if ejected, it will float some distance away from us before settling on the surface."

"Okay. Leanne and I will get right on it and have something by tomorrow."

"Sounds good." Sunul yawned and stretched his arms. "I've got to get some sleep, so I'll be out for eight hours. Let us know if you need anything. We'll see if we can help out. Jar'l will be available while I'm sleeping."

Gina woke Sunul by shaking his shoulder and calling him. "Sunul, something has come up. It's important."

Sunul frowned and squinted, even though the bedroom light was set at twenty percent. "What is it? Did someone get hurt? Was it Rob or Leanne?" He sat up and swung his bare legs out from under the comforter.

"Nothing like that. I got up early, about a half-hour ago and ran the weekly urine tests. All the women are pregnant."

"You, too?"

"Uh-huh. I said all, Dopey."

"Just making sure, Snow." They both laughed. Sunul then inquired, "Are you sure the test is accurate, or is it something we should check further?"

"I'll run another sample in eight hours just to confirm the tests."

"I hope no one has any cravings for things we don't have in the complex. That might be interesting." He grinned at Gina and climbed into clean underwear.

Gina sat on the bed. "Aren't you happy we're going to have a baby?"

"More concerned than happy, Gina. This is something I didn't anticipate in the slightest. Four pregnant women cooped up in the complex might provide for some interesting situations. I wonder who on earth wanted this to take place. Four babies born in space will make interesting headlines though."

"Don't you think we'll make it home for the births?"

"I really don't know. We'll have to see how long it takes to get free of this moon. Once that happens, we can use the salvaged rockets for propulsion, but our speed won't be anything near what it was coming out to the Kuiper belt. We'll have a critical problem; not enough fuel remains for us to move very fast and then slow down as we approach earth. I'm only guessing, but it might take us six months to get back to earth. That's provided we don't encounter any major problems. I wish we had a way to make oxygen; with all the methane out here, we'd have an unlimited supply of fuel."

"Well, finish dressing and we'll give the crew the good news."

Sunul put on his trousers, tunic, and belt, then stepped into his magnetic shoes. "Who should be awake?"

"The Masons and the Griswalts are awake. The Patels have been sleeping for four hours,—if they have been following the regular schedule."

When Sunul was fully clothed, they made their way to the galley where he warmed a tube of bacon and eggs in the microwave oven.

"Ugh! How can you stand that stuff?" Gina turned away from Sunul and started down the hall to the main control room.

Sunul followed, saying, "Do you have a little morning sickness?"

"Not yet. I can't stand to look at that concoction. It looks like yellow vomit."

"It tastes better than that. Try some, you'll like the bacon bits, and you can barely detect the eggs. When I eat from the tubes, I don't look at the stuff that comes out."

When the pregnancies were announced, there was no joy, just disbelief. Gina told them she was going to repeat the tests to confirm the results, but she felt the tests had been accurate.

Leanne asked, "What was in that injection we were given to prevent pregnancy?"

Gina responded immediately, "I checked the vial they gave us. It's an isotonic solution. It sure as hell won't prevent pregnancy. This result had to be planned. We're guinea pigs."

Rob stated, "I'm concerned that we might not have enough food for four more people."

Gina remarked, "Babies don't eat very much, Rob."

CHAPTER 14
WATER AND FUEL TANKS

Sunul sat in silence, barely aware of the voices in the background, but he occasionally tuned into the discussion of the pregnancies, although only momentarily, returning to contemplating the removal of the complex from its entrapment in the methane ice. The sooner they could start back toward the sun, and home to earth, the better. He would have to wait for Rob and Leanne to wake up so he could find out the state of the hair dryers. In the meantime, he would run some simulations on the moon escaping from the gravitational attraction of 5K23. The computations would not cause any alarm by the main computer since such calculations would have been carried out by scientists from the space agency when gathering information for travel to Alpha Centauri. After making preliminary estimates, he would sneak in the data for the complex's mass, instead of the moon's mass, hoping the computer would determine the smaller mass was a programming error. He finished his adjustment to the program and saved it under the name *freedom*.

He felt a hand on his shoulder and looked up to see Gina standing beside him holding a plastic bag about half full of a colorless solid material. "Here, Sunul, hold this." He took the bag and could feel the cold solid. Moisture was gathering on the exterior of the bag.

"What is it, Gina?"

"Something you wished for. Rob said there's plenty more where that came from."

"No kidding? Water is all we need to make oxygen! I'll get Jar'l to design a cell for electrolysis of the water. He'll need some platinum electrodes and a direct current power supply. We'll compress the oxygen and fill the damaged fuel tank after we patch the hole. We can use the shells of the moon engines to carry the frozen methane. Now, I have no doubt, we can get back to earth without the worry of running out of fuel." Sunul stood up, grabbed Gina, hugged her and kissed her eyelids.

"No regular kiss?" she grinned.

"I don't want to get excited; I've got things to do. We're all going to have to work to get us off this hunk of ice." Sunul gave her a swat on the rear and called out, "Hey, Rob, I need to know more about the water ice. We have to mine it as if it's gold."

Rob was sitting at his console, designing a better version of the hair dryer. He instructed the computer to save his work and joined Sunul. As he sat down, he stated, "I'll bet you want to know more about the water that's out there."

"Exactly. How much do you estimate we can recover?"

"More than we'll ever need, even if we recover only part of the oxygen and hydrogen from an electrolysis cell. We'll have to put the gases in disposable containers, expose them to the outside temperature where they'll solidify. Then, we can put the solids in the rocket bodies for storage tanks."

"We don't need the hydrogen, Rob, just vent it to the outside."

"Good, that'll save us a lot of work. We'll only need one recovery procedure. But how are we going to get the methane and oxygen ices into the storage tanks?"

Sunul thought for a moment and then replied, "We're going to move the storage vessels into the cargo bay."

"Yeah, but how do you propose to do that? Those moon engine shells are six meters long and nearly three meters in diameter. We'll have to pull them across the surface and drag them into the cargo hold."

"Exactly. You'll need to make a couple dozen pitons and some hammers to drive the pitons into the ice. Then we'll pull the carcasses across the surface—maybe fifty to one hundred meters at a time. And, we'll need one container for the methane and one for the oxygen."

Rob returned to his station and began designing pitons to be cut from quarter inch steel plate with the laser-cutter/fabricator adjacent to the cargo hold. He also devised clips to fasten a rope to the piton and the astronaut. After calculating the distance to the closest engine shell to be about 365 meters, he realized thirty-five-meter ropes would span the distance between pitons if they were located 30 meters apart. The two nearby faux engine locations would be accessed through wormholes, and each team of two would recover an engine shell.

Leanne had joined Rob in the assembly room to help with the equipment. The fabricator had cut the pitons in about a half-hour. She asked, "Which couples are going to bring back the engine shells? Are you going to ask for volunteers, or should the men do it?"

"Hmm, maybe I should see if anyone volunteers to help. Sunul and I have already spent time in our EVA suits." He smiled and continued, "Maybe the biologists should do some outside activities; they should get some fresh air, they've probably been inhaling too much carbon dioxide in the plant growth chambers."

Leanne bumped shoulders with Rob as she laughed, "Yeah, they can have oxygen or a vacuum. We'll let them choose."

The next time the entire crew was awake, approximately four hours later, a meeting was held and the procedure for recovering the rocket shells was discussed. Surprisingly, Hugh and Triel, the biologists, volunteered to retrieve one of the containers, and the Masons decided to bring back the next nearest engine shell, E4, about a hundred meters father away in the opposite direction from the complex than E1, which was assigned to the Patels.

Rob and Leanne explained how they had envisioned the use of the equipment they had manufactured. No one, except Sunul, could suggest any difficulties with their routine.

"How are you going to see the location of the pitons and the end of your rope? It is pitch black out there except for the illumination from your helmet lamps. Sunlight is negligible out here."

Rob answered, "Good point, something I hadn't considered. I'll give each team a package of diode flashers. After a piton is secured into the ice, attach a flasher to it." He smiled and then said, "Don't put the flasher on the piton and then hit the piton; you'll destroy the diode. Once the diode is activated, just press the side tab, the flashing will continue for about an hour before the battery runs down. Recover the pitons and flashers; we might have to use them later. I'll turn on the lights in the cargo hold; you'll be able to see them from four or five pitons out. Beyond that, the curvature of the moon will interfere."

Sunul commented, "The engine shells are strapped to yokes mounted on the surface. Rob and I will remove the straps for you, so you won't need to carry extra tools. We'll travel through the wormholes; the recovery teams will leave from the cargo hold. Okay?"

Triel asked, "How will we know which direction to travel to reach the engines?"

"We'll start you in the correct direction from the hold. After you set the first piton on a high point, attach a flasher and continue out to the next position. You can continue the line until you see the flasher on the engine shell. When Rob and I get the straps off the shells, we'll attach a flasher so you can make a correction to your angle of travel. Remember to keep your tether lines attached to the rope. If you don't, you might push off the surface. Then, you're in real trouble; there's no way back. The moon's gravity is too small to pull you back to the surface. Remember, we don't have any built-in suit thrusters. No flying through space like Flash Gordon."

Sunul's warning was taken very seriously by the recovery teams readying to make the treks across the surface to the engine shells.

Monel turned to Jar'l, grabbed his arm to get his full attention. "You'll come after me if I float off the surface, won't you?"

"Geez, Monel, you're not going to float off into space. Just keep your tether hooked to the ground cable. You'll be fine. We'll be busy pulling that engine shell over the surface and you won't even think about floating off. Besides, if you did happen to get off the surface, I'd toss you a line and pull you back. Don't worry."

"I still worry about floating off and running out of oxygen; it's like a bad dream."

Jar'l wanted to help calm her anxiety, but what could he do except tell her not to worry and he would come after her? "If you want, talk to Gina. Maybe she can give you something to lessen your fears. We need to be in charge of all our faculties, so we don't make mistakes. EVA work is what we've been trained to do."

"I think I'll be all right once I'm at work. Give me something else to think about."

"Think about the baby. What do you want, a girl or a boy?"

Monel hesitated for a second and replied, "Just a healthy baby; I don't care whether it's a girl or a boy. I remember the last astronaut to have a baby in space, Cynthia Moore. Her baby had all kinds of problems after it was back on earth. I think it had inner ear problems. It had trouble with equilibrium. It took about two months to get the kid over the problem."

After they were in their EVA suits and going through the checkout procedure prior to exiting the complex, Sunul briefed the group. "Keep your mind on your job, we don't want any mistakes. We especially don't want anyone to get hurt. Remember, space is dangerous and unforgiving. Gina has set up the com network so we can all hear what you are saying. Don't turn off your com unit!"

The exiting chamber wasn't large enough for six workers, so the two couples went into the cargo/mechanical bay first, followed by Rob and Sunul. Rob began handing out the flashers, hammers, and pitons while

Sunul attached safety clips to the tethers and dispersed the coils of rope and the towing cables. When the couples were ready with their supplies, they gathered at the cargo bay door where Rob and Sunul pointed them in the proper directions.

Rob instructed, "You will be able to see each other's flashers, so line them up with your own and go in opposite directions. I've attached some mirrors to the outer edge of the cargo doors to reflect light from the bay in your direction. You must use your helmet lights to see where you are going; it is completely black out there. Sunul and I will set out for the engine shells and remove the holding straps. Hopefully, when the straps are removed, you will appear at the sites. We'll help you get started back by attaching the pull cables. Try to avoid the craters, go around them unless they are small—a meter in diameter. If you encounter crevasses, or displacements of the surface, secure yourselves to the ropes and jump them."

Triel was the last to put on her headgear. She hesitated and then asked, "Why can't you and Rob take the pull cables with you through the wormholes? We're loaded down with all this paraphernalia."

Rob replied, "The wormholes are a tight fit to anyone in an EVA suit. We're taking the tools to remove the straps and won't have much room. We can't afford to get stuck in the wormholes. There's little room to work our way free."

Triel smiled, "Okay, just curious. Let's get to work!" Sunul and Rob attached and sealed her headgear, then tapped on the lamp mounted on top of the transparent, fishbowl-shaped helmet, signaling she was ready.

CHAPTER 15
MISTAKES

After the two couples were on their way across the surface of the dark icy moon, Rob and Sunul, armed with ratchet wrenches, entered the access hatches and began their rides to the appropriate engine shells. When Sunul arrived at engine one, he ascended the telescope tower, attached an activated flasher with an additional battery pack at the top, and climbed back down to enter the tunnel to the engine shell.

Inspection of the metal bands holding the shell in place indicated he would only have to remove four bolts, two on each band. After removing three of the bolts, he decided to leave the fourth bolt loose, but in place. He wanted to be sure the shell couldn't move from its location. He spoke into his com unit, "Rob, leave the last bolt loose, but don't remove it. Take it out when the towing crew arrives. We don't want a shell to drift away from us, the other ones are too far away to make an easy recovery."

"Right, skipper. I was wondering if I should stay here until they arrive. That answered my question."

"Don't start calling me skipper, I'm not the commander of a boat. Stick with Sunul, okay?"

"All right. I was just reading a book about an old wooden sailing ship and the crew called the captain, skipper. I thought I'd try it out."

"You did. If you call me skipper again, I'm going to start calling you some dumb nickname."

"All right, but skipper is kind of snappy, don't you think?"

"No. You guys voted me captain, but that's not official."

"Sunul! We've got a problem!"

"What's going on, Jar'l?"

"Monel has drifted off the surface! I can't get a line to her to pull her back!"

"Why didn't we hear her say anything?"

"She's too scared to talk. She's tumbling backwards and she can't see me. What can I do?"

"Talk to her and get her calmed down. It'll take me about five minutes to get to you. I'll get her back. Don't worry."

"Okay, hurry. She's terrified."

Sunul crawled on the dolly and kicked the return lever with his foot. He was back in the cargo hold in thirty seconds. He climbed out of the wormhole and opened a heated cabinet, grabbed two fire extinguishers and made his way to the edge of the open cargo hold. The ground cable was gone. Monel and Jar'l had made good progress before the accident.

"Jar'l?"

"Yeah."

"Where are you?"

"At the fourth flasher."

"Okay. I'm coming out to you. I'm using fire extinguishers as small thrusters. Make sure you're secured to the surface; you might have to catch me."

Sunul listened to Jar'l talking to Monel while he hooked one of the extinguishers to his waist utility belt. He hoped the contents of the fire extinguishers wouldn't freeze before he could get Monel in tow. There was no time to insulate the canisters.

Monel was petrified, her biggest worry had become a reality, but Jar'l had gotten her breathing slowed so she wouldn't hyperventilate. On the surface, Sunul faced the cargo hold door opening, pointed the extinguisher at it and pulled the trigger. The one second burst propelled him into space nearly ten meters. He had to be careful to control his motion from flasher to flasher. Using short, controlled bursts, he moved to the third flasher. Above the third flasher, he again adjusted the direction of the thruster, aiming his body at the fourth flasher. He could barely make out Jar'l's helmet lamp, so he made another slight maneuver.

"I can see you, Sunul. Monel is about a hundred meters out, almost above where we would place the fifth flasher. She's really scared. You should talk to her now."

"Okay. I see her."

Sunul could see the faint light from Monel's helmet, rotating slowly against the almost black background. "Monel, I'm on my way. Try to relax. Put your arms and legs out straight and you'll rotate more slowly."

"C-Can you hurry? My oxygen has dropped below thirty percent."

"I'm almost there. When I bump into you, don't do anything. Then, after you hook to my utility belt we'll start back after I stop our spinning. Okay, I'm going to come from the side and then move in front of you. That's when you snap your belt hook to mine. Watch for my helmet light."

"All right. How close are you now?"

"I'm guessing about ten meters, moving very slowly. I don't want to hit you too hard. I'm on your left."

"Oh! I see you. Thank God!"

Sunul had to have Monel attach to him from behind so he still had unobstructed movement of his arms to point the thruster in the proper direction. Just before he collided with Monel, he had taken a look at the light from the cargo hold. He tried to keep his body oriented so the illuminated opening was visible at all times.

"I'm going to count down from five, Monel. When I get to zero, we'll come in contact. Five, four, three, two, one, zero!"

Without Sunul's instructions, Monel grabbed him and they began to tumble very slowly.

"Are you attached?"

"Yes. Thank you!"

"We're not back yet, Monel."

"I'm not terrified any more. I was beginning to think I would never bump into anyone again, but I was hoping Jar'l would come after me; he promised."

"He was too far from the fire extinguishers or he would have. It would have taken him twice as long to get to you."

"You've stopped our spinning. I can see the lights now." Her normal breathing had returned.

"Good. We're starting back. I'm aiming for the cargo hold. It's easy to see and a big target."

Sunul exhausted the last jet from the first fire extinguisher and handed it to Monel. She clipped it to her utility belt and watched Sunul squeeze the trigger on the second bottle. It took eight blasts from the thruster to get them through the opening and into the cargo compartment. When they touched the floor, Monel let out a giant sigh and sagged to the floor, pulling Sunul with her.

"Hey! I've got to join Jar'l and help with that engine shell."

"Oh, I'm sorry, Sunul. I'll unclip us. I'm staying on the floor and counting my lucky stars. Thank you for saving me."

Sunul got up and extended a hand to Monel. "You're welcome,

but you'd better get inside; your oxygen level is getting low. You can tell us what happened when we get that shell in the hold. You'd better get in the transfer chamber. I'll go through the wormhole and help Jar'l bring back the engine covering."

"What about your life-support? What is your oxygen level?"

Sunul checked his gauges. "Thanks for reminding me. My nitrogen is okay, but I need more oxygen. I'll grab another cylinder before I meet Jar'l."

"Maybe you should take Jar'l some, too."

"Good idea. You should get inside and have Gina check you out. We'll see you later."

Sunul dimmed the cargo hold lights, picked up two compact oxygen cylinders from the supplies cabinet and climbed into the wormhole. While on his way, he radioed Jar'l.

"Monel is safe inside. I told her to have Gina check her out. Gina will probably give her something so she can relax. Her pulse is probably running high."

"Thanks, Sunul. She was really scared, but I couldn't do anything from out here. That was smart thinking. I'm not sure I would have thought of using the fire extinguishers as thrusters. Where are you?"

"I'm in the wormhole, almost to the engine site. I'll meet you on the outside. Have you reached position six yet?"

"Yeah. I just set a piton and attached a flasher. I'm moving on. I should see your flasher before long."

"Okay. I'll be waiting. I brought you some more O2, Monel's suggestion. She seems to have recovered. She's thinking straight."

"Yeah, she's pretty tough. I should get to you in about thirty minutes, if I don't float off."

Sunul laughed. "Hey, I don't want to use up all the fire extinguishers."

Gina was giving Monel a quick physical assessment in the pharmacy cubicle. The tears rolling down Monel's cheeks were obvious.

"You're okay now, Monel. You're safe."

"I know, but I have to tell you something. I think I'm going crazy."

"No, you're not crazy. Drifting off the moon's surface was just an accident. There's nothing wrong with you."

Monel wiped the tears away with her fingers and said, "I don't want a baby. I want to kill it."

"What? You're kidding. All the wives are pregnant. Don't you want a child?"

"No. I want it gone. Give me an aborting tablet, please!"

"Not right now. I want you to relax, you've just been through a scary experience."

"If you don't give me a pill, I'll get one myself."

"No, you won't. They're locked up and I have the key, so lie down and relax. We'll talk about this after the EVA is complete."

CHAPTER 16
TROUBLING THOUGHTS

Gina gave Monel a sedative and after her patient had gone to sleep, Gina reported Monel's strange behavior to Sunul and Jar'l. The men had begun towing the engine shell toward the cargo hold.

They had arrived at position eight, adjacent to a crater about five meters in diameter, but only a meter deep. They had decided to pull the shell through the crater when Gina contacted them.

"Sunul?"

"What is it, Gina? We'll be back in about an hour, can it wait?"

"I just wanted you and Jar'l to know that Monel wants to abort the baby."

There was a moment of silence, then Jar'l's voice came over the com. "What? She didn't say anything to me about it."

"She's asleep now. I told her we'd talk it over later."

Sunul said, "Gina, contact the Patels and find out when they'll be back with the other shell. I think we should all talk about Monel's intentions."

"Okay, their coms have been off. I'll give them a heads-up."

Ninety minutes later, the two engine shells were secured in the cargo hold and the four couples were assembled in the galley.

Gina began, "I've talked with Monel and she doesn't mind sharing her thoughts about wanting to abort the baby. Tell us how you feel Monel."

"I began to think about aborting the baby when I was floating in space. At first, I was just scared of dying out there; running out of oxygen, but after I knew Sunul was coming to get me, a strange feeling came over me. It was almost like someone was telling me to terminate my pregnancy. It was like an inner voice."

Triel raised her hand and Gina called on her.

"I had the same experience, but it happened when we were towing the engine shell back to the cargo hold."

Hugh looked at her and said, "Why didn't you tell me about it?"

"I wanted to talk to Gina first. I thought my mind was getting screwed up because of the long EVA."

Gina surveyed the group and then looked at Leanne. "Have you had any of these feelings?"

"No. I'm kind of happy to be pregnant in outer space." She reached over and patted Rob's thigh.

"Okay. Here's what I'd like to do. Monel and Triel, please record every possible detail of your experiences in the last forty-eight hours. I'll have the computer run a comparison to see what, if any, correlation can be made. I think you have been exposed to something in common."

Monel looked at Gina and said, "I think I know what it might have been."

Nearly everyone said, "What?"

"The water in that plastic bag that Rob brought in from outside when he began melting the ices surrounding the complex."

Rob looked at Triel. "Oh, yeah. What happened to that water sample? Wasn't it kept in the cryostat?"

Gina said, "I put it back in the deep freeze after marking it as outside water ice."

There were a few seconds of silence before Triel said, "I took it out of the cryogenic storage unit when I got two seed samples for the growth chamber. I didn't think it should be in there with potential food items. I was going to put it in a cabinet in the cargo hold, but I forgot. Then I decided to put the water in a small hydroponic tube and added some seeds. That's the last I saw of the bag."

"I was making a clean-up round and threw that bag in the incinerator." Monel looked around, frowned, and continued, "Did I do something wrong?"

Sunul said, "Did you both get water on your hands?"

Monel nodded, "I did."

"Yes. I did, too. I remember drying my hands and discarding the paper towel."

"You think there's something in the water; some kind of bacteria that has been frozen for millions of years?" Rob shook his head and said, "You think that's possible, Hugh?"

"Who knows what might exist out here. Sunlight probably doesn't supply enough energy to make viable life, as we know it, but maybe diffuse starlight and occasional high energy radiation from space could support some type of life. We need to have that water sample investigated. See if any microscopic organisms are present. If life exists, find out if it's carbon based. Gina and Triel should do a complete analysis, making sure the sample is kept isolated."

Sunul nodded and said, "Good idea, Hugh. Triel, wear an isolation suit. I don't want Gina exposed to whatever we're dealing with. Monel, you need to wear an isolation suit too."

"Can I work on the analysis with Gina and Triel?"

Sunul glanced at Gina, who nodded. Sunul said, "Sure, the more minds involved, the better. But keep that sample in an isolation chamber."

Rob and Leanne continued working on the ice melting apparatus and after three hours, reentered the complex to start a new sleep cycle. Rob spoke with Sunul before he went to bed.

"Leanne disabled the fueling robot. It wasn't doing anything useful. She reprogrammed it to hold and guide the warming nozzle. The robot will continue the melting process while we're sleeping. At the current rate of removing the ice, we'll be free in five or six days."

"That means I'd better get to work on a design for attaching the old rocket engines to the complex. You'll have to help with the welding, once I've determined the engine and fuel tank locations. Get some rest Rob. I'm going to take a four-hour rest and then get back to work."

"All right, see you in eight."

"Show me the hydroponics tube containing the water from outside, Triel. What seeds did you add to the water sample?"

Triel moved to a growth rack and pointed. "Everything's in this sample tube, number 117. All the info is on your com unit if you go to Growth Lab #117. I keep all my experiments up to date. I monitor and add data every day."

"Good for you. I used to have several different investigations going in my chemistry lab and would forget some of the details. Then I had to repeat the experiments. I learned quickly. With patients it's a little different, there's no room for errors."

"I'm running ten research trials simultaneously, so I don't remember all the details. I have to keep good records. If you have any questions, just ask."

Gina was already accessing the data on sample 117 and said, "Right." Her examination of the data took about ten seconds. Then she created a file of her own on the lab computer: GB-Analysis-117.

"Let's filter off the organic solids from the seeds first, then we'll run a molecular sieve. I want to get a particle size distribution of the filtrate."

Triel said, "Okay. Monel will carry out a spectral analysis of the size partitioning."

Gina said, "I want to look at the ..."

Monel interrupted, "infrared and ultraviolet wavelength regions."

"Exactly, Monel. You read my mind."

"I think we had the same idea, Gina. You wanted to see if the organisms, if they exist, can absorb electromagnetic energy and perhaps communicate."

"Exactly. Let's look for emission of radiation at longer wavelengths than our scanning energy. Triel, have you ever programmed nanobots?"

She nodded, "Once, in an inorganic robotics lab, but they were very limited in abilities. They had less than 2,500 atomic mass units."

"What was their function?"

"They mined silver, gold, and other precious metals from obsolete circuit boards. A battalion of 5,000 could clean off a copper board in a couple of hours. Very efficient little critters. We didn't have a sophisticated bot-assembler though, nothing like the one we have here in our lab."

"Okay. As soon as we get the wavelength analysis, we'll build some bots to carry out investigations of the atomic structures of the aliens."

"If we have any alien entities, that is. I still have the desire to rid myself of the baby. I'm wondering if it's primarily a physiological or psychological effect."

"Maybe we'll be able to eliminate the problem with drugs. If that doesn't work, we'll send in a squad of killer-bots intravenously to destroy whatever it is."

An hour later, Triel was describing the size analysis to Monel and Gina. "There's the usual background scatter of low mass fragments and ions, similar to low molecular weight hydrocarbons, slightly above noise level. I believe that clutter is from the seeds, but there is a reasonably well-defined system of peaks centered on atomic mass 67,900. I've isolated everything from mass 67,000 to 69,000 and carried out a census. Only a few of the masses are duplicated. That's kind of curious, don't you think?"

"Hmm." Gina leaned back, stretching her arms and said, "What's the molecular weight of hemoglobin?"

Triel answered immediately, "Sixty-four thousand. What are you thinking, Gina?"

"What can these things exist on? They have to have an energy source in addition to light. Most of their environment is methane, water, and some trace inorganics. Can you run an analysis for metals on the masses in that cluster? I'm thinking there will be some iron and platinum present. Check and see."

"Okay, I'll use the laser ablative mass spectrometer and see what I can find. It'll take about ten minutes."

"I'll be reporting our initial findings to Sunul. As soon as you get the results, find me. We need to get to the bottom of this quickly." Gina turned and walked toward the main computer station where she could usually find Sunul.

When she arrived at the main console, Sunul and Jar'l were discussing the time record on the communications with earth.

"Is there an automatic signal being sent to earth and when does it occur?"

Jar'l scratched his head and said, "Yeah, but the broadcast time varies from day to day."

"Can we hack into the com system and change the time the signal is broadcast?"

"No way. The signal is sent from a transmitter on the surface that's controlled by the main computer. We can't get into the central processing unit; we've already tried that and failed."

"Yeah, that's right. I have another idea. Can we build a secondary transmitter next to the one that is now in use? We could shield the one controlled by the CPU and rebroadcast from the secondary. We can then repeat the broadcast with our own time record added."

"Say, that might work. There would only be a few milliseconds delay in the signal until we start back toward the sun. The earth receiver would never know the difference because of our orbital variations. I'll get right on it. As soon as we break out of the moon and start back, we'll be able to mark the signal, so the time of transmission indicates we are still in orbit in the Kuyper belt."

Gina was listening intently and realized the entire crew would have to make sure to contact earth using the secondary transmitter or the complex's true location would be given away. The conniving officials would detect the messages from the deiced ship as the astronauts traveled toward the sun unless the transmission times were altered. Would officials try to destroy the returning ship and claim an accident resulted in the loss of eight young Kuiper Belt crew members? She wrote a message, made paper copies for each crew member, and added the following: Please contact me in person acknowledging you have received the message. Don't reply using your individual com units. We don't know if any of our devices are being monitored from earth, the moon, or Mars.

It took less than an hour for responses from everyone. They all recognized the importance of disguising where they were located on their return trip.

CHAPTER 17
CHECKLISTS

Sunul gathered the crew and made sure that communications with regard to the complex being removed from the ice and returning toward the sun were handwritten. Their regular communications with earth should continue though. He stated, "We are making a checklist of every procedure that must be accomplished before we escape from 5K23m in the complex. If you have anything to add, please inform Gina or me of your thoughts."

Some discussion ensued, primarily about the deicing. Rob informed the crew, "We have about half of the complex exposed. I expect in another week, we should have the entire structure free of the ices. I have one of the old empty fuel tanks full of solid oxygen. We'll need another half-tank to supply all our requirements. I'll need some help lashing the complex to the moon to keep us from separating too soon."

Sunul added, "We'll need to use one of our engines to separate us from the moon. I'd like to be able to turn the engine ninety degrees so after we've separated, we can still use the thrust for accelerating toward the sun."

Rob had already been envisioning the separation. "I want to use one of the remote telescope structures for the engine mount, Sunul. I just have to design a swivel so we can rotate the engine through ninety degrees."

Jar'l and Hugh both volunteered for the EVA to secure the

complex to the moon before the deicing was complete. Sunul and Monel began construction of a parabolic dish aerial to send signals to the repeater transmitter located on 5K23m. Most of their work was done in the sickbay after bringing in some tools and materials from the cargo hold. Sunul drew plans so Rob would know where to attach the aerial to the outside of the complex. Extra ice, about a cubic meter in volume, would have to be removed to create a cavity large enough to contain the aerial.

When Sunul brought in materials from the cargo area, he dismantled one of the robots that was refueling the external moon rockets which had been discovered to be non-functional.

He built a low energy transmitter from the robot's transceiver. As he worked on the transmitter, Sunul realized other parts of the robot could be used to construct a swivel for the outboard engine.

"Rob, I have a gift for you."

"What's that?"

"The rest of the robot I dismantled. You can use it for the swivel, can't you?"

Rob thought for a couple of seconds and said, "Yeah! That'll work. We can actuate the rotation mechanism remotely, too. Great idea, Sunul! I'll have to do some welding and drill some holes to attach it to the top of the telescope pyramid. That'll require an EVA for two of us. But I'm a little worried about the stress from the rocket thrust. We'll have to be careful."

"The stress when we pull free from the moon will be radial and it won't be much. We can use that thruster after we've got the ship moving with the impetus from the engines attached to the body of the ship." Sunul's statement reassured Rob that his engine mounting would not be subjected to severe stress.

"Okay, boss." Rob looked at Sunul and smiled. Sunul just shook his head. "That's almost as bad as skipper, Rob."

The weekly physical for the women verified the pregnancies. Monel and Triel both reported that thoughts of interrupting their pregnancies had passed. They both seemed content and were looking forward to being mothers. Gina was skeptical and ordered blood, urine, and fecal tests for both women. She was discussing the results with Sunul.

"I couldn't find any platinum in their blood, Sunul."

"What about the urine and fecal results?"

"Also, negative. I'm having them record hourly body temperatures and watching for changes in eating habits. Something that was in that water sample affected them, I'm positive. I'm going to determine what it was or is."

"Why not do an elemental body scan for heavy metals? Do it on all four women."

"Okay, but iron might camouflage the other metals. I'll set the instrument to only look at elements above atomic number seventy-seven. That well include platinum in the scans. Hopefully, we'll be able to detect it. I hope all four of us can hold still for five minutes."

"I know you'll do the best you can. Report what you find, if anything."

"I'll have the results tomorrow."

"All right. Interrupt me when you get the data. I'll be working with Rob on the engines."

Sixteen hours later, Gina had the results and was waiting for Sunul to finish an EVA with Rob. They had completed and tested the mechanism that would rotate the outboard engine. They came into the complex for a break and a meal before they attached the engine and the flexible feeder lines to the fuel tanks.

"Well, Sunul, are we going to test the engines before we try to break away from the moon?"

"We have to. I don't want to be out there floating around with a wrench in my hand, tumbling head over heels hanging onto the engine mounts. We'll give each one a two second burst to see if it functions, wait a second and try it again. If all three work as planned, we're ready to start back toward the sun. Jar'l said he and Monel are ready to go."

"What about Hugh and Triel?"

"Hugh said they're ready at any time, just give them ten minutes to secure lab equipment."

"I'm scheduling a crew meeting for eight hours from now. We'll go over any last-minute operations, make an engine test, and if all goes well, we'll leave this ice ball for good."

"All right. I'll double check all of our modifications to the outside of the ship and make sure no ice has reformed on the skin. Then, I'll take nap." He smiled and said, "Don't worry, I'll set my alarm."

Gina joined Sunul after she watched Rob walk away from her husband.

"I've got the results on the element scans."

"What'd you discover?"

"Platinum is located in the embryos."

"You and Leanne, too?"

"No, just Monel and Triel. Leanne and I have normal embryos, thank God."

"Do you envision any problems caused by the platinum?"

"I've searched all the medical files and couldn't find one iota of info about platinum in embryos. Apparently, it has never been studied. Perhaps it has never occurred, other than trace amounts in isolated sites. We have to keep observing the two women to watch for deviant behavior. But if the metal is in the embryos, the mother shouldn't exhibit any effects. I'll watch them."

"Sounds good. We're almost ready to leave the Kuiper belt. We'll all meet in eight hours. Could you please send paper messages to everyone?"

"Consider it done."

"Thanks, Doc." Sunul tried to give Gina a high-five but she missed his hand on purpose and laughed.

The eight hours passed quickly. Following some frantic activity, most of the crew slept for at least four of the eight hours. Hugh and Triel were a few minutes late but apologized. They were involved with isolation of the tube containing the first water sample obtained from outside the complex. Triel had been observing the container for the past ten days and had noted the formation of a root-like structure. They had transferred the specimen to a larger container and when they irradiated the new vessel with ultraviolet light to sterilize it, the adjacent root structure moved and fluoresced. They had sealed the new container and specimen in a double walled glass isolation vessel to guarantee its security. The extra care they had taken made them a few minutes late for the crew meeting.

Sunul smiled and said, "I think we're ready for our next journey. We're going to aim for Mars and borrow the return ship that is in orbit around the red planet. Actually, there are two earth-return (ER) ships in orbit, one for equipment, completely computer controlled and the other, which can be piloted by crew or flown by computer. We'll borrow the latter."

Jar'l commented, "So we're going to one of the lunar colonies, rather than earth itself?"

"I'm not sure yet. We might have to put it up for a vote when we get there. It might depend on the babies. Gina has identified platinum in the embryos Monel and Leanne are carrying. We'll have to evaluate the situation when we reach the moon. We don't want to risk the earth's population with some sort of unknown virulent virus or other medical problem. We might have to quarantine the two babies for an unknown amount of time. Monel and Triel have talked this over with Gina. They understand the risks."

Hugh spoke up, "What are we going to do with this hulk? Put it in orbit around Mars and let it die a fiery death in the atmosphere?"

Sunul smiled, "Another crater on Mars might improve the look of the planet, who knows? I suppose, if we have to, we could take it to the moon. They could ferry us to the surface. We'll decide on the course of action when we get there."

No one else had anything to say, so Sunul gave one last recommendation: "Everyone don your EVA suit and strap yourself in when you're ready for lift-off. Rob and I are not sure what level of stress the ship will be subjected to as we move the complex away from the ice. If we spring a leak, we'll be ready for loss of pressure. You have ten minutes to get ready, but we won't leave anyone behind if you're a little slow." He grinned. "I'm not sure about all of you, but I'd like to get off this ice ball."

Gina and Sunul went to their quarters and climbed into their EVA suits and headed back to the reclining launch chairs. As they were getting seated and inspecting each other's pressure suits, Gina commented, "Did you notice what Monel and Triel were doing when you were briefing us a few minutes ago?"

"Well, I noticed they were both chewing gum."

"It wasn't gum, Sunul. It was paper. Monel was tearing bits of paper off one of my memos and eating it. I think Triel was doing the same thing."

"They were swallowing it?"

"Uh-huh. I wonder why."

CHAPTER 18
BREAK AWAY

Sunul had set the clock holographic display at ten minutes when the crew had dispersed to climb into their EVA suits. Everyone had returned and was belted to their reclining seats clutching their headgear, ready for rapid attachment to their body protection in case of an unexpected loss of pressure. The men seemed to be relaxed, but the women appeared to possess some anxiety, perhaps thinking something was bound to go wrong and what would happen to the life within them. Gina asked if any of the astronauts wanted something to ease their anxiety. They all declined.

When the clock displayed ten seconds, everyone leaned back, most with their eyes closed, and took a few deep breaths before Sunul ignited the outboard engine. At first, it appeared nothing had taken place, but after a couple of seconds, the complex began to shake and creak, as if a strong gust of wind had made an old wooden house emit squeaks and shudders from a threatening wind.

When Sunul slightly increased thrust, there was a single popping noise and the complex began to move. The vibration sensations were suddenly gone and Sunul said, "We're free of the ice, now we're going to move away and orient the ship toward the sun. I'd say hang on, but it isn't necessary, our contraption will gradually pick up speed until we reach about one thousandth the velocity of light. Then I'll shut down the engines and we'll coast toward the sun, picking up speed—just like a comet."

Monel was doing some mental calculations and spoke up, "Sunul, at this rate, it's going to take us about a year to get to Mars, and we'll have to slow down to orbit the planet. Am I correct?"

"About eleven months, Monel. But I plan to use the gravitational attraction of Neptune to speed us up, and remember, the sun will be pulling us, too. I've calculated it should take us roughly five months to get to Neptune, and then four to five more months to reach Mars, about the time when you ladies will have your babies in diapers. Look forward to it, maybe they'll be the first toddlers learning to walk on the surface of Mars. The return trip from Mars to earth is common, about a week. They have nuclear engines with high metal content fuel, unlike what we're dealing with."

"Can we use Saturn and Jupiter to speed us up?"

"No, Monel. They're too far out of our way."

"But Sunul, even without the aid of Jupiter and Saturn, we'll be moving so rapidly, how will we slow down for Mars?" Monel didn't want to give up asking questions. Jar'l had said she was very intelligent.

"Rob and I thought of that. This ship can be divested of its less important parts. If we can jettison more than half the mass of the ship, the rockets will be used to put on the breaks. Rob thinks he can use some of the unwanted mass to feed our engines, giving us more thrust to help slow us. According to our present quantity of fuel, we should be able to slow down if we jettison half our mass. We might have to use the giant planets to slow us down. After we pass the asteroids, we'll go into an elliptical orbit around Mars and brake some more using Mars' gravity and drop into a nearly circular orbit. Good question, Monel."

Leanne was talking to Hugh and she turned toward Sunul. "Can you display our position on the main screen?"

"Sorry, Leanne, but if we do that, we risk the Space Agency discovering our intentions. We can't afford to use the computer that way. I'll compute where we are each day and send you a voice message. You'll know when we are passing each visible planet on our route. Also, you'll see them from the observation ports. I know you're disappointed that it will take us so long to get back to earth, but I'll attempt to make the journey as quickly as I possibly can, and without any more danger than we've already experienced."

Jar'l commented, "Sunul, we have to fire the main engines in fifteen seconds."

"Right. I'm making one last burn to get our orientation correct." Two seconds of thrust from the outboard engine could be felt. Then Sunul sat back and waited until Jar'l said, "Now!"

The entire crew could feel the acceleration forcing them into their seats as the engines attached directly to the sides of the cargo hold began pushing the structure toward Neptune. Since Neptune's revolution about the sun occurs in 165 years, Sunul's vectors had been computed easily; the planet had not moved significantly since they had passed it on their trip to the Kuiper belt. He only made slight adjustments to the values used when travelling from Neptune to 5K23m. He had used the directional coordinates from the main computer and reversed the sign of the outward-bound vector on his hand-held calculator.

Following the fifteen-second burn, the acceleration forces were negligible. Gina released her security straps and moved over to talk with Monel and Triel.

"I've been observing both of you since we started back toward the sun. What are you eating?" She already knew they were chewing on bits of paper but wanted to know if they were aware of it.

Triel frowned and said, "Oh, it's just gum."

"May I look at the note I sent everyone earlier today?"

"Sure. It's in my pocket." Triel reached in her pocket and withdrew a piece of paper with more than half torn off around the edges. She handed it to Gina and said, "I don't know what happened to the rest of it."

"I believe it's in your mouth, Triel. You and Monel have been eating paper for the last half-hour."

"No, it's just gum, Gina. I'll show you." She spit the white saliva-rich wad of paper into the palm of her hand and held it out to Gina. "See."

"Touch that with your finger, Triel. Does that feel like gum? What flavor is it?"

Triel looked perplexed. Apparently, she really believed she was chewing on a piece of gum, but now she realized it wasn't sticky and had no flavor at all. It was not what she thought. Monel had realized the same thing after following the same actions as Triel.

"Why would Triel and I be eating paper, Gina?"

"That's my question. I'm wondering if whatever is in that water sample is causing some irrational behavior, like wanting to end your pregnancies and causing you to chew or eat paper."

Triel reacted, "Doesn't that paper have silica added to it?"

"Yes, but why would your body need silicon?"

Monel followed with, "Aha!" Her mouth was agape. "Last night Jar'l ate some of my fries and had to spit them out. He said they were so salty he couldn't eat them. I had salted the potatoes. Calcium silicate is added to salt, isn't it?"

"You're right, Monel. You both seem to have a desire for silicon, in one form or another. Let's mention this to the men and see if they can come up with a reason. I can't think of any medical reasons for it. The body has only a tiny amount of silicon in it and it doesn't seem to have any function. It's probably an impurity from eating foods grown in the ground. Silicon is a common element found in the soil on earth."

Gina sent a handwritten memo to all four men reporting what the women had discussed. About an hour later, Hugh suggested an experiment. Lock up all paper products and salt. If the two women are being driven to find sources of silicon, the rest of the crew will report that behavior. If they find another source of silicon, Gina will scan their bodies for silicon to see where it is being used. "Is everyone in agreement?"

No one voiced any opposition, so all paper and salt were given to Gina. She locked the items in the secure pharmaceutical cabinet and gave the key to Sunul, who put it in his personal locker and changed the combination. Four hours into the journey, Sunul used his com unit and sent a message to the crew informing them of the ship's progress. He asked them to reply when they received the message. Within ten minutes, he had received return messages from five crew members. Monel and Triel had not replied. He talked with Jar'l.

"Jar'l, would you borrow Monel's com unit and check the integrated circuits?"

"What are you thinking?"

"Neither Monel nor Triel have returned my request for a reply. I'm wondering if their units are functioning. Check their coms for me. Call me back from their units."

"You got it, boss."

"You, too? You've been talking to Rob, haven't you?"

"Yeah. He said it was all right to refer to you as boss."

Sunul laughed, "He's trying to get you in trouble, Jar'l. I told him just the opposite. I've got to think of something foolish to call him, an embarrassing nickname. Let me know if you come up with anything."

"Okay, Sunul."

"Thank you."

After thirty minutes of waiting for messages from Jar'l, Sunul sent a text message: 'Jar'l, any progress?'

Jar'l responded, 'I've talked with Monel and Triel. Their coms are not functioning. I'm coming back to my workstation to dismantle their devices. See you in a minute.'

Jar'l, carrying a small plastic container, about the size of a shoe box, appeared in the passageway from the living quarters. He waved to Sunul, sat down, opened his utility box and extracted two com units. As he triggered the release code from his electronic access gun, the units popped open. To his surprise, the processors were missing from both com devices.

"Hey, Sunul, the receiver-transmitter chips are missing. No wonder you didn't get a reply from Monel and Triel. There's no way they could use these units."

Sunul walked over to Jar'l and looked at the internal circuits. The master chips were missing. "So how did the women gain access to the guts of these units?"

"You've got me. They shouldn't be able to get them open without my access device." Jar'l held up his small gun shaped unit, about the size of an antique computer mouse from the early part of the twenty-first century.

"Monel must know your password, Jar'l. Maybe you said it in your sleep, or she knows you better than you think. Has she ever exhibited any penchant for clairvoyance?"

"Yeah. Come to think of it, she does finish my sentences occasionally. More so than any of the other women I've known."

"I'll bet you've known quite a few, huh?"

"No more than you have, my friend. You think they have been consuming those chips because of the silicon in them?"

"I don't know, but I don't think they could swallow those chips whole, they'd have to break them into pretty small pieces and wash them down."

"Let's keep watching what they eat and alert Gina if we see anything out of the ordinary. I'd like to find out what stomach acid would do to a pulverized com chip. I hope the alien species in the water haven't changed their biochemical processes. We might be in for some behavior we can't possibly understand. I hope we don't have to place Monel and Triel in quarantine. If that's necessary, I'll go with her. I imagine Hugh would go with Triel, too."

"I'd expect that of both of you. But when you are eating together, watch what she puts in her mouth."

"I'll do that. I'd like to know what is going on, just as much, or more, than you."

CHAPTER 19
PEPPER

"Do you realize that wanton destruction of your com devices is a violation of your oath when you joined the space agency?" Sunul was talking to Monel and Triel, showing them the com units missing the multifunctional integrated circuit. "Being out of contact with crew members can be a danger to you and the others on the ship if an emergency occurs."

"I don't understand why you are accusing us of doing that, Sunul."

"Can you explain how you opened your com units?"

"Sure. It was accidental. Triel and I were talking when we received your message. We were thinking of another source of silicon. I don't know why; we just have this desire for the element in any form. We looked at our coms and knew there was silicon in the circuits, but we didn't know how to open the units except with Jar'l's device. We were just holding the units, and pressed SEND to reply. Then we both said, "I wish we could open these. They both popped open. We were totally surprised but could see the master chip. We extracted the chips and ground them up in the food processor."

"After we ground them up," Triel said laughingly, "They looked like pepper. That's when you showed up and began to ask us questions. We were on our way to get something to eat that we could add pepper to. Now that I think about it, the whole thing sounds a little crazy, but at the time, it seemed very logical. We both thought that, didn't we?" She looked at Monel for support.

"I did. Can't Jar'l fix the units?"

"Yes, but then you'd do it again, wouldn't you?"

"I suppose we would. Is what we are doing a craving, due to pregnancy? How would elemental silicon be useful to the babies? How can silicon get into our blood? Is stomach acid strong enough to break down silicon? Hmm. Maybe we have an enzyme that came from that water."

"That's what Gina might figure out. I want both of you to have another elemental body scan to find out where the silicon is going. Then maybe we'll have some answers to our questions."

Triel said, "Do you mind if we get something to eat first?"

Sunul hesitated for a few seconds, but then replied, "You might as well get your silicon fix. Wait for an hour to let digestion occur before you do the scans. I'll tell Gina what we want to do. Go ahead and put some pepper on your food. Gina will expect to see you in an hour."

Ninety minutes later, Gina returned from the infirmary. Monel and Triel were close behind. Sunul called for the crew to assemble after seeing the looks on the faces of the three women. When everyone was seated around the main console, Sunul asked, "What's the verdict, Gina?"

"The element scan showed nearly all the silicon is located in the embryos. It looks like it is concentrated in the vicinity of the platinum. We'll have to repeat the scan at nine weeks. We'll know more then. The embryos will be much larger, and we'll be able to pinpoint the location of the silicon."

Hugh spoke up. "Are we going to supply the women with whatever they need as far as elements are concerned?"

"I'll take care of that, Hugh. We might have to confine them to their quarters. We don't want Monel and Triel to start munching on the computers." Everyone but Gina had a good laugh, but Gina had thought it through. She was very serious. "You think that's amusing. I suppose it is but give it some thought; it could put us in great danger. We can't afford for any of our major equipment to fail. That could mean we might all perish."

The crew was now listening intently. Even Monel and Triel realized the significance of what Gina had said. Triel volunteered, "I'd like to warn you of Monel's and my desires for unusual additions to our diet, but the behavior is not abnormal to us. What can we do? We both thought we were making pepper from the chips in the com units."

"It sounds like those platinum containing entities are influencing your thinking. They must be causing your strange behavior, forcing you to acquire certain elements for assembling something in or around your babies. I hope it isn't something we'll regret allowing to take place." Sunul looked at Monel and Triel. "Don't get mad at the rest of us if you catch us watching what you are doing. We want everybody to be safe."

The two women nodded. They understood what he was saying.

The next week was hectic for the travelers. The makeshift spaceship passed through a dispersed swarm of pea-sized rock particles which punctured the walls of the complex and caused some loss of atmosphere. An emergency siren sounded three times in a twelve-hour period. Rob and Sunul located the ruptures quickly with the aid of the computer pressure sensors and sealed the holes with VAC-SEAL spray until Rob could weld small aluminum alloy circles to permanently close the small vents. There was no way to avoid such punctures, the skin of the complex was not built to travel unshielded through space. Comet refuse and asteroid debris was scattered throughout the solar system in unpredictable locations. When Sunul calculated the return trip toward the sun, he had purposely plotted a course slightly above the plane of the solar system to diminish the chances of particle penetration of the ship. They had been lucky so far, but Sunul tried to maintain optimism that baseball sized, or larger particles would not strike the ship. But he knew probability might not be on their side for very long.

Two months had passed since the crew had exited what they considered to be their icy coffin. Sunul had received a message from earth asking if there was something wrong with the main computer. Gina, Jar'l, and he discussed what they thought was the reason for the question from earth.

"I think we need to examine our time stamping of the computer's messages. I'll bet the retransmission of the computer's automatic signals are not correct, they're the normal signals from 5K23m's position, about eight hours, but we're not there anymore."

"I think you're right, Jar'l. We made a stupid error. We forgot to account for our motion toward the earth and the changing propagation times. I'll fix our program and send the amended routine to 5K23m. Then we'll send a message to earth and see what their response is. Hopefully they won't be suspicious."

"Why not tell them we had a problem with the master computer, and it had to switch central processors to a set of the backups. That might have influenced the data sent."

"Good idea, Jar'l."

It took eighteen hours to receive an acknowledgement from earth. Jar'l was showing the message to Sunul. "They're asking what we thought happened to the central processor. I sent a return message that we detected a beam of x-rays from outside the galaxy. Didn't they have any problems on earth?"

Sunul commented, "That will cause them to inspect satellite data from earth and mars. When they don't find any problems, maybe they'll decide to drop it. Maybe we'll be in luck and they'll find a supernova that they didn't notice."

Sunul's assumption was correct. There were no more inquiries from earth.

After four and a half months travel toward the sun, the crew began watching Neptune draw closer. The ship was only two weeks away from the giant. Of greater interest was Gina's report on the pregnancies. Triel and Monel looked big, as if they were at eight months, but Gina and Leanne appeared to be of normal size. The last scan of all the women hadn't indicated a great difference in the fetus's size, but in the last month things had changed significantly.

Gina was consulting with Sunul, "I'm going to do an element scan of Triel and Monel and also do an amniocentesis for each of them. They've asked about the sex of their babies, so that will be a normal procedure, but I want to find out why their bellies are so large. I don't understand why their babies have grown so much in the last month."

"Do you think the silicon they ingested would have caused a growth spurt?"

"I can't imagine why it would. The only thing I can think of is that the silicon might somehow have altered their DNA. I'll detect any abnormalities when I look at the amnio samples."

"What about their body weights? Do you keep track of them?"

"Not really. They should be keeping those records. I'll ask to see them. I haven't noticed them eating more than normal meals for a pregnancy though. Maybe they're raiding the freezers when the rest of us are sleeping. I'll look at the galley records, too. Those are automatically updated whenever the food supply is accessed."

Two ordinary days passed before Gina called a crew meeting after talking with Sunul.

As the crew assembled, Gina accessed the holographic projector and loaded several files from her hand-held laboratory computer.

"Okay. I have some data for you to see." She spoke into her lab-com and a three-dimensional picture of a male fetus appeared above the main console. "This is Monel's baby.

As you can see, it is fully formed, and as near as I can tell, is ready to deliver. In contrast, this is my baby, not completely developed, but the same age as Monel's." A green dot roamed Gina's and Monel's fetuses simultaneously, indicating the differences between the two images. "The reason I used these is images is that both fetuses are male. Leanne's and Triel's babies are both females. Now you know the sexes of all four babies."

Triel said, "What about the position of the silicon and platinum? Did you detect their locations?"

"That's the next thing I want to show you." Enlarged images appeared showing silicon in blue and platinum in red. The blue image resembled a computer chip and the platinum appeared in a root-like structure, but only in Monel's baby's tissue. Gina's fetus showed no red or blue coloration.

Triel gasped, "That's like the structure in the laboratory test tube. It looks like a plant root. Where is it in the baby?"

Gina zoomed out and everyone could see the structures were in the baby's brain.

"Oh, my God, Gina. Can those structures be removed?" Monel and Triel both had their hands to the sides of their heads as they observed the foreign formations in their baby's heads.

"Not with the technology available on our ship, only back on earth at one of the cancer centers. We just have to carry on as if nothing has happened, just treat the young ones like any others. Maybe we won't notice any problems. Those structures might be benign." Gina spoke into her lab-com and a graph appeared.

"These are the DNA analyses. Jar'l and Monel Mason's baby's DNA shows some striking differences from what is expected from the parent's. The strangest characteristic is they have twenty-five pairs of chromosomes, two more than normal. If I didn't know who the parents are, I would say Jar'l and Monel are not the parents. All of the crew have twenty-three pairs."

"So how are the differences in DNA going to affect the child? Should Monel and I worry about some deformities? Will our babies look normal?" Triel was very concerned.

"From all the information I can see in the data, your children should look normal in every way. Because of the abnormalities in the brains, I have no inkling what to expect. Our information from the DNA library on board is not complete enough to anticipate the results of this DNA analysis. At least the data do not indicate any known form of disease or physical abnormalities. I think we have to wait and see. Just hope for the best."

CHAPTER 20
NEPTUNE'S BABIES

"I feel like I'm going to pop any moment, Gina. Can't you give me something so I can give birth now?" Triel was very frustrated. Her baby had been kicking and punching for nearly a week. "I had a dream that the baby looked up and said, 'Can I come out and play now?'"

"I want to deliver, too! I'm going to need a wheelbarrow to carry my belly if I get any bigger." Monel was arching her back to make her protruding stomach seem even larger.

"Okay, ladies. If you don't deliver tomorrow, we'll induce labor. But I've been thinking, the babies might transmit whatever they have in their systems if they drool on either Leanne or me. I've talked it over with Sunul and Jar'l. They think it would be a good idea to keep the babies in isolation until we know if they can transmit the platinum/silicon problem. We'll have to sample their bodies and their waste products for at least ten days before we can let them inhabit the rest of the ship. The two of you and your babies will be quarantined for two weeks, not forty days, in the storage unit adjacent to the laboratory. We'll set up the room like a hospital suite. You and your babies should be comfortable. You can help me get the room ready today. Any problems with that?"

Monel and Triel both shook their heads. They recognized the danger of exposing Gina and Leanne, carrying normal babies, to a contagious perhaps alien disease.

"Let's get started." Gina began walking toward the dispensary. "We'll set up three beds, the newborns can share one of them. I'm sure Rob can fashion some type of railing to keep them from falling on the floor, although with little gravity, a tumble wouldn't hurt them."

Monel said, "Do you think they'll fight? We might have to keep them in cells." They were laughing as they entered the lab and started moving supplies from the storage unit to make room for the sleeping area.

A half-hour into the transformation of the storage room, Monel yelled, "It's coming!"

Gina helped her into one of the newly made beds and stepped into the dispensary to get a few surgical instruments. When she returned, no more than fifteen seconds later, the baby's head could be seen. Triel was holding Monel's hand and saying, "Remember to breathe, Monel."

Gina took over and when the next contraction occurred, she said, "Push!"

Triel started to laugh. Gina looked at her in disbelief. "What's so funny?"

"I was thinking the baby would reach out, grab you, and pull you in."

Monel was pushing again, and the baby slid out onto the sheets and started making a clucking noise. His eyes were open wide and seemed to be focused on Gina.

"Is he all there, Gina?"

"Yes, Monel. He's perfect, a beautiful baby boy. I'll clean him up and give him to you. How do you feel?"

"Like a heavy weight has been taken from my shoulders. Thank you for your help."

"You're welcome, but you did all the heavy lifting. I'll be right back with your son. Have you guys chosen a name for him?"

"Jar'l wants Licon, but I like Tinsil."

Gina wore a hazmat helmet and rubber gloves when she returned with the baby. She placed the newborn in Monel's arms and smiled. It was the first baby she had ever delivered, and although a little scared at first, she now felt more confident. As far as Gina knew, she was the first person to deliver a baby in the vicinity of Neptune, two billion eight hundred million miles from the sun.

"Gina, he keeps making a clucking sound, I thought he would be crying, not acting like a chicken."

"Give him something to suck on, Monel. Maybe he's hungry."

"Really?"

"What do you think those things are for? They're not just to attract men!"

Less than a quarter hour later, Triel sat up on her bed and yelled, "Oh, my God! I think my baby is coming!"

Gina came running from the dispensary, pulling on gloves and donning her hazmat helmet. Ten minutes later, Triel's baby had arrived and was wrapped in a pink blanket in her mother's arms. Triel's baby was also making the strange clucking sounds.

Gina was listening closely. Monel's child would make a series of sounds and after a second or two, Triel's baby would utter a similar series of noises. "Triel, have you chosen a name for your baby?"

"Yes, I like Miranda. It's one of the moons of Uranus. Miranda was discovered by Kuiper in 1948. I found that info on my com unit last night. I couldn't go to sleep so I looked for names for girls. Hugh said it was fine with him."

"Sounds good. Miranda Patel." Gina asked the two women, "Have you noticed when one of the babies is making that funny sound, the other is quiet, almost like it's listening to the noises?"

Monel reacted, "You actually think they're communicating?"

"I know that's hard to believe but count the noises. I always hear eight sounds in a grouping. It's my guess they are talking in binary, eight bits per word or byte. That's just like early computers. What I hear is a few clucks, an inhalation, then more clucks and inhalations; almost like a cluck is a one and an inhalation is a zero."

Triel said, "What would that mean? Let's ask Jar'l and Sunul to listen to the baby babble. See what they think. Do you think they already have a language? Could they have been communicating before they were born? That's hard to believe. I'm beginning to wonder if we have some children that are geniuses, before they can walk, or talk to us in English."

Gina sat for a moment pondering what Triel had said. "I'll bet Sunul will want to try to communicate with them with a computer if what we propose is actually going on in their tiny heads."

The two babies began another chat sequence and Monel said, "I'm recording what they are doing, or saying. Sunul can have the main computer run an analysis and we'll find out what is going on—I hope."

"Good idea, Monel. I'd like to know if we'll have to quarantine the babies before we get too attached to them. But I don't like to think of keeping them like caged animals, either." Triel was looking at her baby and almost crying over her thoughts. "That damned water!"

Monel sent the recording to Sunul who ran a language recognition program and reported to Monel and Triel. He walked into the dispensary and peered at the newborns. "These little ones are making all the funny noises?"

Gina said, "Yes. They're pretty cute, huh? What did the computer say the noises represent?"

Sunul hesitated and then said, "Well, I guess I'd better tell you." He looked at the women as if what he had to report was very serious. "The computer report says it's nothing but baby talk. It doesn't mean anything."

He laughed and said, "There's not enough data to be able to analyze it. You'll have to give me a lot more info."

Gina scolded Sunul for leading them to think the noises were something important or dangerous. "Your next injection is going to be with an extra-long needle, Sunul."

Triel said, "I get to administer the injection. I hope it's in your behind."

"And I get to do the one after that," commented Monel. "Maybe the other cheek."

Sunul scanned the smiling faces and said, "I think I hear the main console calling. Bye."

He waved, did an about face and strode back to the crew assembly room. He smiled as he returned to his command console.

"Did somebody tell you a joke, Sunul?"

"No, Jar'l. The joke was on me." Sunul took his seat and looked at his preliminary data on his com unit. "Have you got those calculations for the Neptune course correction completed yet? Neptune's disc is getting larger every day. We'll have to be right on to get the maximum increase in velocity from the close approach."

"They're almost ready. You'll have to take over to make sure we miss the planet's satellites and almost graze the atmosphere."

"Okay. I'm glad we don't have to use the main computer. We'd have alerted the earth long ago. Have there been any more transmissions from earth?"

"Nope. I don't think they have a clue yet, but some amateur astronomer with a camera might detect us when we get near Jupiter."

"Only if it's a rich amateur with a twenty-inch scope. We'd be awfully hard to detect until we get near Mars, we're too small and our reflections would be erratic. If they see us, I hope they'll think we're an unexpected comet, or an unknown irregularly-shaped asteroid."

"Those ideas wouldn't last long; they'd compute our orbit and discover that we're headed toward Mars."

"You're too pessimistic, Jar'l. I don't think we'll be detected until we tell them where we are."

"I hope you're right, Sunul."

As the ship approached Neptune, the crew secured themselves at their console seats, except for Monel and Triel. They were with their babies, belted to their beds in the isolation ward. They had made carriers for the children and those were secured to their chests, babies strapped tightly in their pouches. Sunul had warned everyone that the acceleration forces might be fairly strong. Most crew members recalled the automobile laws of the early twenty-first century requiring occupants to wear seatbelts. They were no longer necessary.

The babies had been jabbering away, more so every day, but no one, even with computer assistance, had been able to make any sense of their seemingly random noises, except for the patterns of eight clucks and breaths. Jar'l had analyzed several recordings but had discovered nothing. His conclusion was the same as Sunul's; it was just baby talk, but why was it in sequences of eight? However, Miranda had begun saying mama to Triel. Monel had remarked that her son, Licon, had uttered two words: "too hot." At least that was what she thought she heard from the little guy who now weighed slightly more than twenty pounds.

CHAPTER 21
ARTIFICIAL SATELLITE

Monel and Triel noticed the babies had become silent, not moving their limbs, fingers, or toes as they normally did. They appeared to be totally absorbed in listening, as a medium might be perceiving something happening or about to happen, a clairvoyant.

Monel picked up her com unit and called out, "Jar'l, Sunul, I think something is going to happen!"

Sunul was concentrating on directing the engine thrust and had no time to respond to Monel's loud frantic cry. He glanced at Jar'l, who spoke into the unit in his breast pocket, "What are you shouting about, Monel?"

"It's the babies. They're acting very strangely. I think they know something is about to happen."

"We all know what it is, Monel. Relax. Sunul is taking us in a close approach to Neptune in a few minutes. Try singing to the babies. That should calm them down."

"They are calm, Jar'l. That's the problem! You don't understand! I think they know something is going to happen, maybe not an ordinary event."

"Well, let us know when it happens. Then we'll take care of it." He shook his head, "What's next?"

Sunul had just made the last course correction before skimming through the tenuous outermost atmosphere of Neptune. The crew felt the acceleration and the slight change of direction, then the rockets kicked in and forced them into their seats. About twenty seconds later, the ship was rocked by a collision with a foreign object causing the ship to start rotating slowly.

Jar'l stared at Sunul, "Jesus, what was that?"

"Something hit near the cargo hold. I'm having to use the engines to stop us from spinning. Give me a minute." Sunul was adjusting engine thrust on two of the engines and had the spinning stopped when the computer announced, "LOSS OF PRESSURE IN THE CARGO HOLD, PANEL ELEVEN! CARGO AREA HATCH HAS BEEN SEALED. ACCESS THROUGH THE FORWARD ENGINE ROOM ONLY. EVA SUITS REQUIRED." The warning was repeated in text on all the consoles in flashing red letters.

"Rob, can you investigate what hit us?" Sunul had unbuckled his restraining harness and was running a diagnostic on the cargo hold. According to the rapidity of the pressure drop, the object they had run into was estimated to be at least a meter in diameter. Several wall sensors had been damaged. The computer couldn't give an estimate of the object's mass, visual evidence was necessary. Sunul figured it was probably a piece of rock that was tumbling through space and was attracted to Neptune by gravitational forces. The collision had occurred within the range of Neptune's moons which have erratic orbits about the large planet. Most of the sixteen moons were probably captured from the Kuiper belt by the planet's gravitational force.

"I think I'll go with Rob, Sunul. He might need some help."

"All right, Jar'l. Keep your com units open. Let us know what you find."

"Right. I'll keep you advised."

Twenty minutes later, Sunul was going to ask if Rob and Jar'l needed help, but Rob's baritone voice cracked with a report. "It's an old satellite, guys; something from last century. Its batteries are dead; it probably hasn't functioned in decades."

"Can you tell where it originated?"

"NASA, about 1990. One of the side panels was broken open. Jar'l muscled it off and we have access to the guts. The circuit boards have 1989 stenciled on them."

"Can you pull it into the cargo hold?"

"Let me give you some of the serial numbers of the components. See if you can get a diagram of it from the computer. I can't tell how big it is; only part of it penetrated. It might have aerials extended or even a dish attached to the outside."

Sunul could hear heavy breathing from Rob as he was tearing something off the satellite to get a better look inside.

"Jar'l, hand me a pair of wire cutters. There's a box blocking my vision."

Sunul listened to the conversation from the cargo hold as he entered serial numbers from the components. He had completed entering the second serial number when a picture flashed on his monitor. It was a radar satellite for mapping the surface of Neptune, RMS3, launched in 1991, expected lifetime: ten years. It had been dead for nearly eighty years.

"Got it, Rob. It's a radar mapping satellite from 1991. It should have some panels and a dish antenna on it. It's about one meter in diameter, three meters in length and the aerials extend about three meters, opposing each other. The dish is on the major axis."

Rob answered, "I'll have to go out to cut off the panels; they're useless anyway. We'll have to cut open the hull to get it in here. Is it worth it?"

Sunul puzzled over the problem for a few moments and said, "Take out all the radar equipment and get the dish from the outside, then jettison the rest and close the hole. If you can revive the radar unit, we can avoid future collisions. Okay?"

"You got it, commander." Then he laughed.

"Thanks for not saying boss, Rob."

"You're welcome. I'll keep you updated on the radar unit. I imagine it will take a couple of eight-hour shifts. I'll get Leanne to help me. With her assistance, it'll be functioning a lot faster."

"Okay, the sooner the better. We don't need any more collisions."

The crew of eight adults, two children, and two fetuses was nearly halfway home. The journey had taken slightly more than five months. The sun was beginning to have an increasing influence on their speed. The remaining twenty-eight and a half astronomical units would be covered in about sixty percent of the time already invested in the trip. Sunul sat at his console trying to think of a way to slow the ship as it moved faster and faster toward Mars, the next stop on their journey home.

Saturn and Jupiter were not going to assist braking unless both planets were in advantageous positions. From his console, his calculations showed that only Jupiter's gravity was going to be useful as a brake, and it was gradually moving out of a very useful position. It would not exert enough force to slow the craft for insertion into an orbit around Mars. Mars' gravity was just too small for the final slow down, there just wasn't enough fuel to put on the brakes.

Sunul leaned back, sank into his cushioned seat and scratched his head. Gina had come into his view as she entered the command station from the dispensary, having just left the quarantined room and removed her hazmat uniform.

"I got it!" he exclaimed. "You did it, Gina!"

"What'd I do?"

"Remember that day when I told you to take Saturn's mass out of your equations? Recall, seven months ago, when we were cadets training for this mission?"

Gina sat down beside Sunul with a puzzled expression. She was thinking back to the episode with the scorpion and she suddenly remembered. "Oh, yes, you were watching that sexpot put on an exhibition."

Sunul grinned, "Yeah, but the importance of that is you had included both Saturn and Jupiter in your trajectory to speed up the spacecraft. But now, we can use the same path to slow us down, an S shaped trajectory. I'm going to call it Gina's maneuver."

"But what I did was a mistake!"

"Only for that problem. This situation is different, but similar. This time, it's not a mistake, it's the correct solution. I'm not sure I would have thought of it if you hadn't done it that day." He sat back and blew a kiss to Gina. "That's why I married you."

Gina laughed. "You're full of space debris, Sunul!"

"That's better than some things I've been told I was full of." He motioned for her to sit beside him and when she did, he patted her bulging stomach and kissed her left ear. "How's our baby these days?"

"He's just fine. He's started kicking me every once in a while."

"You're sure it's a boy? When did you find out?"

"Don't you remember the pepper incident? Our baby is a boy, for sure. I confirmed the earlier data today."

"That's great, Gina. How much longer do we have to wait? I figure about three months."

She thought for a moment and said, "Uh, that's about right. Start thinking of a name, but not something weird, please!"

"I've got one already, Miles. Miles Sunul Burke, what do you think?"

"That's okay. I was thinking William, but I like Miles. What about place of birth? Will it be Mars?"

"I think that will be the closest planet. We might even be on the surface for the birth."

"That would be great! But there's no way to land this pile of junk on the surface, Sunul. You know that."

"You've forgotten about the beta group, Gina. They're living on the surface, but there are at least two craft in Mars' orbit. Contrary to our group, they have some redundancy in equipment. There's another lander and at least one ferry for transport to earth. I've been thinking we might borrow one of those ships."

"When will we know the ship we'll take?"

"That will depend on how all four babies are doing. If we have to keep Monel's and Triel's kids quarantined, we'll have to go to the surface. We can't afford to go to earth with them if they could conceivably change the DNA of the human race. You and Leanne and your babies could go back to earth. But, if members of beta group also have children, we might be in a predicament."

Gina was thinking of a way out of the dilemma. "Could brain surgery be performed on Mars?"

"I doubt if they would have the equipment or the expertise, Gina."

"Jeez, Sunul, I want to help Monel and Triel."

"I do too, but we've got a lot of other things to think about before we get to Mars. Let's not get ahead of ourselves."

CHAPTER 22
PREPARATORY WORK

Gina, Monel, and Triel were working together to accumulate information about the two babies born less than an hour apart. After nearly three weeks of recording data, the only significant difference between the babies and normal human newborns was their body temperature, ninety-six degrees Fahrenheit, about three degrees lower than average.

There were other deviations, but the women had concluded part, if not all, of the differences could be attributed to the enhanced intelligence quotient of the mothers. Both babies were, according to growth tables, double normal size and weight. However, most astonishingly, was their language development; they were both talking with vocabularies more like three-year-old children rather than three-month-old babies.

Why was becoming a word the women were beginning to dislike. Every waking hour there seemed to be an endless solo shared by the two youngsters, occasionally a duet, of whys. Neither Monel nor Triel could imagine being a preschool teacher, but they were coping without losing their tempers. They had always thought patience was a virtue to be valued, but now they were in doubt.

"Gina, how is it the kids can speak in sentences and have so many questions at such a young age?"

"I really don't know, Triel. What is Miranda asking about now?"

"Both Miranda and Licon want to know where they are and where they're going. Monel and I gave them an astronomy lesson and drew some diagrams to illustrate where we are, but we couldn't really tell them where we're going with any certainty. They really want to know. They keep asking where we are going and if they are going home. They asked why we are in this cage."

"Have you told them earth is home?"

Triel nodded and said, "I don't think they believe me. They don't really know what a planet is and why it moves around a star."

"I've been thinking about some things. Would you like to try some nanobots to see if those structures in their brains can be removed without surgery? Let's ask Monel if she wants to try it."

"I don't want to hurt the little ones, but I think we should try. Let's ask Monel what she thinks."

After putting the babies together in their makeshift playpen, the three women moved to the opposite corner of the room to have a private conversation. Gina and Triel told Monel what they had discussed.

Monel watched the little ones as she scratched her forehead and looked at Gina. "If we destroy the platinum complexes, what do you think will happen?"

"I really don't know, but here's what I think occurred. Very close to the time of fertilization, you two ladies came in contact with the water sample from 5K23m. The platinum tetramers were suddenly exposed to an energy and component rich environment that allowed them to proliferate, but there was a limited amount of platinum, so it was used as a manufacturing center to synthesize two additional chromosomes. Those additional chromosomes are apparently responsible for the rapid development of your children."

Triel whispered, "So you think the platinum isn't doing anything now?"

"I think it was just a template to get things started. I believe it is dormant now."

"Hmm. What about the silicon? Remember the clucking sounds my Licon was making?"

"Yes! Miranda was doing the same thing. We still don't know if they were talking or making some sort of connection with a friend." Triel smiled. "Kind of like texting. Remember, on those ancient telephones."

Monel grinned. "I think they were warming up their vocal cords and ears, or more likely, giving us something to worry about. You know how smart they are."

Gina said, "So what do you think? Should I make some bots to retrieve the platinum?"

"I don't mind if you try it on Licon. Will you label the bots so we can track them?"

"Sure. I'll dope them with some Iron-59, and we can follow the beta emission. The bots will decompose in a few hours and come out in the baby's excrement along with the platinum."

Monel frowned, "What about the radioactive iron?"

"It decays to stable cobalt. It will be excreted, too."

"Okay. Let's try it and see what happens. How about you, Triel?"

"I want to see what happens with Licon before I subject Miranda to the procedure. I hope you don't mind, Monel."

"No, that's all right with me." She looked at Gina and said, "When will the bots be ready?"

"It will take a couple of hours to program the synthesizer and another couple of hours to manufacture them. I should be ready in about five hours. I'll try the bots on a test strip containing platinum before I give them to Licon." She turned to go to the lab but was stopped by Triel.

"Gina, could you please get us some magnetic material so we can make some shoes for the babies? They want to walk on the floor, but they're restrained to the playpen, so they don't drift around the room."

Gina was surprised. "You really want them to be walking around?"

"They want to walk like we do, on the floor. We wouldn't turn them loose to roam around, but it would stop some of their incessant questioning if they could look out one of the observation ports. We could lift them up to look and we could show them around the ship. They are very curious and want to see where we are. I think they would begin to comprehend why we are confined to the ship. They would be able to see Saturn, Jupiter, the sun, and the stars. In our opinion, our diagrams are woefully inadequate.

"I agree, Triel and I would be able to get them accustomed to gravity and they would be exercising, developing their major muscles."

"All right, I'll get you the materials you'll need. You can make shoes while I program the synthesizer."

As Gina moved around the ship gathering the elements for shoes, she found that all four men were in a four-hour sleep cycle, a rare occurrence for normal activity. Leanne was working on the final steps toward a functioning radar system, and the new mothers were tending to their baby's needs, most of which concerned body waste. Gina could hear laughing coming from the nursery as Monel and Triel tried to keep obnoxious fumes from contaminating the air conditioning filters. Gina delivered the shoemaker's supplies and then began programming the nanobot-synthesizer.

Gina's program was red flagged when submitted for execution. She had hoped it would be accepted and production of the nanobots would proceed without delay, but the necessary iron-59 isotope contained in the synthesizer had been depleted to a very low level and would have to be supplemented from the ship's main reactor that provided power to the complex. It would take at least eight hours before the nanobot-project could be resumed. Gina donned a radiation protection suit and moved into the reactor core access room to instruct the robot attendant to prepare a sample of iron-59 adequate for the number of nanobots she wanted: 5,000, a minimal dose. The mechanical attendant sent a message to Gina's com unit that the sample would be ready in ten hours.

On her return to the main console, she stopped by the nursery and informed Monel and Triel of the delay. They would administer the nanobots to Licon following the next eight-hour sleep cycle. At the console, Gina investigated the probabilities of a forty-six chromosome human reproducing with a fifty chromosome individual. The computer returned a notice of incompatibility: the chance of a fully functioning offspring was zero. She spent a few minutes contemplating the results and then opened the file containing the babies' elemental scans for silicon and platinum. She asked, "Results if the silicon and platinum structures are surgically removed from these living beings." Gina waited for a couple of minutes before the following message was displayed: THE ORGANISM WILL NOT ENDURE, SEVERE RETARDATION AND LOSS OF MOBILITY.

She said aloud, "Well, so much for surgical removal, let's see about nanobot removal."

Gina began programming but soon ran into problems. The nanobots' self-preservation routines precluded them from scavenging silicon contained in computer chips; barriers prevented the microscopic robots from degrading silicon in printed circuits, so they couldn't destroy computers from the inside. She quit trying to circumvent the problem after a half-hour of dead ends. She would have to wait for Jar'l or Sunul to see if there was a work-around they knew of. She decided to inform Monel and Triel of her findings.

As she started toward the nursery, Leanne called to her from the electronics' workstation. "Gina, the radar should be functional now. I made the final connections to the backup monitor and one of the reserve com units. Where should I place the system controller, near Sunul's station?"

Gina mulled it over and answered, "That would be fine, Leanne.

Anyone can access it there. There's a universal mount in the wall cabinet next to the hallway to the galley."

"Okay. I'll install it and get it functioning. I think Sunul will need it as we approach Saturn a couple of days from now. Rob and I upgraded the resolution achieved by the antiquated planar circuits by installing three-dimensional circuitry. We were able to increase the frequency by nearly fifty percent."

"That's great, Leanne, but Sunul and Jar'l will appreciate what you have done more than I do."

Leanne laughed and said, "Rob will let them know all the details, probably much more than they want to know. He's proud of what we did together."

"Sunul is proud of what we did together, too."

"Oh, yes! Rob is proud of that, too." Both women laughed.

Gina returned to the reactor and cancelled the radioactive iron-59 routine by deleting the last program entered into the robot's procedure queue before going to the nursery. When she arrived at the quarantine room, everyone was asleep. She checked the vitals of the babies and returned to the command console to wait for Sunul. She looked at his twenty-four-hour schedule and found he should be back from their quarters in eighteen minutes, time for her to play a game of chess versus the computer. She was playing at level seven, ten was the highest.

CHAPTER 23

UPSETTING SOUNDS

Sunul immediately spotted the radar control unit when he arrived at the main console. Leanne had gone to bed, so he would have to wait for two hours before Rob would be available to provide details on the new unit at the command station. Leanne had left a note that Rob was on a six-hour sleep cycle. Sunul was standing and brought up the display to show the ship's position with regard to Saturn's, the first close approach initiating the craft slowdown using Gina's maneuver.

The holographic display allowed him to walk around Saturn to imagine all possible orientations of the rings, the moons, and the planet that would allow the ship to continue on toward Jupiter without requiring too much fuel for steering and further slowing as the ship approached Mars. He surveyed the 3-D image from many angles before returning to the console to program a couple of trajectories that might work. He would use the most efficient one, the one that required the least fuel.

As he sat in the command station chair, anticipating a future message from earth inquiring about the use of the computer for such complicated calculations, he thought of a reply that would not create suspicions. He said aloud, "I'll tell them I was thinking about a problem we had during our training and I was investigating various alternative solutions. The same problem would arise if we ventured all the way to Alpha Centauri." He looked at the console clock and added twelve hours, the earliest time earth could contact the ship after receiving transmissions sent from 5K23m.

Pleased with his proposed answer, he interlaced his fingers behind his head, smiled, leaned back, and relaxed, thinking about how he wanted his answer to be interpreted. His response should convince the Earth command that the alpha crew believed they were travelling toward Alpha Centauri surrounded in ice inside 5K23m. He was thinking how his responses to earth's inquiries would add to their surprise when the commanders find out the ship is headed back towards Earth, the return journey nearly three-fourths complete.

Hoping Rob would soon arrive from his sleep cycle to show him the operation of the jury-rigged assemblage of circuits removed from the ninety-year-old satellite, he went to the galley to get something to eat; his stomach had been growling for the last half-hour. As soon as he ate, he planned on going to the exercise room to ride a minimum of ten miles on the resistance cycle. While his meal warmed, he selected a recording of a piano concerto which began permeating the galley with soothing 200-year-old music. He had no idea the piano-orchestral selection would cause an uproar. He sat down with the hot meal and opened the plastic bag.

Monel came running into the galley yelling, "Sunul! Turn it off! The kids are going crazy!"

Startled, he loosened his grip on the meal as he looked at Monel. The pouch began spinning as it floated away from him, squirting its hot jelly-like substance into the air. He ignored the flying food and moved to the entertainment controller on the wall and pressed the music-off button. "What's all the commotion about, Monel? Aren't you supposed to be in isolation with Triel and the babies?"

"When the kids heard the music, they started shrieking with that clucking noise and thrashing their arms and legs. The music must have triggered something. They were sleeping until the music started. Oh, Gina told us we can come out of isolation, there's no danger to anybody."

"Hmm, she neglected to tell me. She was asleep when I woke up. I wonder how the music impacted the kids."

"Me, too. They haven't been clucking in several days—since they started talking."

"They're talking? Geez, nobody tells me anything."

Monel was looking at the food drifting around the room and said, "You need help cleaning that up?"

Sunul laughed, "No thanks, I know where the vac-bags are. As soon as I get another meal and eat, I'll visit you in the nursery. I want to talk with the kids. How many words do they know?"

"I think several hundred. Their minds are like data cubes, everything they hear, they store. They pronounce the words correctly, too. It's amazing."

While the replacement meal warmed, Sunul corralled the gobs of the first one and disposed of the vac-bag. Out of habit, he started to turn on the music, but as he reached for the music-on pad, he jerked his hand back saying, "Oops, I almost did it again." After his last swallow of coffee, he took the twenty steps to the nursery and watched Monel and Triel interacting with their children. Licon and Miranda were much larger than he had imagined, having only heard of their rapid development from Gina. Both children looked like two-year-olds, rather than being only a few months of age.

Sunul decided to try an experiment. He began to whistle. Licon and Miranda stopped playing immediately, looked at Sunul, smiled and began walking toward him—without the help of their mothers. They sat at his feet and he stopped whistling.

Licon said, "More," and Miranda followed with "Yes." Sunul smiled and pulled out his com-unit in which he had loaded some orchestral music just for this occasion. He said, "Play selected music," and turned the unit towards the two toddlers. Licon and Miranda started screaming and clucking as they got up and ran toward their mothers. When the screaming began, Sunul stopped the music and walked over to the children. "I'm sorry, Licon. I'm sorry, Miranda." He patted them on the head, looked at the mothers and commented, "Now I think I understand what happened when they heard the music."

"Please don't do that again, Sunul. That music must hurt their ears." Triel glanced at Monel for support. Monel nodded and then said, "What was that all about?" Sunul couldn't help noticing the frowns directed toward him.

"The music doesn't hurt their ears, ladies, it's overloading their little brains. They are programmed to remember everything they hear, but the orchestral music has so many frequencies from different instruments, they can't store it all. It's too much information—too fast. When they can't process fast enough, they react with screams and somewhat spasmodic movements, or they flee from the source."

Monel looked worried. "Do you think they'll get over it?"

"Sure. As they get older, they'll differentiate between phenomena and ignore the things that aren't important, just like we do."

Triel started to laugh, "My problem is that I ignore the important things and remember the garbage. I think that's why I majored in botany, I didn't need a lot of math, only enough to get by. I always liked playing in the dirt." She stooped down and picked up Miranda and walked over to Sunul. "Show her your com unit but play back a message from one of the crew; no music, please."

Monel brought Licon over and held him up so he could see what they were doing.

Sunul played back a message from Hugh. Miranda grinned and responded, "Daddy!" She looked around and said, "Where Daddy?"

Sunul held the com and told Triel and Monel to say something into it. They spoke the names of the babies and Sunul played it back for the kids. They both smiled and seemed to realize that the com unit was a recording device. Licon pointed at the com and said, "I like," and smiled. "Do again. What it called?"

Sunul didn't have time to answer before Rob's voice came over the unit. Everyone was slightly startled by the unexpected voice. "Sunul, I want to show you the radar system. Please come to the command center."

"Okay, ladies, I've got to go. We'll be nearing Saturn in about a day. You might let the kids watch through one of the viewing ports, we'll be going between the planet and the rings—might be exciting for them."

Triel exclaimed, "What a good idea! Thanks, Sunul. Will you have enough time to warn us when we pass close to the planet?"

"I'll let you know about an hour before we start the maneuver. You'll have enough time to get ready. I've got to go." He turned and walked away, but looked back and said, "Better get the kids used to the com units. We don't want them to be afraid of the units because of the music."

Rob was waiting at the radar-monitor station when Sunul walked into the command center. Rob raised his arm and beckoned to Sunul without looking up from the monitor exhibiting the radar sweeping the volume of space within 10,000 miles of the ship.

"Detect anything, Rob?"

"Nope, clear sailing. I'm shutting the system off so you can see how to bring it on-line from a wait mode or power-off state. Oh, it's not connected to our system computer; I had to use the central processor from the satellite. Unfortunately, the clock speed is only 100 megahertz, but that wasn't too bad for 1990."

Sunul watched Rob bring the radar system online and remarked, "That procedure is about the same as running an old microwave oven, pretty easy after it was plugged into a wall socket. I kind of wish we still had those things."

Rob snickered, "More like a new toaster. Set it on the countertop, drop in the bread, and tell it what shade of brown you want. I'm working on an update for the system. We should have at least a two-gigahertz clock speed when we get past Saturn. I'd like to have it before then, but I don't have enough time to complete the programming. Leanne is almost finished with the circuitry."

"Could I help with the programming?"

"No, but thanks for the offer. You'd have to know the circuits and it would take me longer to get you trained than if I do it myself. Besides, don't you have to steer us through the rings?"

"I'm almost ready for that. The course corrections aren't very complicated, they'll need a little tweaking as we pass between the inner rings and the planet's atmosphere, that's all. Your radar will come in handy then."

A little over twelve hours later, Jar'l and Sunul were talking about the approach to Saturn.

"Saturn has at least seventy-three moons, Sunul, but nothing to speak of within the inner rings. We only have to be aware of the moons' positions as we approach the system, a few of the moons are moving retrograde and they're small with largely eccentric orbits. The radar will detect them around fifteen seconds before we would collide. Is that enough time for you to react with the ship?"

Sunul leaned back in his command chair and scratched his head. "I'm going to need more computing power, Jar'l. Our com units can't handle it. I'll have to have the simulation program running on the main computer with someone to enter the velocities and positions of any close satellites. You or Rob will have to be feeding radar data to the program so I can avoid any problems. This hulk we're in can't change velocity vectors very rapidly, but I can rotate the ship to avoid close calls."

"You'd better have Rob handle the radar. I can help with the engine ignitions to keep us from going too far into the atmosphere. I have no desire to burn the ship up in the gaseous envelope of the planet."

"Yeah. I'd rather not end up as a meteor, either. You can handle the fixed engines and steer the gimbals, I'll take the swivel engine, and Rob will enter the radar data." Sunul glanced at his watch. "Rob should be here in about an hour. I'd like to run a simulation with him entering radar figures, a little practice for the real thing. We'll rotate the ship 360 degrees and then get aligned for the encounter. I've estimated the close approach to occur in about three hours."

CHAPTER 24
COLLISION PREVENTION

Rob entered the command station sixty-five minutes later. Sunul beckoned to Rob and he joined Jar'l and Sunul in front of the radar console.

"What is it? Something wrong with the radar?"

"No, radar Rob, we need your help for the near approach to Saturn." Sunul had finally found a nickname for Rob. Sunul grinned and slapped Rob on the back. "What do you think of your moniker?"

"Not bad, boss, better than just Rob." Following the laugher, they turned to more serious talk.

"Jar'l and I want to run through the close approach procedure. We need you to feed the radar sightings into the main computer. Jar'l and I are going to steer the ship through some avoidance maneuvers in case we're on a collision course with one of Saturn's moons."

"Okay, I'm ready. We'd better alert the rest of the crew. Tell them to secure themselves so they don't get thrown around." Rob recorded a message on his com unit.

"Right. I was going to alert Monel and Triel about the upcoming passage between the rings and atmosphere. They want the kids to watch. I'll send them a message right now." Sunul spoke into his com and warned everyone to get prepared for the close approach in about two hours, and Rob was going to warn them of the upcoming practice maneuvers.

Then Rob sent his message for the crew to take positions to keep from banging into bulkheads when the ship rotated in a few minutes. He looked at Sunul, "Ten minutes?" Sunul nodded and Rob advised the others when the practice maneuvers would begin.

Rob decided to make the simulation activity as difficult as possible for Jar'l and Sunul. He decided to have two small moons on a near collision course with the ship. One object, a kilometer diameter retrograde moon, and the other, a much smaller prograde object, having twice the velocity as the first satellite, would come within 100 meters of the ship and collide with the larger satellite. Then the pilots would have to avoid the imaginary fragmentation products from the collision.

As Rob finished the momentum calculations and determined likely orbits for the collision products, Sunul stated, "One minute until simulation begins." Although Rob's calculations were done on his com unit and were only approximate, he was sitting in front of the radar unit ready to enter the data into the main computer. He was watching the three-dimensional radar as if he were actually observing the imaginary satellites. A very faint signal had just appeared at the far edge of his screen at a distance of approximately 9,700 miles. Its signal indicated it was a fairly small object, but he would have watch for it and alert Jar'l and Sunul of its presence if it approached within a thousand miles of the ship. If it came any closer, they would not have time to respond and avoid it, provided the ship was moving on an intercept course.

Rob began entering false signals and Sunul started ship rotation to provide the smallest cross section to the lesser fake moon as the object was rapidly approaching. "Jar'l, get ready to provide a two second burn toward the planet, then I'll stop the rotation."

"God, Sunul, I can't do that with only one burn as we rotate. You'll have to stop the rotation first. The gimbals' movement is too slow for rapid reactions."

"All right, in five seconds, give a two second burn toward the planet."

"I can do that, no problem."

Rob gave them the position of the larger, retrograde moon as it was going to cross in front of the ship as it moved toward the planet. It was not necessary to rotate the ship, just move it ahead of the satellite. Jar'l responded quickly with a five-second burn.

Before Sunul and Jar'l had a chance to relax, Rob announced, "Ah, guys, there's a real object coming at us, coplanar with the rings, about 1,200 miles away. We'd better get out of the way. Jar'l, you'd better move us out of the plane of the rings, fast! We've only got about ten seconds or we're dead meat."

Jar'l reacted quickly and used all of the ten seconds to move the ship, the size of a six-story cylindrical building, below the rings, the easiest direction to avoid a possible collision and still be in position for Sunul to guide the ship on the close approach trajectory.

Sunul watched the object from one of the observation ports as it passed by. He returned to his station to rotate the ship into the proper orientation to pass between the innermost ring and Saturn. The fixed engines would be doing the majority of the work.

"Was that object one of the known moons, Rob?"

"I don't believe so, Sunul. It was approximately 250 feet wide and 600 feet long. I think it was a captured comet. I'm estimated the size from the strength of the radar reflections. I could be off by fifty percent in both estimates. It looks like it won't be back for some time, the orbit is highly eccentric."

"From what I observed, I think your estimates were right on. It was covered with small craters. I wish we could harvest some rock from one of those objects. That would allow us to generate more thrust from our engines, the methane and oxygen burns aren't giving us enough kick, and I think we'll be low on fuel by the time we reach Mars."

Rob suggested, "Let's try to do some mining when we get to Jupiter. We should be able to steal some useful mass from a small moon."

"What do you think, Sunul? Will we be going slow enough to match speeds with one of Jupiter's moons?"

"Hmm. My immediate thought is no but let me do a few calculations." Sunul had to determine how much of the fuel present would be consumed in the slow down and the benefit of the increased mass from the higher density matter obtained from mining. There would be a benefit to cost calculation that would not be easy. He would have to estimate the density of the matter they could excavate and transfer to the cargo hold. For his calculations, he chose a density of three, about 185 pounds per cubic foot on earth, typical of basalt.

The results of Sunul's program indicated the only possible position on their path back to Mars and Earth would occur at the asteroid belt. They would still be moving too rapidly after the close approach to Jupiter, so the next option was the asteroids, about 105 million miles outside Mars' orbit. Sunul's calculations indicated the crew would have to mine nearly ten metric tons, 22,000 pounds of material, or about 119 cubic feet of asteroid rock, but if they parked in an orbit alongside a minor asteroid, they would exhaust all but twelve percent of their remaining gaseous fuel. If the mining was not successful, they would be unable to slow the ship to orbit Mars, and the return to Earth would be impossible. He was forced to call a crew meeting.

The gathering was going to be postponed until after the close approach to Saturn, which was less than an hour away. In another thirty minutes, Saturn's atmosphere would fill the view from the observation ports. Monel and Triel had to be told to get their children situated so they could observe the passage of the ship between the innermost ring and the planet.

Sunul made an announcement with his com unit so the mothers could get ready with the children. He rocked back into his command chair and watched Monel and Triel guide the little ones to the observation windows. They were out of earshot so he couldn't hear what was being said as the women pointed at objects that could be seen outside the ship.

Licon pointed at something and the women began to laugh, then Miranda pointed and Sunul read Triel's lips. She had said, "Those are rings."

Sunul directed his full attention to the computer which was counting down to the initial rocket burn. Jar'l had taken his seat adjacent to Sunul and was watching the minutes and seconds counting down from 15:00 minutes. Upon reaching zero, all three rockets would burn for five seconds. The ship would rotate 180 degrees, and Jar'l would begin the ignition of the fixed engines for a burn of eighteen seconds. Sunul was to give the command to Jar'l.

Sunul made another announcement, "You have thirteen minutes to secure yourselves and others before we fire the engines to slow us down and change orientation as we briefly pass through Saturn's outermost atmosphere. The ship might groan and vibrate some, but don't be alarmed."

Sunul watched as Monel and Triel carried the children away from the viewing ports to the isolation room where all four could be safe from jostling about in the ship. Hugh and Leanne came into the command station and lashed themselves in place. Gina showed up a few seconds later.

Sunul said, "How's the radar look, Rob?"

"The rings are giving a good signal. We're clear of anything so far. I hope we don't encounter too much friction; we might lose the radar dish. It's not too sturdy out there. Can you keep it shielded by the ship?"

"I'll try to keep the antenna oriented away from the planet until we've passed through the plane of the rings."

"Do what you can."

"Don't hesitate if you get any signals as we move through the upper atmosphere."

"Right, boss."

Sunul didn't have time to respond to Rob's use of boss, the clock had counted down to eleven seconds. There was no time for banter.

When three seconds showed on the clock, Jar'l called out, "Here we go!"

Zero on the clock caused Sunul and Jar'l to punch their start engine buttons simultaneously. The vessel groaned, began to rotate and the thrust from the fixed engines pushed everyone back into their reclined, cushioned chairs for a brief three seconds. As Sunul stopped the rotation, he said, "Three, two, one, hit it Jar'l!"

The main engines forced everyone into their chairs a second time and after eighteen seconds the engines shut down. There was silence for a few seconds and then the loss of pressure siren began sounding. Before the third gong was heard, the computer announced, "Pressure drop in the botany section—five seconds until main hatch is sealed. Temperature dropping."

"What is it, Hugh?" Sunul wanted information quickly.

"We must have struck something. There's been a catastrophic failure of the ship's hull. I'll try to get in there and seal the puncture. Rob, you'd better come with me. We've only a couple of minutes before we lose all of next month's food!" He yelled at Jar'l, "Turn off that damn gong!"

Hugh asked, "EVA suits?"

"Yeah! Suit up as quickly as you can. Bring two seal patch packets and a roll of Fiber-Strong, there might be more than one hole." Hugh was headed for the botany lab as he gave directions to Hugh.

Jar'l and Sunul were watching the radar and making some slight adjustments to the ship's trajectory after skimming Saturn's atmosphere. Apparently, the radar was not damaged, but whatever had struck the ship must have come close to the radar antenna, it was mounted near one of the external support rings for the growth chamber walls.

Gina and Leanne had released their safety harnesses and joined Jar'l and Sunul at the command console. Gina stood beside Sunul and said, "Did we slow as much as you calculated?"

"I don't know yet. We'll have to use the radar and measure our velocity with a reflection from one of the moons. Can you do that, Jar'l? I've got my hands full here." Sunul smiled and reached out to Gina's protruding stomach and rubbed it. "How's the little one doing these days, dear?"

Gina placed her hand over Sunul's and replied, "About two more months in the oven," she smiled. "I'm beginning to feel that Licon and Miranda will be teenagers when Leanne and I give birth. I'm starting to worry about the older babies attacking the younger, defenseless ones."

Sunul said, "I wouldn't even think about that. You'll be able to observe the differences in growth rates and brain power between Monel's and Triel's babies versus Leanne's and yours. We'll all keep our eyes out for baby attacks, but I hope the older ones will welcome the younger ones, maybe even care for them. Their interactions should make for a great publication in one of the medical journals. You could write a book about it and submit the first chapter when we get to Mars."

"Sunul, you're always so practical." She rolled her eyes back. She had only contributed one research article to a journal and had never considered writing a book about anything, but now that the idea was planted, she would have to keep it in mind. She would record her thoughts in her com unit. The unit's memory was capable of recording at least ten novels.

"Your statement about my being practical reminds me, we have to have a crew meeting as soon as the food-growing chambers are back in working order. We have some big decisions to make."

"Are they about Jupiter?"

"No, after Jupiter. When we get to the asteroid belt."

CHAPTER 25
BOUND FOR JUPITER

Sunul spoke into his com unit in his right breast pocket, "Rob, what's the status of the puncture in the growth chamber?" Sunul and Jar'l were standing together to go over the data Jar'l had extracted from the radar signals, as they waited for a reply from Rob.

"We got in here as fast as we could, Sunul, but Hugh says we've lost about thirty percent of our vegetation. Most of the plants can't tolerate freezing conditions for very long. Fortunately, the growth medium doesn't freeze until the temp drops to about ten below zero, so the root structures are still viable. I had just harvested everything about six hours ago, so we didn't lose any matured crops. Some of the leafy material has freezer burn.

"The hole in the hull was nearly a foot in diameter. We had to use five sheets of Fiber-Strong to cover the hole after we trimmed away the sharp edges. Then we covered the opening with a layer of PeneSeal membrane. We're about to attach an aluminum alloy plate over the fiber and membrane. I'm getting ready to weld the plate in position. The fix will be ugly, but nothing will leak through it."

"Do you have the projectile?" Sunul hoped nothing else had been damaged.

Hugh answered, "Yes. I'll store it in the cargo area. We can examine it later. It's about the size of two hardballs fused together. It must have been moving pretty fast when it hit us. It ripped through the hull like it was crepe paper. It crashed into a wall cabinet and scattered some lab equipment, hit the floor, and then slid under one of the workstations. I think the magnetic floor material kept it from bouncing around. Most of the kinetic energy was absorbed by the hull."

Jar'l said, "So you think it's magnetic?"

"Oh yeah, it has an affinity for the floor. It looks like a meteorite with high metallic content and only about fifteen to twenty percent stony material."

Sunul observed, "Too bad we don't have a cargo hold full of that material. We wouldn't have to stop and do any mining. That chunk might not have been going very fast, but we were. As soon as you guys finish up in there, we need to have a crew meeting. How much longer will you be?"

Sunul could hear Rob's breathing; he sounded relaxed. "Maybe thirty minutes. We've got a small mess to clean up while the pressure returns to normal. When the temperature reaches about sixty degrees, we'll open the hatch and join you."

"Okay, I'm not in any hurry." Sunul sat back and ran his palm over his rough chin whiskers; he hadn't shaved in two days. His laser shaving tool had only been used once in the past week. He had been absorbed with planning calculations for the close approaches to both Saturn and Jupiter and had spent most of his awake time carrying out computations. Fortunately, the mathematical work was complete. Now the meeting with the crew had to be carried out. They had to be advised of the risks of fuel expenditure and mining an asteroid before continuing to Mars.

Sunul had forgotten to check with Jar'l about their current velocity. He looked at Jar'l to see if he was busy. Jar'l waved a sheet of paper at him and moved from the radar unit and sat down next to him. Sunul could see some data was circled in red ink.

"How much did we slow, Jar'l?"

"About twenty-eight percent. Here's before and here's after." Jar'l pointed at two numbers.

"Damn! I thought we'd get into the high thirty percent range. Jupiter will have to contribute a larger slow-down than I had estimated. We've got to get our speed down to about 50,000 miles per hour after our close approach to Jupiter or we won't have enough fuel to dock with an asteroid and carry out mining. Maybe we can swing around Ganymede or Callisto if one of them is in the right orientation."

"What's the velocity of an asteroid, Sunul?"

"About forty thousand mph. We've got to slow our ship down by expending some fuel. We need to talk with Rob and see how much of this scow we can jettison. I'm afraid we're going to have to drop at least twenty percent of our mass so we'll have enough of our present fuel to park and take on heavy fuel."

"There aren't many alternatives, huh?"

"Not that I can think of right now. That's why we need to have a meeting."

With everyone assembled, Sunul explained the situation and asked if anyone wanted to comment. He looked around at the crew and Rob said, "We'll have two empty fuel tanks to jettison, but that's not much mass."

Hugh chimed in, "What if we discard the botany lab? I'll bet that would castoff about twenty-five to thirty percent of our mass."

Triel frowned and grabbed Hugh's arm. "Hugh, we can't give up our source of food, Miranda and Licon are eating solid food now." She turned to Sunul and asked, "When will we arrive at the asteroid belt?"

"In about nine weeks. We have to catch up to Jupiter and carry out another close approach and then move toward the asteroids. Can you stockpile enough food for another month after dumping the growth lab? It will take us another month to arrive at Mars. The orrery computer program indicates Mars will be catching up to us while we're mining the asteroid belt."

Triel sighed and leaned back, with Miranda held against her stomach. "We'll have to ration our supplies. If we cut our food intake to about two-thirds, we'll be all right."

Gina frowned and looked at Leanne, who was exhibiting a similar expression of concern.

Leanne said, "Gina and I can't cut our calories by a third, we have to eat for our babies; they're due in about two months."

Hugh spoke up, "What about the medical synthesizer? Can't necessary vitamins be made in the medical lab?"

"Well, I suppose we could do that. Leanne and I will start taking doses to supplement our decreased food intake." Gina glanced at Leanne and she nodded and said, "We can't afford to waste anything edible, so add any bits of food you don't eat to the source materials bin on the synthesizer."

Gina added, "And don't jettison body wastes. We'll run excreta through the sterilizer and recycle it in the synthesizer. We'll reclaim sodium, potassium, calcium, magnesium, and iron for sure. Chloride and sulfate salts will also be conserved."

Monel asked, "Can you show us the positions of the planets in their present positions and the vectors and times involved in each transition?"

Sunul carried out the calculations on his com unit and then displayed the results on the holographic viewer with each transition in a different color. Using that procedure, he could avoid informing earth of the return of the ship. Not utilizing the main computer would prevent alerting earth of the computations, keeping the team's real position cloaked. Items displayed in the ship were never part of the data sent to earth stations.

Everyone had their eyes locked on the display as Sunul traced the motion of the ship along the predicted path to Mars. When the ship's position reached Jupiter, Sunul switched off the display and informed the crew of the options.

"So, we don't have enough gaseous fuel to maneuver into orbit around Mars. However, we could skip Mars and go directly toward Earth. Earth will be in nearly the same position when we started our journey. Mars is nearly opposite the Earth on the other side of the sun. If we take on fuel from the asteroid belt, we will be able to accelerate or slow down as we see fit."

Monel asked, "What about our food supply? How long will it take to visit Mars and then return to Earth?"

"That's a big problem with the food situation the way it is now. I expect if we go to Mars and then Earth, we will be in this tub for another six months."

Gina said, "We'll all be dead, Sunul! We'll have to skip Mars and go straight to Earth. Maybe they'll send a ship with food and fuel to get us into orbit and then ferry us down a few at a time."

Jar'l was thinking of something else. "What if the Earth doesn't want us back? Will they try to destroy us as we approach and say they had to protect Earth from a collision with a comet or an asteroid?"

Sunul remarked, "Let's not get ahead of ourselves. We'll solve that problem when we get back to Earth's orbit. I think there are some reasonable people at the space agency."

The couples began murmuring, discussing the situation. About a minute passed before Sunul spoke up, "I've been thinking about the food situation." Sunul looked at Triel and Hugh. "Is there any great reason to have all the growth chambers in the present location? Can't we move the larger arrays into the hallways and the entertainment complex, and the smaller units into our private quarters, maybe even the galley?"

Hugh and Triel smiled and Triel said, "Great idea, Sunul! We'll begin work moving the equipment. Rob will have to help us fasten the chambers to the floor and walls of the various rooms and hallways." Hugh commented, "We might only get about three-fourths of the plants moved, but that should be enough to sustain us for nearly a year. We'll still have to ration some items. But we won't have enough room to put the cattle out to pasture."

Everyone laughed for a moment and then Gina pretended to be annoyed. "Are you talking about us, Hugh? Leanne and I are not that big."

"That was only a joke, Gina. I was thinking about a farmer on a Montana cattle ranch."

Sunul said, "You'd better be careful, Hugh. Your foot is getting awfully close to your mouth."

CHAPTER 26
NEARING JUPITER

Twenty-five days later, the ship was approaching Jupiter, but still about ten days away. The four large Galilean satellites could be seen without optical aid, although they were still only tiny disks or crescents. Sunul entered their positions into his simulation program and found that Ganymede and Callisto, the more massive moons, were going to be in favorable positions to assist with the ship's braking maneuver, if he could jockey the ship into an optimum approach trajectory. It would require using all three engines and another ten to twelve percent of the remaining fuel. Slowing to mine an asteroid might be a nail-biting rendezvous problem. Without fuel to maneuver the ship, the sun would control the final part of their journey. Luck would determine whether they could return to Earth or alternatively, plunge into the sun.

After completing the simulation, Sunul sat back to relax and watched Hugh and Rob as they attached the last of the vegetation growth racks to the wall leading to the galley from the entertainment center. The interior walls of the games area reminded him of pictures of the outside of century-old medieval castles covered with ivy and bright yellow-green mold dappled with bright yellow and red splotches of roses and wildflowers. He had to smile as he thought of how the crew had, without exception, attacked the multifaceted job of reorienting the growth paraphernalia without any but minor complaints. As the days passed, the crew began to form special interests in some of the plants, taking over some of Hugh's and Triel's duties.

The vegetation specialists had exhibited great patience as they directed the movement of the apparatus. The new positions of the growth racks had caused the botanists some concern over the lack of organization of the vegetation, but they recorded maps on their com units. They posted the printed maps on the bulkheads for everyone to see.

Sunul made an announcement over the ship's intercom, "Rob, we need to talk."

Five minutes later, Rob entered the galley where Sunul was eating lunch.

"What is it, boss?" Rob was carrying a cutting torch and some cable, and his face had a slightly sour look. Apparently, Sunul had interrupted progress in one of Rob's projects.

"Have you been thinking about how we're going to separate the growth lab from the rest of the ship?"

"You interrupted those arrangements. I was making some explosive bolts and getting ready to carry out an EVA to mount the explosive charges on the hull around the joining seams. I'm going to wrap some cable around the outer hull, so it breaks off as a unit instead of in sections. I'm afraid if it doesn't come off cleanly, the residual chunks might damage the remainder of the ship as we put on the brakes."

Sunul hesitated for a moment and then replied, "Good thinking. I should have known you had something planned. Will we be able to explode the charges from inside the ship?"

"That's what I have planned. It will take two of us to do it, though. We'll have to be close to the seams to carry out the transmission. One com unit doesn't have enough power to penetrate the hull where the seams are located, but two will do the job if they are fully charged. I've built some amplifiers to strengthen the signals. I didn't want to use a remote laser to set off the charges; the laser would be sacrificed, plus it could be dangerous when the explosions occur. Besides, we'll need all our lasers for mining."

"If a section of hull remains in place, Rob, I think we can dislodge it with our side thruster. If that doesn't work, we can use an EVA and remove it with a torch." Sunul looked at the cable Rob was carrying over his shoulder. "Sorry I interrupted you. Do you need any help out there? I've got some time available. I'd like to jettison the growth lab in twenty-eight hours and reorient the ship. Will that give you enough time?"

"No problem, I should have it ready to go after one more work-sleep cycle, but if you can help from the cargo door, it will speed things up by a few hours. I've been making trips back and forth to pick up equipment and it's taking more time than I had originally planned."

"All right. I'll meet you in the cargo hold in fifteen minutes. I'll get suited up."

Rob headed for the cargo bay and Sunul started for his quarters, passing the galley where Licon and Miranda were standing on the swing-out barstool cushions. Triel and Monel were holding the youngsters so they wouldn't drift from their seats and float away. Licon swallowed and said, "What is your name, mister?"

Sunul smiled and replied, "Sunul. Who are you?"

"I am Licon. This is Miranda. We are friends. These are our mothers." He pointed at each of the ladies.

"I'd like to stay and talk, but I'm busy right now. Later."

Licon responded, "Yes, we will talk later." He dipped his spoon into what looked like pudding and filled his mouth, smiling at Monel and waved his spoon at Sunul.

Sunul entered his quarters as quietly as possible, trying not to wake Gina. She was lying on her back and seemed to be sound asleep, her swollen belly looked as if she had just eaten a large watermelon, whole. Sunul had to get his headgear, so he held his breath and lifted the bubble shaped helmet from its storage shelf.

"What are you doing?"

"Jesus! You scared the crap out of me. I thought you were sound asleep."

"I've been trying to sleep, but I'm so uncomfortable and I keep thinking of how painful it's going to be. Giving birth is something I planned on doing later in life, and not in a stupid, make-shift spaceship. I thought I'd be on earth with a regular doctor and support nurses."

"Well, think of the ship as a tent; we're on a camping trip in the woods at Yosemite. There isn't a doctor within miles and I'm the only one to help you through it. We can do this together."

"Oh, my God, Sunul. That makes it even worse. Now I won't sleep for days."

"Can I get you a sedative? It will relax you and you can sleep while I'm in the cargo hold helping Rob."

"What's he doing?"

"He's getting ready to remove the growth chamber section of the hull to lighten our load. It will take less fuel to slow us down if we reduce our mass. But you know all about kinetic energy."

"You're not going outside the ship, are you?"

"No. Don't worry. I'm just going to get tools for him. He's on a tether and I'll hook up to the cargo hold wall."

"Okay. I'll take one of those tiny pink pills and go to sleep, if I can. Get me up in a couple of hours, whether I'm sleeping or not, okay?"

"Yes, doc."

"Nurse?"

Sunul turned, smiled, and looked at Gina. "Yes?"

"Give me a kiss."

He kissed her lips and then her belly. As he backed out of the room he said, "Go to sleep!"

Sunul and Rob worked together for just over two hours before taking a break. As they waited for the pressure to stabilize in the airlock, Sunul asked, "What more do you have to do out there?"

"One more explosive bolt to install and then I'm through outside. I've got to do some cutting on the inside hull where the bolts will blow. It should take me another hour after I come back in. Then I'm going to sleep for about six hours. I'm starting to feel a bit rundown."

"Yeah. Those EVAs take it out of you. I always worry about being struck by something when I'm out there."

"I know what you mean. But we're still pretty far from Jupiter so it's relatively safe. When we get within a million miles, things could get a little hairy. The amount of space junk starts to increase as we close in on the orbits of the outer moons."

"Sunul, I just picked up a low-level signal from Earth to the Mars' station. You need to hear this." Jar'l's voice had boomed over the intercom. Then the message was repeated in Sunul's headgear. Although Sunul was holding his EVA helmet on his lap, Jar'l's announcement sounded as if it were an echo. The digital chamber pressure display indicated normal; the protective lock disengaged, and the hatch door swung open. Sunul turned to Rob and listened as the EVA suit closure was released, then Sunul released Rob's suit seal. As soon as they donned their uniforms, Sunul departed for the command console, leaving Rob to complete the internal amplifier circuits on the inside hull near the explosive bolts.

"What's the origin time stamp on that message, Jar'l?"

Jar'l looked at the Earth time indicator on the main console. "Ah, about an hour ago."

Sunul thought for a moment and said, "What you received must have been a retransmission from one of the Earth orbiting wide-angle transmitters. If it had been a line-of-site broadcast, we would never have picked it up. What does it say?"

"The Distant Orbital Infrared Satellite detected an erratic signal approaching Jupiter. Earth is asking the Mars' station to focus on Jupiter with optical telescopes to see if they can find an asteroid that was recently pulled from orbit." Jar'l smiled, "They're looking in the wrong direction. They have no idea we're on our way back!"

"That's right, but in a few hours, they're going to see some strange infrared signatures when we put on our brakes again. I'll bet we can eavesdrop on some messages if our exhaust heat is detected. Let's hope that Jupiter's atmosphere will conceal some our presence, but we won't be able to stay in Jupiter's shadow very long. Someone in the agency will have thought of us and wonder if we know anything. Let's make sure we have all our transmission data corrected to our Earth-known distance in the Kuiper belt. We don't want to encourage any suspicions."

"Right. I'll check with you before we forward data to our relay transmitter on 5K23m. I'll have Monel verify our time calculations. She's very good at intricate detail work. I'll watch Licon while she goes over our computations."

CHAPTER 27
JUPITER AIDS THE SLOWDOWN

"Sunul!" Gina sounded irritated. She was standing in the opening to the galley chewing on something, staring at her husband, and holding her swollen stomach. Sunul knew he was in hot water; he had forgotten about waking Gina from her nap.

"I'm sorry I forgot to wake you, Gina. Jar'l picked up a message from Earth to the Mars' station. Someone noticed our engine exhaust signature taken by an infrared satellite camera, but they don't know what it is. We expect another request for the Mars' station for info after we pass close to Jupiter. We won't be able to hide all our engine exhausts. I'm trying to figure out the burns that will be hidden from detection, or at least minimize the hot exhaust clouds that the IR satellite might detect. I'm assuming the IR satellite isn't very far from Earth, but maybe it's in a super-lunar orbit."

"You think the Earth techs will figure out what's going on?"

"Nope. I'm going to have Rob place a charge on the hull we're jettisoning. I think it will provide a distraction from our hot exhaust gases. I'll have him set the charge to detonate when the hull remnant hits the atmosphere. I just have to reorient the ship so the growth section will fall into Jupiter before we hit the brakes again."

"Hmm. Very clever. Now I understand why you forgot about me.

Too many crucial things on your mind."

"I'm really sorry, Gina. Were you able to get some sleep?"

"Uh-huh, about ninety minutes. Miles woke me up with some kicking."

"Another month?"

"I think so. Where will we be?"

"After this slowdown, it will take us about a month get to the asteroids. After a day of mining and with more massive fuel aboard, we can speed up, another two weeks to Mars."

"Sunul, I don't think I can keep the cork in the bottle for six weeks, urgency might take over any day in the next few weeks." Gina laughed and held her stomach like a bundle of clothes from the dryer."

Sunul grinned and said, "Don't squeeze him out, Gina. Let nature takes its course. How is Leanne feeling?"

"She hasn't said much, she just goes about her business as usual. I don't know if you've noticed, but she isn't as big as I am."

"Rob mentioned that earlier today, when we were working, but they're having a girl; maybe she'll be a little nymph."

"I think we're going to have a giant bruiser." She wrapped her hands around her belly as if to hold it up. "I'm glad we're not on Earth, I'd have to get a grocery cart to haul my stomach around."

"I remember my mother telling me I weighed ten-and-a-half pounds when I was born."

"Oh, your poor mother. You were a real load!"

"My sister weighed in at nine pounds."

"You have a sister?"

"Sh." He put his right index finger to his lips. "I don't want anyone to know. I lied on my application. Her name is Priscilla. She's an artist, lives in Paris with her husband, Francoise Girard, and their little girl, Gisele."

"What else have you hidden from me?"

"I wasn't hiding it; it just never came up. There's nothing else. I thought it was time to let you know we can send pictures of the baby to family. Speaking of load, I've got to talk with Rob so we can put an explosive charge on the section of the ship we're jettisoning. I'll talk to you some more later." Sunul gave Gina a kiss and disappeared down the hallway toward the cargo hold.

Gina wanted to talk to the other women about pain. How had they handled it? Did they depend on medication? Gina couldn't remember prescribing any pain meds for any of the other women. She touched Leanne's tab on the main console and found that Leanne was sleeping. Her vitals were all normal. It had been a week since her pregnant friend's last checkup. Gina was a little disappointed, she wanted to inquire about Leanne's health and that would give her a reason to ask about pain. Leanne had been busy for the last couple of days moving the growth apparatus from the soon to be jettisoned chamber to the hallway walls and the activity areas. She hadn't asked or made any remarks about pain.

Monel's and Triel's tabs indicated both women were scheduled for a sleep period in thirty minutes. They followed almost identical schedules so the children could be together for the majority of their physical and mental activities. The location sensor indicated the two women were in their compartments with their children. She headed toward Monel's and Jar'l's quarters. As Gina approached the residents' units, she could hear Monel's voice getting louder and more excited. The door was fully open.

"No, Licon! You can't go outside the ship."

"Why not? Plenty of room for everybody."

As Gina stepped to the open door, a tone sounded indicating to the inhabitants someone had appeared outside their quarters. Monel and Licon turned their heads to see Gina fall through the doorway and crumple to the floor.

"Gina!" Monel dropped to the floor on her knees and lifted Gina's head. "Licon, give me a pillow." Monel placed the pillow Licon had pushed off the bed, then Licon dropped to the floor and joined his mother next to Gina. Monel straightened Gina's body so her swollen belly was up. Licon placed his hands on Gina's tummy and rubbed with both hands, pushing in slightly.

Monel said, "Licon, what are you doing?" She was both surprised and amused at her little boy's actions.

Gina opened her eyes, squinted at the bright ceiling lights, frowned, and was trying to sit up, but Licon pushed on her shoulders and said, "Stay on floor a little longer, then the little boy inside will be fine, you too. He was crooked."

"What happened to me?" Gina's eyes were fixed on Monel.

"I think you fainted. Licon said the baby was crooked. It must have caused an attack of extreme pain. It came on all of a sudden."

"Licon? What did he do? He's too little to know anything."

"Well, he massaged your belly and said you and the little boy will be fine. Somehow, he knows things. The other day I bumped my knee. He wasn't even with me. Later in the day he asked how my knee was."

"You must have been limping."

"No, I'd forgotten all about it. My knee wasn't even sore. Funny thing, Miranda does some of the same things with Triel, and the kids have a connection, too, what one knows the other one knows. It occurs almost instantly."

Gina was standing now, holding onto the door casing with one hand steadying herself. "What I came by to ask was about pain when you gave birth to Licon."

Monel shook her head. "Gosh, I don't remember any, but there must have been some. I remember you telling me to push and then it was all over. I hope your experience will be as trouble-free as mine was."

Gina said good night, withdrew from the room and returned to the command center. She had a feeling of euphoria; pain was the farthest thing from her thoughts. She tuned in the conversation between Sunul and Rob, listened for a few minutes, found the exchanges boring, and checked to see any messages had come from Earth or Mars. It had been months since there had been any contact with the beta group. Gina was wondering how many of the women in the beta group were pregnant.

"Gina? Are you at the command center?"

"I'm here, Sunul. What do you need?"

"Please start the simulation program for Jupiter. It's labelled J611. I'll be there in a few minutes. Rob and I have been discussing the Jupiter breaking routine and I need to go over it one more time. I overlooked something."

"Okay. I'll have it ready for you."

"Thanks, dear. Are you feeling all right?"

"Never better. When you get here, I'll tell you about an experience I had about thirty minutes ago."

"A dream?"

"No, something special from Licon."

"Now you have my imagination moving at light speed."

When Sunul arrived and was seated beside Gina, she told him of her fainting spell and the strange feeling of well-being after having been touched by Licon.

"That reminds me of the Superman stories. He had x-ray vision."

"The feeling I had was as if I had taken a euphoriant or had been put under with nitrous oxide, but it didn't happen until I was wide awake and walking back from the Jar'l's and Monel's living quarters."

"Great! Now we have to worry about the kids controlling our thoughts and perceptions."

"I don't think we need to worry about that. I think it was a result of him massaging my stomach to move the baby to a more comfortable position, but I'll avoid any contact with him until after I have the baby. Maybe he can't communicate with non-pregnant women."

"We'll have to do some experiments with the kids to investigate their abilities. But if they can read minds, that will be difficult. Why don't you ask Triel and Monel to try some things and observe the kids' reactions."

"I'll talk with the mothers when the kids are sleeping."

"Sounds like a plan. I've got to get to work on the simulation of the breaking maneuver. We'll talk during dinner. Then, I've got to get some sleep. I've got to be alert for the maneuver. It's going to take place in about nine hours."

Sunul had gotten up after sleeping for six hours. He ate some breakfast and carried his hot drink container to the main console. The count-down clock registered fifty-seven minutes.

He spoke into the intercom and alerted everyone about the upcoming jettison explosions and the breaking maneuvers. He wanted the crew and children to be secured within ten minutes of the procedures.

"Rob will be initiating the firing sequence of the explosive bolts. There will be six rapid-fire explosions. You should feel two vibrations of the ship: the first, when the bolts fire, and the second, when the hull section releases from the remainder of the ship. Rob tells me that we shouldn't be alarmed if we hear some metal snapping. However, if the ship pressure drops, have your breathing apparatus handy.

"Unless you are taking part in emergency procedures, remain in your harnesses. We will begin a slow-down maneuver a few seconds after the hull section has been uncoupled. There will be some g-forces that might cause loss of balance. I don't want anyone to get thrown around."

The ship approached the north pole of Jupiter, accelerating as the giant planet's gravitational forces began to tug at the Kuiper Belt ship. The explosive bolts blew as planned and the hull that had contained the food growth labs decoupled and began tumbling toward the planet's clouds. When at a safe distance from the ship, just as the refuse touched the clouds, Rob sent a signal and an explosion rocked the jettisoned portion of the hull. The crew heard nothing, but could see a flash of light, almost like lightning back on earth, but longer lasting. The ship's interior lighting returned to normal.

"Everyone ready? Here we go!"

CHAPTER 28
DESTINATION: ASTEROIDS

In less than three hours, the ship had slowed significantly by completing an S-shaped trajectory around Jupiter and its most massive moon, Ganymede. Jar'l was watching the ship's velocity and gave Sunul a thumb's up. The maneuver was successful but not without some concern to the travelers. The ship had groaned and strained the air-conditioning unit when they passed briefly through the upper clouds of the huge planet. The ship with its ten occupants, soon to be twelve, was continuing toward the asteroid belt, still coasting, but being accelerated by the sun. Sunul said, "You may release your seat belts and roam around the cabin. Next stop will be the asteroid belt for in-flight refueling."

There was some laughter and smiling by the crew as they related to Sunul's announcement, similar to that of an airline pilot back on Earth after a passenger plane had reached cruising altitude. Sunul continued with more flight information. "We should arrive at the asteroid belt in a little over three weeks. We have no choice but to refuel. Our reserves are down to slightly over twelve percent. That's enough fuel to dock with an asteroid, but not enough for us to land without mishap on Mars."

Rob and Hugh moved from their cushioned travel chairs and sat down beside Sunul.

"Hugh just asked me how much rock we're going to need to ensure we'll have enough fuel for the remainder of our trip to Earth. I don't know how to make that estimate, Sunul."

Rob's concern showed in his face. He appeared frustrated as he waited for Sunul's reply. He was rubbing the palm of his left hand with his right thumb, a nervous habit he had always exhibited when he felt at a complete loss to formulate an answer.

"You can help me do the calculations, Rob. We'll make our best estimates and add twenty percent to give us some leeway. We've been using low density fuel since we left 5K23m and we're going to run out before long. We've got enough to allow us to dock with a medium sized asteroid, and that's it." Sunul looked at Jar'l. "What's our current velocity?"

"Give me a minute." Jar'l turned to the radar unit and timed a reflection from the surface of Ganymede, trailing behind them. "Between 220,000 and 230,000 miles per hour, Sunul."

"Thanks. Okay, Rob, let's get to work."

The two men worked together for about fifteen minutes before Sunul asked, "What's the volume of the cargo hold?"

"Completely empty: 480 cubic meters, but we've got those nearly empty gas tanks from our old ship in there. I'd estimate we have about 300 cubic meters of free storage space."

Sunul thought for a moment and replied, "If we cut the fuel into cubes, one meter on an edge, we can only stack them three units high or we won't be able to handle them. That means we'll use the old tanks as fuel and have room for about 150 cubic meters of denser fuel."

Rob perked up and asked, "How do we get the solid fuel to the engines?"

Sunul smiled, "That was my next question for you."

Rob clapped his hands and stood up. "I've got an idea, but it'll take a couple of weeks to assemble what I'm thinking of. I'll need some help with an EVA, actually, several EVAs. I'll sketch my idea and go over it with you tomorrow."

When Rob was ready to reveal his plan, Sunul was busy reviewing positions of asteroids, trying to find a target for their mining expedition. He was monitoring the use of fuel, gradually slowing the ship, but having to fight momentum and the acceleration from the sun, his calculations indicated they were going to run out of fuel and overshoot the asteroids. He needed fuel. Sunul wasn't aware that Rob had joined him at the console. Sunul spoke into the PA system, "Rob, please come to the main console. We need to talk."

"I'm right here, boss."

"How long have you been here? I didn't see you sit down beside me."

"Maybe five minutes ago. You were totally absorbed in a computation, so I sat down and waited."

"All right, show me what you want to construct."

Rob held his com next to Sunul's and said, "Copy feed."

Sunul looked at the feed sketch on his com unit and asked, "Why the figure eight track?"

"It's not quite a figure eight; the track's not closed at the middle. The only robot feeder we have can't go in reverse, so I have to make a circular track pinched in the middle. The feeder will take a hopper of fuel, travel to rocket A, dump the load and return. Then the robot will pick up another hopper and take it to rocket B, dump and return. This way the robot can function continuously without intervention."

"Looks good. The feeder will run continuously on the outside of the track and outside the ship, except when it takes on a new load. The cargo hold will remain open?"

"Yes. We have no choice. In fact, we can remove the cargo door and feed it to the engines."

Sunul glanced at Rob and smiled. "I was going to ask you what part of the ship we can sacrifice to use for fuel. We're going to need every atom we can find to feed the engines to slow us. We've got to reduce our velocity by eighty percent to dock with an asteroid. We'd better make a list of things we can sacrifice as fuel."

"I'll make the feeder track from the empty fuel tanks. The remnants will be fed to the engines. They'll make good snacks for the rockets."

Sunul smiled and thought for a moment. "We might have to dismantle all the internal doors and use them as fuel, too."

Jar'l commented, "Are we going to need the engine attached to the rotation mechanism? It's got a significant mass. We can use the other two engines for steering as long as we don't have to make any sudden changes in course."

Rob and Jar'l were watching Sunul as he considered sacrificing the engine that possessed the largest directional thrust capabilities. Sunul didn't react as quickly to Jar'l's suggestion as expected. Sunul's mind was buried in several layers of thought. He couldn't afford to make a bad decision and sacrifice twelve people.

"Let's not use that engine for fuel, only if we have no other choice. I'd like reserving steering ability as long as possible. If we can't slow down significantly by the time we're converging with the asteroid belt, we'll have to forfeit the engine. Let's see if we can slow down by giving up other things first."

"All right. Sounds good to me. I'm going to start assembling the track for the robot feeder. It's going to take me several days to make the parts and another couple of days to install it on the outside of the ship. I'll let you guys know when you can help with the EVAs."

Sunul replied, "We'll start dismantling interior parts of the ship and transferring the pieces to the cargo hold. Let us know where you want us to store the materials."

"Just pile everything near the interior door. I don't want to have to work around junk as I construct the robot-track."

"Okay. Let's get to work." Jar'l tossed a screwdriver and wrench to Sunul and they moved into the recreation complex. The game console was going to be the first non-essential item to be scrapped, after that, they would remove all doors. The loss of privacy would have to be tolerated.

It took nearly thirty minutes to remove the console and cap the optical fibers. Jar'l wanted to retain the integrity of the light pipes in case the crew needed them for another device that they might damage as they dismantled the interior of the ship. Unfortunately, structures thought to be made of metal were constructed from plastics sheathed with a thin layer of aluminum and reinforced with a composite of cellulose and polymer fibers treated with fire retardant. More massive elements would have to come from other sources. Sunul began to think that the growth chamber that had been jettisoned had been disposed of too soon.

The men began removing the doors to the crew's quarters by surgical cuts through walls with lasers to uncouple the motors and locks. As the first door was removed and carried to the cargo hold, Sunul heard Gina cry out.

"Sunul! The baby's coming!"

Sunul could hear the urgency in Gina's voice, so he dropped the door outside the cargo hatch and ran to his quarters. Monel and Licon were standing next to Gina. They all heard another cry for help, "Hugh! It's time!"

It was Leanne. The day before, she had mentioned to Gina that she knew the birth was imminent. It was almost like they had planned for simultaneous births, the yells for help had come about ten seconds apart. Hugh passed by the doorway with part of a large strawberry sticking out of his mouth and rubbing his hands on his close-fitting gray tunic.

"Put ladies on the floor beside each other." Licon seemed to be taking over. Sunul looked at Monel and said, "Does he know something? He's only a few months' old."

Monel raised her open hands to both sides of her face and said, "Let's do what he says. He always has a good reason. He's extremely clever. Somehow he knows things we wouldn't expect of him."

Sunul knew it would sound strange, but he called out, "Hugh, bring Leanne in here and put her on the floor beside Gina. Rob's in the cargo hold."

"What?"

"You heard me, bring Leanne in here and put her on the floor!"

Licon pointed at the floor and said, "Blanket." Then he looked at Sunul and said, "Put the lady on blanket."

Sunul complied, laying Gina on the blanket. Hugh appeared at the doorway carrying Leanne and Licon pointed at the floor. "Other lady here." Licon pulled on Monel's pant leg, looked up at his mother, and said, "Get Miranda."

Triel had heard Licon's immature, but demanding, voice and appeared holding Miranda on her hip.

Carefully, Licon stepped between the two women on the floor, sat down, and beckoned for Miranda. Miranda sat facing Licon and the kids grasped the pregnant women's hands. Monel and Sunul positioned themselves to catch the babies. The room became quiet except for the subtle sounds of breathing. Licon looked at Gina and said, "Close eyes." He repeated the same words to Leanne.

Miranda and Licon began to hum, similar to the clucking sound they had made when babies, but not in unison. Sunul took Gina's stethoscope and listened to Miles' heartbeat. It was synchronous with Licon's humming noises. Curiosity guided Sunul to check Leanne's baby's heartbeat. It was in synch with Miranda's humming. Sunul looked at Monel and shook his head in disbelief at what was transpiring. Sunul said, "Gina, are you all right?"

"Yes. I'm floating in a cloud above the base hospital in Houston. I feel wonderful; the clouds are like giant mounds of cotton."

Leanne volunteered, "I'm floating, too, but not in a cloud. I'm in a pool of warm water. It's beautiful here. I think I'm in Yellowstone Park."

Licon and Miranda stood up and said in unison, "The babies will come out now."

Leanna and Gina pushed, and the new babies were delivered into the waiting hands of Sunul and Monel. Hugh handed Sunul a pair of scissors and some towels to wrap the new members of the makeshift spacecraft.

Hugh was transfixed. "That was amazing! If I hadn't seen it, I wouldn't have believed it, not in a lifetime. Licon and Miranda have some unbelievable abilities. How could they do that?"

Monel said, "It's kind of wonderful. They amaze me, too, but I'm a bit worried what they'll be able to do when they get older. They might not fit into our society on Earth. Triel and I think they might have to be left on Mars. Of course, we'd stay with them until they reach maturity."

Hugh reacted, "You mean you wouldn't let them visit earth? That would be a pity. I think Triel and I want to take Miranda to earth to see the cities and the national parks."

Monel argued, "But Hugh, if the government finds out about Licon and Miranda, they'll be taken from us, poked and prodded, x-rayed and studied innumerable ways. They'll probably be quarantined. I don't want Licon to experience that. When he realizes what is going on, he might act violently."

"Maybe you're right. I'll have to discuss it with Triel. I need to know what she thinks. We might have to stay on Mars and out of the limelight."

CHAPTER 29
MINING

Ten days had passed since the new births. There was a celebratory mood in the ship; all four couples had healthy children and Sunul had announced that it appeared there was going to be enough fuel to dock with a large asteroid in about ten more days. Rob had completed the track for the robot refueler, and it had been successfully tested. Triel had baked a cake, although she didn't get the batter quite correct for the low gravity environment. The cake had almost overflowed the oven. She was disappointed, but the angel food-like cake was delicious even though it looked more like swollen Swiss cheese.

"Leanne, what have you named your little girl?" Jar'l was curious to see if the Griswalts had chosen the name of a giant planet's moon for their daughter.

"The mythological name of Jupiter's wife is Juno, but Rob and I thought Juno sounded more like a boy's name. We've decided on Junette: Juni for short."

Miranda was tugging at Triel's pant leg. "Mommy, the new babies are broken."

There was a sudden hush to the festivities. Everyone's attention was drawn to Miranda.

Gina asked, "What do you mean, Miranda?"

Miranda smiled and said, "Licon and I can't talk to them. We think their hearing is not working. We will show you."

Gina was holding Miles in her lap and Leanne was feeding Juni with a squeeze bottle as Rob held their baby. Licon stood in front of Miles and touched the baby's knee. Miranda followed Licon with Juni. Miles and Juni were both smiling at the older children. Licon and Miranda began their clucking sounds simultaneously. Neither of the new babies reacted to the rhythmic noises except by squirming in their parent's arms.

Licon and Miranda turned and looked at the adults. "See, they aren't talking to us. We don't think they heard us. Their ears are not good." Miranda nodded, agreeing with Licon.

Gina looked as if she didn't have the patience to give a long explanation to the older children. She glanced at Sunul who had just thrown up his hands. He was admitting his first defeat. "Monel, do you want to handle this?"

"I'll try, Gina. Feel free to chime in anytime."

Monel began by trying to explain DNA, but the children could not grasp what she was saying. They sat there expressionless as she tried to explain about chromosomes. Jar'l came to Monel's aid with some basic binary mathematics. He hoped they would understand computer math. After about ten minutes of drawing on his com tablet, he finally said, "The new babies don't understand the way you and Miranda do, Licon. It will take them much longer before they will be capable of doing mathematics. Babies grow very slowly, especially with their mental and speaking ability. When they are seven or eight years old, they will understand what you do at this time. You have a great advantage right now, but they will eventually catch up." As he was talking, he hoped the content of his last sentence was true.

Licon and Miranda seemed to understand. Miranda said, "We will take care of them so they will be able to learn more quickly than other babies. If they cry, we will figure out what is wrong and fix it."

Gina had to make a comment. "Don't give the babies anything to eat unless you ask one of the adults first. Okay?"

Licon nodded to Gina and said, "Okay. Come Miranda, let's play our game."

Gina turned to Monel, "What game do they have?"

"It's like rock, paper, scissors, but more complicated. From what I've figured out, it's about stars, planets, and moons, but I don't understand it."

Sunul laughed, "I hope they don't take over the ship when we're asleep."

While the next ten days passed, the space vehicle began a gradual slowdown as the internal hardware from the ship was fed into the two main engines. At 165,000 miles from the asteroids, Sunul asked Jar'l for a velocity measurement.

"Our present velocity is approximately 45,000 miles per hour. That could be off by a thousand or so. I'm targeting asteroids and most all of them are rotating. The reflections are not very strong, sometimes only twice the background signal level."

"That's close enough. Another 5,000 miles per hour has to go. We're going to have to cannibalize the variable angle engine to have enough thrust to slow us to that extent. There's not much else in here that we can do without. Get ready for an EVA with me. We have about two hours to spare before hitting the brakes again. We're going to pull that engine into the cargo hold and dismantle it."

"What about the radioactive core, Sunul?"

"I was going to ask you about that. Can we dismantle the core and use it for fuel, too?"

Jar'l snickered. "Not unless you want to blow up the entire ship. The ion chambers are surrounded by electromagnetic collars which are energized by the radioactive core. If we tamper with the magnets, the core will try to compensate and probably go critical. We're talking about at least a twenty-kiloton explosion."

"Hmm. So, when we get to the magnets, we'll have to store it until we're clear of the asteroids. How much of a delay should we use when we blow it?"

"Thirty minutes should be enough. We'll be accelerating to about 50,000 mph, so we'll be about 2,500 to 3,000 miles away by the time it explodes."

"We can't leave it on the rock we're going to be mining, so we'll eject it perpendicular to the plane of the asteroids. The radioactive materials will be dispersed in all directions. No one will come in contact with anything injurious."

"We'll probably hear some radio chatter about the explosion. Earth telescopes will see the flash." Jar'l smiled at the thought of amateur and professional astronomers wondering what caused the burst of light.

Sunul was thinking about the explosion they had created just before they grazed Jupiter's atmosphere. "Do you think anyone saw the blast of the hull we jettisoned?"

"I haven't heard any comments from Mars or Earth. Maybe they missed it."

"That's good. We want to leave as few trails to follow as possible."

Sunul and Jar'l spent an hour of EVA struggling with cables and wrenches. Their investment finally paid off with the front half of the third engine secured to the interior floor of the cargo hold. Rob had rigged a winch to pull the engine into the hold as Jar'l and Sunul carved it into properly sized pieces the robot feeder could transport to the remaining two engines. Jar'l supervised the removal of the core surrounded by the magnetic collars. The core was secured to the floor of the cargo hold after it was placed in a dormant state. Jar'l likened it to hibernation. They covered it with polymer foam to protect the magnets from being damaged, to preventing nuclear detonation inside the spacecraft.

Back in the control room, Sunul initiated the final braking maneuver that would allow them to dock with an asteroid. He decided to slow the ship more than necessary so they could observe several possible landing sites and speed up when necessary. Sunul was thinking of choosing a minor chunk of rock less than a couple of miles in diameter and, if possible, very slowly rotating. Jar'l was watching the radar signals as the ship approached the belt of tiny planetary objects.

Sunul commented to Jar'l, "See if you can find an object that has an elliptical orbit and is moving toward the sun. We'll hitch a ride for a few hours before heading to Mars."

Jar'l studied the radar screen for about fifteen minutes before coming up with one prospective mining site. It appeared to be an irregular mass having its longest axis several hundred yards in length and moving slowly toward the sun. "Got one! But it's rotating a little fast."

"We might have to take what we can get, Jar'l. I can't find anything visually except the object you just referred to. It's only a mile or so ahead of us. Let's take a closer look."

Sunul nudged the ship forward until they could see the rock clearly from the observation ports. The chunk of stone looked as if it had broken off a larger object, perhaps a minor planet that had collided with another massive object; there were some small craters on one slightly curved surface.

"I think we'll try for it, Jar'l. Get Rob in here so he can see what we have to land on."

As Sunul jockeyed the ship toward the large chunk of rock, Jar'l called Rob on his com unit. Rob didn't have to reply, he was already moving toward the command console when he heard Jar'l's message. Waving at Jar'l and smiling, he joined Sunul at the nearest observation port.

"Where would you like to land, Rob?"

"On the crater strewn part, boss. Cutting through the raised sections of a crater will be easier than trying to slice out sections from a flat area." He moved his face closer to the port window and continued to scan the craters. "Oh, I just finished fashioning something that will help us dock and also get the fuel into the ship."

"So, that's why you haven't been seen for a while."

Rob chuckled, "Yep. I think you'll like what I made. There, I see a great place to land." He pointed so Sunul could see. "Over there by those craters that overlap."

"Got it." Sunul glanced at Rob, "Get ready to secure us to the rock."

Rob was dressed in his EVA suit except for his helmet. He turned and moved toward the cargo hold. Sunul heard the airlock close and moved back to the command console. He then announced, "We're planning to land on an asteroid. Better hang onto something for a few minutes, it might be a bit bumpy."

The ship rotated about fifteen degrees and rolled so the floor of the cargo hold was almost level with the asteroid's surface. Sunul matched the spacecraft's speed with that of the space rock, tapped the engine firing button a few times and heard a crunching noise as the ship and the asteroid came in contact. There was a thump and then another one. Two noises that he had never heard before.

"Jar'l, what was that?"

"You've got me. Must be Rob's invention."

Sunul observed the surface of the asteroid through the transparent port. Nothing was moving. The ship was bound to the rock. The foreign noises had to have come from Rob's handiwork. He must have secured the ship to the space rock with his new device.

"Hugh! Do you want to help with the fuel?"

Sunul's com unit blared, "Do you want dinner tonight?"

"All right, chef. Jar'l and I will help Rob start lasing chunks of rock. I hope tonight's meal is a good one, plenty of protein. We're going to need it."

Jar'l and Sunul prepped for their EVA and met Rob in the cargo hold. Rob showed the newcomers how he had attached the ship to the asteroid. He had used the charges of his explosive bolts to fire hardened steel-alloy barbed rods into the stone surfaces. The rods were tied to cables which were pulled until taut by winches in the cargo area.

Rob lowered a ramp to the center of a five-meter-wide crater, looked at Jar'l and said, "We need to hook up to the core of engine three. The lasers will need a power boost for all the rock carving we're about to do."

The three men gathered around the foam-covered power unit and Jar'l knelt at one end, stripped off a handful of foam and looked up at Rob. "We need to attach power cables to the lasers and turn them on. The core will automatically feed us the power we need. Don't worry about using up the power, there's enough to last five years at maximum output."

Rob had to laugh. "I think that should be sufficient, buddy. Let's get to it." Rob gave one end of a cable to Jar'l and attached the other end to his laser cutter. He pointed it at the rock surface and pulled the trigger. Sparks flew as the beam sliced into the rock, melting it like warmed chocolate. He guided the laser light across the surface and cut a rectangular piece of rock about fifty centimeters on two sides and a meter long. He shut off the cutting tool and pushed the solid out of the way.

"What's that weigh on earth, Sunul?"

"Umm, about 600 pounds, but you can lift it here without much effort. The only problem is the sharp edges. Don't snag your suit. I don't have any tire patches with me."

"I thought of that, boss. I've got one more winch to drag the rock into the hold. Attach this cable and I'll pull it into the ship. Just make a lasso noose around the rock and get out of the way."

Rob walked up the ramp and disappeared for a moment. The cable became taut and the rock began to slide up the gangplank into the ship. As soon as the chunk of fuel was at the top of the ramp, Jar'l began cutting another segment. Sunul moved about five feet to Jar'l's side and started another cut. Rob ran the winch and stacked the rock in the hold while the other men sliced thick slabs of rock from the crater wall. Rob estimated they had accumulated twenty cubic meters of rock in half an hour.

Rob spelled Jar'l after an hour and then Jar'l replaced Sunul and continued cutting large blocks up to a meter on an edge for another half hour. The crater wall had been completely removed and they had lowered the floor of the crater nearly two meters when they struck denser, much harder material. Sunul was anticipating more strenuous work.

"Hey guys, I'm low on oxygen and I'm getting hungry. How about going in for an hour? I think another two hours of cutting and we'll be finished." Sunul didn't need to say anything else, the laser photon beams were turned off and the cutting guns were placed on the crater floor in a quiescent state.

"Hey, Rob. We're coming in for dinner. We'll be ready to eat in about fifteen minutes."

The tinny sound of Rob's voice came over Sunul's tiny EVA suit speaker, "We'll be ready for you. We've been listening to the rumbles of the rock being dragged into the cargo bay. Sounds like you've been pretty busy."

It was the first time in many days that the entire crew and children had eaten together. Rob explained what they had been doing and he tried to explain the mining procedure to Licon and Miranda.

Licon said, "Can we watch?"

"You'll have to ask your mother. There's only one view port that allows observing activity in the cargo hold. Your mom will have to hold you up. Maybe we can find you something to stand on. How about that?"

"I'd like that."

"Me, too!" Miranda glanced at Triel for approval.

"Okay, Miranda. We'll find a way for both of you to watch."

Rob added, "I'll set up a light so you can see on the surface of the asteroid. When we're cutting, the laser light allows us to see what we're doing."

Sunul reached into his pocket and pulled out a small piece of rough-edged stone. "This is what we're cutting into. It's very hard, so the lasers are having some difficulty."

He passed the sample around and when it came to Gina, he said, "Please run an analysis of that, would you?"

She frowned and replied, "Right now?"

"Yes, please."

"Okay, but you have to hold Miles."

Sunul smiled and said, "Do I have to?"

Gina shook her head and held Miles out to Sunul. She expected him to grab the baby like Miles was a sack of potatoes, but Sunul surprised her and supported Miles, wrapped in his baby blanket, and held him in the crook of his arm.

"Well, wonders never cease."

"Gina, please run the analysis. I don't want to have to change Miles."

Ten minutes later, Gina had the results, but for a moment, she stood out of sight and watched Sunul with the baby. She could see the baby's smile when Sunul talked to him. Sunul appeared to be enjoying the time with his son. She stepped into the command station and announced, "Sixty-three percent nickel, eight percent palladium, and twenty-five percent platinum. The remainder is aluminum silicate. That amount of metal is worth a pile of credits back home. Platinum sells for about 2,200 credits an ounce. I checked with the computer. How much is there?"

Sunul grinned and said, "We could all be rich. I'll bet there's several hundred pounds of the stuff. We can cut it out of the rock and stash it for our return to Earth. But we might have to give it to the government."

Jar'l said, "After how they've treated us? I'd like to show it to General Ohland and stick it where the sun doesn't shine."

That brought on a chorus of laughter and some more outlandish comments that the children wouldn't understand.

CHAPTER 30
NEXT STOP: MARS

The amount of platinum containing rock was larger than Sunul originally thought. It had to be cut in two before loading into the ship. Sunul concentrated on it while Rob and Jar'l worked on the rock surrounding the rarer metal. After three hours they called a halt to the mining operation, the cargo hold was full. They left a narrow pathway between blocks of rock for access to the robot and the airlock. Back inside the ship, the men decided to sleep. Only Monel was awake, monitoring the radar and internal sensors of the spacecraft. The ship was still firmly attached to the asteroid.

While she was keeping track of the ambient conditions of the ship, a transmission notice registered on the main console two hours into the sleep period. She was a bit reticent to look at the Earth message at first, but when it appeared in red capital letters above the console, she read the entire message. She decided to let Sunul respond. She wasn't sure she had grasped the significance of the communication.

She sat in Sunul's chair a little confused. After mulling over the message for about ten minutes, she decided to wake Sunul. Monel pressed on Sunul's alert button. Ten to fifteen seconds passed before she heard Sunul's voice on the intercom.

"What is it, Monel? Has something failed?"

"No. A message from Earth arrived a short time ago. I think you'd better take a look."

"Okay, I'll be right there."

When Sunul arrived at the control center, Monel pressed the repeat message button and the Earth message reappeared, this time in blue, for a redisplaying of the communication.

Sunul said, "Shit! They must know where we are!"

The message was: How long would it take you to get to Mars from your present location?"

Monel slid out of the command chair so Sunul could use the computer. She watched his fingers dance across the command keys. Then watched him sit back and begin talking.

"Computer: Distance to Mars from our current position in the asteroid belt."

"Approximately 2.65 astronomical units. Do you desire any further information at this time?"

"Thank-you. Not at this time."

Sunul reached for his com unit, carried out a few calculations, then activated the transceiver to Earth. He entered, "Approximately 74 hours at c/100. We have to accelerate and then decelerate. Why?" He looked at his watch and sat back, trying to completely wake up. Another quick calculation and he got up, glanced at Monel and said, "We'll get an answer in about forty-five minutes. I'm going back to bed."

"Shall I wake you?"

"Umm, yes. Feel free to read any messages. We'll start for Mars as soon as we know what's going on."

A half-hour later, Sunul returned to the command console. Monel looked at the console clock and gave Sunul a little frown.

"Couldn't sleep?"

"Yeah, I kept thinking about Earth knowing our every position.

I'm pissed that I didn't anticipate the computer constantly broadcasting our position. The entire ship must be serving as an aerial."

"None of us knew, Sunul. Don't blame yourself. Jar'l and I should have known, if anyone, we're the communications people on board."

"I'm going to wake up Rob. He has to release us from the asteroid. When he cuts the cables, we'll roll and dump the engine we used to power the lasers. Then we'll power up the main engines and move away from the rock."

The message from Earth arrived forty-seven minutes after Sunul replied to the agency's question. It mentioned the beta group on Mars needed medical help. Their injured surgeon needs an operation. Earth is near conjunction with Mars; too far away for a surgeon to arrive in time. Gina has the knowledge to operate.

"Send a reply, Monel. Tell them we're on our way. I'm getting Rob up so we can get out of here."

Ten minutes later the entire crew was awake and secured in their travel positions. The children were firmly fastened to beds in the nursery. Rob punched a button on his console and the crew felt a small jolt as the ship began to drift away from the asteroid.

Twenty seconds later Jar'l announced, "We're 200 yards off the asteroid, Sunul. Roll the ship any time. Ready, Rob?"

"Aye, aye, sir." He gave a big smile to Jar'l.

Sunul rotated the A gimbal ninety degrees to its extremity and pulsed the engine. As the ship began to rotate, Sunul said, "Hit it, Rob."

Rob pressed the selected cargo eject button on his operations panel and everyone heard a thump from the cargo hold. "Let's get out of here, Sunul. Full power to both engines!"

Sunul had aligned the gimbals and applied maximum thrust to the two engines. As the accelerometer reading climbed, a bright flash of light could be seen coming from the side viewports.

Rob said, "Too bad, that was a good engine."

Hugh laughed, "Get over it, Rob. It wasn't one of your children."

Rob grinned and replied, "You know what I mean. That engine supplied the power for us to mine the asteroid. Now we have enough fuel to get us back home, with some to spare."

"What about the ore, Rob? Are we going to have smaller pieces so we can carry it off the ship?"

"I'll start working on that today, Hugh. I'm going to cut it into pieces we can carry on our person or put in our luggage. Let me know if there's any particular shape you want. I can even sculpt it into decorative pieces if you like, but not too complicated, please. I can't make delicate cuts with a laser torch."

Gina was very quiet, thinking about something no one else had asked. "Is that ore radioactive? If it is, I'd rather not have it near Miles."

Triel had a Geiger counter in her bio lab equipment. "I'll scan it, Gina. I haven't used the instrument yet. Do you have any more of the sample Sunul gave you?"

"Sure, I'll get it for you. I only used a few milligrams for the analysis."

The sun was growing in size and brilliance as the ship moved toward Mars. The solar disc still looked small, but much larger than the tiny disc of Mars, which looked like a reddish star. Sunul plotted an intercept course, and when the ship was at the halfway point, he rotated the craft 180 degrees and started slowing the spacecraft. Nearly two days remained until the ship had to match velocity with the red planet. Sunul asked the computer to plot the trajectory. He began monitoring the ship's position hour-by-hour, comparing his calculations with those appearing on the console.

The planet and the spacecraft were going in opposite directions, so the ship would have to swing around the red planet and go into orbit, avoiding the two small Martian moons, Phobos and Deimos. Sunul could not imagine a problem with the satellites, but he made sure the ship's computer had considered the positions of the moons when the trajectory was being calculated.

"Computer: Have you considered the position of the Martian base in your calculations?"

"Yes, Sunul. The ship will pass directly over the Martian colony's dome."

"Sunul." He looked away from the console toward the origin of the voice. It was Gina carrying Miles on her hip.

"Triel said that sample carried only background radiation. It's safe."

"That's good to know. How are you and Miles doing?"

"We're fine. Do you know who on Mars needs surgery?"

"No, but it must be their chief medical officer. Otherwise, why would they need our help? Do you remember the name of the beta group's surgeon?"

Gina bit her lower lip, threw her head back, closed her eyes, and suddenly said, "Yes! Her name is Shania Estwick. But I don't know her married name or who she was dating."

"Boy, you sure worked hard for that name!" Sunul smiled and addressed the computer.

"Computer: Send a message to Mars. We would like to know the extent of the damage to the injured person. Ask for Shania to reply."

A message was received from Shania about thirty minutes later. "I have an extremely aggressive form of lung cancer. I believe I can recover if my left lung is removed. When can we expect you? Shania Winslow."

"Computer: Reply to the last communication. Fifteen hours. Dr. Gina Burke." Sunul then motioned for Gina to join him at the console. She sat down with Miles and said, "I'm going to spend most of the remaining time studying the removal of a lung. The computer's medical knowledge is very complete and up-to-date. You might have to help me, Sunul."

"All right. I'll review the computer files you examine. Read rapidly and forward them to my file, please. I'll be working on possibly landing this ship on the surface. We might not be able to use a shuttle to land. I don't know what will be available. I hope the colony won't be as isolated as we were on 5K23m."

CHAPTER 31
MARS

Gina and Sunul missed the next sleep period as they prepared for the surgical procedure and landing on Mars. Six hours before they would circle Mars and orient the ship to land near the dome that covered the Mars colony, the Burkes decided to get some sleep. Sunul was reviewing the computer's final calculations when he fell asleep in the command chair. The console alarm had been set to wake him two hours before the ship entered into a synchronous orbit above the colony, or alternatively, the computer had reversed the ship's orientation in preparation for landing. Sunul would have to make that decision after evaluating the Martian environment.

He woke suddenly, reached to his chest and felt what he first thought was a pillow, but it was Miles wrapped in a blanket. Gina was standing next to the command chair steadying Miles to prevent him from falling. When Sunul grinned, Miles lit up with a big smile.

"What time is it?"

"Your alarm is set to wake you in ten minutes. I didn't think you'd mind missing a little sleep to talk."

"No, that's okay. What's on your mind?"

"I've been mulling something over and I thought I'd see what you think. I'd like to take Licon and Miranda with me to the colony. They might be of assistance with diagnosing Shania. They might also reduce the normal quantity of anesthesia. I might be able to communicate with Shania during the surgery."

"Gina, I don't know what the situation will be for reaching the surface. There might be a shuttle of limited capacity. The crew will have to vote to decide if we are going to take the ship to the surface. Landing this hulk is going to be dangerous. The probability for a positive outcome might be extremely low. You have a good point though about the kids. We'd better call a meeting; we can't change our minds at the last minute."

"Shall I call the crew together?"

"Yeah, we'd better get it settled. I'll give them our options."

During the meeting, Monel talked with the base about transportation to the surface. There was a shuttle in orbit that could only handle three passengers. It could only be used when a supply ship came from Earth. The shuttle had to be refueled from the supply ship. That information had simplified the decision for the crew. They would attempt a soft landing on the surface, not far from the colony. Sunul and Jar'l would take over from the computer during the last thirty seconds of descent and manually guide the ship to the sandy surface.

A Martian crawler was available that resembled an old Volkswagen bus moving on continuous belts of rubber plates. Following the landing on the surface, the robot driver could taxi the entire crew and luggage in one trip across the sand to the dome. There was no reason to risk the life of a human when journeying across the arid landscape without an oxygen atmosphere. However, a human driver could override the robotic driver if necessary.

Sunul issued an order. "Everyone must be in their EVA suits when we land. If we lose pressure, we will only have a minute or two to patch any cracks in the ship's hull. A major rupture will be catastrophic."

Leanne and Triel asked simultaneously, "What about the children?"

Hugh answered, "There's only one room remaining with doors

that can be sealed, ladies. It's the bathroom." Hugh looked at Rob. "Can you fashion something to secure the kids to during the landing? One of us can stay in the bathroom with the children."

Gina volunteered, "I'll take care of them. Rob, fix the toilet so I can strap myself to it."

Everyone had a laugh, each person apparently thinking of a funny situation that resulted in a person having to be tied to a toilet.

Sunul added, "Make those straps strong, Rob. I don't want my wife slipping off the john. That's a story I wouldn't like to get spread around the solar system."

"If that happens, Sunul, I'm blaming it on you." Gina blew him a kiss, got up, and headed for the nursery to start preparing the children for landing.

"We've got about ninety minutes before things start happening. You'd better get prepared; it might be rough when we hit the surface. Jar'l and I will try to make it as smooth as possible."

The next hour was frantic with most of the crew multitasking. Sunul and Jar'l had little time to do anything but go over the planned trajectory, checking for the positions of Deimos and Phobos and accounting for the rotation of the planet. Sunul wasn't convinced the computer was making the calculations properly, so he had to check for errors with the simulator program. Jar'l double checked to make sure nothing was overlooked. With twenty-five minutes before the engines were to fire, Sunul issued a warning: "You must be in final positions in twenty minutes. The ship will not have to rotate until we pass Mars, then we're going in with the engines pointing at the horizon. There will be some heating of the external surfaces, but the environmental system should keep us comfortable. When we touch down, it will be bumpy as we slide across the surface. Remember, we don't have wheels, skids, or fins."

Jar'l reminded the crew, "If the loss of pressure alarm sounds, let Rob and Hugh handle it. Stay cool. Keep your helmet secured until the alarm is silenced. Oh, one more thing. Stay away from the cargo hold. The robot and the fuel blocks might be in disarray and I don't want anyone to be crushed. Those cubic meter blocks of fuel each weigh more than a ton. Remember, the gravity on Mars is thirty-eight percent of Earth's. Your leg muscles and bones are not used to your weight for extended periods of time. Try not to stumble when you move around. We don't need any broken bones."

The babies were crying in the bathroom, but Miranda and Licon seemed to be enjoying the preparations. They were looking forward to playing on the surface of a big ball. Gina was checking the restraints on the little ones and left them for a moment to wish Sunul and Jar'l good luck. She gave Sunul a peck on the cheek and returned to the bathroom. She closed and sealed the door and said a prayer.

Hugh and Triel were taking last minute adjustments to the growth chambers along the walls to keep from losing any of their food producing plants. They were anticipating a rugged landing, so they had sealed the chambers to prevent spillage. The chambers would need to be transported to the interior of the domed colony to provide food for the crew's stay on Mars. Although Hugh and Triel didn't know the capacity of the crawler, they expected the transport of the plants to the dome would take several days.

Sunul's voiced boomed over the public address system: "Five minutes. Take your stations and hang on!"

Jar'l was calling out the altitude: "Twenty thousand, fifteen thousand, twelve, eight, five, three—"They could feel the rockets firing and the force increasing on their bodies, pressing them into their cushioned chairs. "One thousand, five hundred, one-fifty."

"Rotating the ship." Sunul called out as he watched the altimeter reach eighty miles and then begin to increase as the ship swung around Mars. Sunul felt the ship continuing to rotate, so he tried to move the gimbals to counter the rotation. It was too late. He couldn't get the ship in the proper attitude to continue the slowing process. They would go into an elliptical orbit and try to enter the atmosphere on the second pass. The computer output indicated the next burst from the engine would occur in fifty-eight minutes.

He announced, "We missed our first opportunity. You can relax for about fifty minutes."

"Want me to assist you next time, Sunul?" Jar'l was continuing to monitor the ship's position on the radar screen, but he glanced over at Sunul for a quick check, and then resumed monitoring the radar screen.

"I think you should. If we can handle the gimbal positions quickly enough, we should be able to ski across the sand on the next pass. I'm writing a subroutine to help us keep the gimbals accurately positioned on entry. As we lose altitude, the ship and gimbals are not pointed in the same direction, otherwise we start to tumble. The problem is with our center of gravity. Our makeshift spaceship wasn't intended or assembled to make a planetary landing."

"What do you want me to do?"

"You run the gimbal on engine B, I'll take engine A. Just change the gimbal angle to follow what the subroutine tells you. It will be a gradual adjustment, not anything rapid. Just don't overshoot the angle or we're in big trouble, we'll dig a deep hole in the Martian surface."

Jar'l sat back and observed the radar signals from both moons. They were not going to offer any threat to the landing. That was one more thing to forget about. About twenty minutes went by in silence before Sunul spoke.

"Okay, we're ready, Jar'l. Ten minutes from now we'll drop into the atmosphere. The engines are going to be opposing the gravitational attraction and our inertia, so the g force plus the engine thrust will be very strong. Keep your hands on your control panel, just use your fingers to change the gimbal angle; kind of like typing on one of those antique typewriters you see at a museum."

"Too bad we don't have gyroscopes to help with an inertial guidance system. The engineers didn't put any of them into our ship. We weren't supposed to be doing this." Jar'l smiled and continued, "They didn't anticipate you being on the ship, Sunul."

"I'm going to be interested in what the mission commanders will say when we arrive on Earth, if we get back in one piece."

"Losing confidence, Sunul?"

"This is not the same as making love the first time, Jar'l. No one has ever done this before."

"Ninety seconds, everyone. Hang on!" Jar'l pressed the intercom off setting and wiggled his fingers. Sunul was watching his panel for the first gimbal instructions. A slight vibration could be felt as the engines started applying thrust to slow the ship. As the thrust increased dramatically, Jar'l had to exert more muscle power to his arms to keep his hands on the controls. The vibrations increased and both pilots, eyes riveted on their instrument panels, began adjusting their gimbal controls.

Triel yelled, "Is everything all right!"

"We're okay. Let them do their thing." Hugh's white knuckles indicated he was probably thinking about the landing as much, or more, than his wife. The pressure on his body began to lessen, but the engines appeared to be at full throttle. About ten seconds later, there was no sound, no vibrations, nothing, and then the ship hit the Martian surface. A scraping-grinding sound from the hull started and didn't seem to lessen in any way for at least fifteen seconds. Sudden silence and no feeling of motion signified the landing had been successful.

"Welcome to Mars! This is communications engineer Nial Conners. Do you need immediate assistance?"

Jar'l answered, "No. You are speaking to Jar'l Mason. It's good to hear a voice from the Mars' station. When can you come to get us?"

"Party of eight?"

"No, party of twelve." There was no reply for at least ten seconds.

"Could you please explain?"

"Sure. Eight adults and four children under one year of age. Let me ask you a question. Are any of your colony recently pregnant? I mean in the last week?" There was another pause, this time for about a minute.

"Until you can further clarify your situation, we cannot send a crawler to transfer you to our facility."

"So, you don't need a surgeon? Is that correct?"

"We do need a surgeon, but if one of your party has a communicable disease, we cannot admit your entire group to the dome. Is the surgeon infected?"

Gina had opened the bathroom and could hear the exchange of words. She motioned for Triel to come to watch the children and she joined Jar'l and Sunul at the command station.

Gina smiled at Sunul and whispered, "Let me talk to . . . what's his name?"

Sunul said, "Nial Conners."

"Nial, this is Gina Burke. I'm the surgeon. Can you have someone in an EVA suit escort me to the colony? Infection is not our concern. Once I am able to communicate with your entire group, you will understand our concern about pregnancies. It should not be a problem."

"We'll send a crawler and stop 100 yards from your ship. You will walk to the crawler in an EVA suit. Bring any necessary instruments with you."

"I cannot do the surgery without one of the children. We have no EVA suit for a child."

"You must bring a baby with you? I don't understand."

"The child is not a baby. Physically, he is the size of a three-year-old." Gina was beginning to lose her patience. "Nial, send someone to the ship in an EVA suit. That person will have to enter the ship through the cargo hold. That's the only intact airlock we have. If that person is worried, he or she can stay in the suit until we explain the situation. Then I will come to your facility if you let this child accompany me. Does the crawler have an airlock?"

There was another delay. Then Nial's voice was heard again. "All right, I am sending Corey Daniels in a crawler. It will be about twenty-five minutes. You are a little over a mile from us. The crawler has an external airlock that will fit over your main hatch. We will not need to use the cargo system."

CHAPTER 32
SUGGESTED TREATMENT

The crawler was right on time. A female voice came over the intercom announcing the arrival. Some tapping sounds could be heard inside the ship as the airlock was being attached to the hull. A couple of minutes later, someone rapped on the outside wall, and the voice said, "You can release the seal on the main hatch now. The pressure in the crawler should be nearly the same as inside your ship."

Rob moved to the hatch, with some difficulty, crawling up the curved hull wall, and pressed the release panel. There was a slight hiss and the hatch swung into the ship. A tall redhead, without her EVA helmet, was standing in the hatchway smiling.

"Welcome to Mars, everybody. I heard you had a long trip. I'm Corey Daniels. Can you give me a rundown of your situation?"

Sunul took over and introduced the crew. They were standing beside their travel positions, trying to get used to Mars' gravity. After the landing, they had to stand and flex their leg muscles to adjust to the stronger gravity than their magnetic shoes provided when in space.

"May I see the children?"

Monel entered the bathroom and came back holding the two babies. Licon and Miranda followed, trying to walk as before, but falling to their knees, laughing at their clumsiness.

"Feet are heavy," Licon stated as he watched the tall Martian. He had never felt the tug of gravity before. "I'm am Licon and this is Miranda." He pointed at Miranda, turned to Corey and said, "We are happy to meet you, Corey Daniels."

The redhead wasn't sure how to react, but a few seconds later, she said, "I'm very happy to meet you." She watched as Miranda made a strange noise, something she had never heard before, almost in a whisper to Licon.

Licon smiled at Corey. "Miranda wants to ask you something. Is that all right?"

"Yes. What is it?"

Miranda seemed a little bashful. She struggled for a couple of seconds, apparently forming what she wanted to say, and asked, "Do all Martians have red hair?"

Corey smiled when Monel and the others laughed. "No, Miranda. I'm the only one."

"Oh, then you are special, like Licon and me."

"How are you special, Miranda?"

"We can do things."

"Can you show me?

"We can multiply numbers. Tell me a number."

"Six."

"Now tell Licon a number, but don't tell me."

Licon moved to Corey and she whispered, "Seven," so quietly no one else could hear.

Miranda responded immediately with, "That's an easy one, forty-two." Miranda and Licon laughed. "We can do other things, too."

Gina clapped her hands. "Okay, kids, go play while we talk."

Corey had a blank look, cocked her head and looked at Gina. "You have to explain that little trick."

"That wasn't a trick, Corey. Let me explain those little beings."

Fifteen minutes later Gina said, "Now you know the whole story. I haven't tested their saliva for platinum complexes that might, for want of a better word, infect someone recently pregnant.

I believe it would occur within a day, or perhaps hours, of conception. Otherwise the foreign complexes could not keep up with normal cell division. They would be overwhelmed and cast aside by the human body."

"Why haven't you tested their body fluids?"

"It didn't occur to me that the presence of the older children might cause a problem. We only knew about seventy-two hours ago that we were going to land on Mars. I don't see having Licon and Miranda in an operating room would be cause for alarm. We could isolate them from the population until after tests could be conducted."

"We can do that. Our operating suite has an isolated, controlled-atmosphere system."

"Good, that's settled. Do you have to contact the colony?"

"That's not necessary. I have the authority to allow entry to the dome. Who will be going with me?"

"The kids, their mothers, and me. Is there room enough?"

"No problem. I could take all twelve of you. However, let's take this one step at a time.

If the results are satisfactory, I'll send the crawler for the rest of your party. They won't mind staying another day or two on board the ship, will they?"

Sunul and the others had been listening to Gina and Corey during the entire exchange. Sunul looked around at the crew and could see no one objecting. "I think that will work. We've been in this hunk of junk for about a year already. Another day or so won't make any difference. All of us would like to take a real shower though." Everyone applauded.

As soon as the crawler was loaded with passengers, the remaining crew members were told to close the hatch. The airlock was deflated, and the taxi backed away, breaking the seal.

"Hey, Hugh, what's for dinner?"

"A vegetable plate, a vegetable protein burger, kale, a multivitamin capsule, and water. Hopefully we won't have many more meals aboard the ship. It will be interesting to find out what the Martians are eating."

Hugh commented, "Since Leanne is the only woman on board, let's give her some help with the babies. We should make up a schedule of two-hour shifts. Does everyone know how to change diapers?" His question resulted in a chorus of boos and Leanne laughed, which brought on a bout of hiccups. She went in the galley to get some water and help Hugh.

Travelling in the crawler was fun for the children, but Gina was contemplating the details of the lung removal and hadn't watched the colored sands through the viewports. By the time they had reached the eastern entrance to the domed city, she had decided to introduce the children to Shania Winslow before any mention was made of the impending operation. Gina had to make sure Licon and Miranda physically touched Shania. Their impressions could be very valuable; perhaps surgery would not be necessary. Licon and Miranda might be able to do something more than lessen the need for anesthesia.

When the crawler entered the eastern airlock, Gina noticed an architectural drawing of the complex on the wall that depicted the hatch to the dome. The dome had an entrance at each compass direction and looked like an igloo when approaching the covered city. The drawing indicated the diameter of the dome was 100 yards. The height was eighty feet at the center.

The city inside looked more like an old-time trailer park that existed over a century ago. The buildings having been made from portions of spent rockets from Earth. However, it was exceptionally clean and well organized. The streets were named after rocket pioneers and early astronauts, all having passed long ago. Their names were painted on the corners of appropriately positioned buildings. There were no well-wishers or greeters of any persuasion; in fact, the city did not seem to be inhabited.

"Sorry that no one is here to greet you travelers, but we have to be extremely cautious about bacteria brought into the city. Our atmospheric quality control has failed before. We'll walk to the surgical suite. Shania and her husband will be glad to see you."

The alpha group women and two children followed Corey to the center of the enclosed city. Licon and Miranda suddenly tugged on their mother's hands and pointed above their heads. A man in a hovercraft was moving along one of the seams of the dome squirting something from a wand. It looked like he was spraying for termites, but that was impossible.

"What is that man doing?" Licon was pointing over his head.

Corey replied, "He is fixing an atmospheric leak. Over time, the contractor's seal comes loose from vibration and pressure differences. He puts a synthetic rubber sealant over the leaking seal. He's up there about once a month. We can't afford to lose any oxygen."

They walked another fifteen yards before Corey said, "We're here." She ushered the group into what looked much like a doctor's office on earth.

"Hi, Bert! These are our new visitors from the Kuiper belt."

Gina introduced her group and asked, "May we see Shania?"

"Sure, she'll be right here. She's treating a broken wrist. One of the maintenance men had an accident. Come with me to an isolation room. We do surgeries there."

Physician's assistant Bert Scott guided the group to an opaque plastic-walled room equipped with zippered doorways on two sides. There were three chairs and the women sat down. Licon and Miranda looked around and sat on the floor beside their mothers. The wait was short, less than a minute, and a woman about the same size as Gina entered and sat on the examination table. She appeared to be out of breath and wheezing.

"I'm Shania. Please introduce yourselves."

Following the introductions, Gina explained the presence of the children. "Licon and Miranda are six months old. They are gifted in several ways. Although they appear to be three or four years old physically, they are much older mentally. I want to see if they can help before we carry out any surgical procedures. Do you mind if we conduct an experiment?"

"I don't understand the disparity between their age and their stature."

"Join the group. We don't know that either. We just know they have some abilities that we cannot explain. Would you like to take part in a séance-like investigation? It won't hurt or alter you in any way permanently. As a fellow physician, I can guarantee it."

"Well, all right. I'll try almost anything—once."

Gina spoke to Licon and Miranda explaining that Shania had a sore in her chest. Gina asked if they could investigate the problem. Licon and Miranda put their arms around each other in a huddle-like position and spoke in rapid clucks.

Shania asked Gina, "What are they doing?"

"They're talking about you. Wait a minute."

Licon and Miranda separated, asked their mothers and Gina to stand and move the chairs close together in a triangle.

"Please sit here, Shania Winslow." Licon pointed at one of the chairs.

After the Martian doctor was seated, Licon and Miranda crawled up on the other chairs and grasped hands, Licon's left to Miranda's right.

"Please hold our hands, Shania Winslow."

Shania reached out and grasped the children's hands to form a continuous ring.

"Now we must relax." Licon looked at Miranda and they began to cluck, slowly at first, but then increasing the frequency until the clucking became a hum.

"Oh! I feel like I'm having atrial fibrillation. My pulse is very high." Shania's voice was pregnant with concern.

"Don't worry, Shania, they won't hurt you." Gina was still reasonably confident no harm would result from Shania's interaction with the children.

The high frequency hum changed to a low frequency clucking which seemed to be a normal pulse rate, and then stopped. Licon and Miranda put Shania's hands back on her lap, got down from their chairs, and joined their mothers.

Licon looked at Gina and said, "Her red water needs some of ours, just a little bit."

Shania frowned, "They want me to receive some of their blood? I don't know about that. What do you think, Gina?"

"Okay. I think I know how we can do this without any risk. I'll take a milliliter of your blood and mix it with a drop of Licon's or Miranda's. We can monitor the reaction, if any, with a microscope to see if there is any clotting. But what I would like to do is take a sample of your diseased lung tissue and mix it with a drop of their blood. I think that would tell us more. What do you think?"

"I'm not too cool with a biopsy, Gina."

"I'll sedate you. You won't feel a thing. Where are your x-rays?"

"I'll get them for you, just a moment."

Shania stepped out of the room for less than a minute and returned carrying a memory module which she plugged into the operating room computer. She opened a file and displayed a three-dimensional x-ray of her lungs.

"Do you have a 3D projector?"

"Yes, I'll route this file to the imaging system next door. Come with me, Gina. The others will have to stay here in isolation."

"I'll need a graduated probe so I can measure some distances."

"No problem, I have what you need." Shania waved a twenty-centimeter pencil-shaped ruler fitted with a micrometer guide.

CHAPTER 33
AREOLOGY

Shania led the way to the adjacent building to the north. Gina noted the sign above the door:

AREOLOGY. She wasn't sure of what that meant until she stepped inside and saw the maps covering the walls.

"Surprised you, huh?"

"I didn't realize you were studying the geology of Mars."

A tall, thin man with sunken blue eyes appeared and welcomed them to his laboratory. He was well over six feet tall and had a full head of graying hair and bushy white eyebrows.

"I'm Dr. Kaiser. How can I help you?"

"I sent over some x-rays. Dr. Burke and I would like a three dimensional analysis of them. We also would like to get an exact dimension rendition. We want to carry out a biopsy of the patient's lung tissue."

"I don't believe we've met. You are?"

Shania replied, "I'm Dr. Winslow. I believe you know my husband. He's a seismologist."

"Oh, yes. You must be Shania. He has often mentioned you. He's correct, you are very pretty."

"Thank you, doctor. Could we see the holographic projection?"

"Oh, yes. Come this way."

The two females followed Dr. Kaiser past a long table half-covered with bones to the back of the room.

"You've brought samples from Earth?" Gina couldn't help noticing the array of bones.

Dr. Kaiser turned and said, "Those specimens are from Mars, young lady. They're over a million years old, some sort of a monkey-like vertebrate. Could be an ancestor of yours." He smiled and broke out in a fit of laughter. "Actually, they're from some sort of sea creature that might have walked on land." He opened a large refrigerator-like cabinet and said, "Load your x-ray data into the console and an image will appear in the center of the structure. You can adjust things by voice command. There is an instruction book on the table." He walked away saying, "Good luck with your measurements."

Gina said, "Thank you, doctor." She watched as Shania requested her file and the holographic image of her torso appeared.

Shania requested, "Lungs, please."

Gina asked Shania to remove her shirt, which she did. She handed the ruler to Gina and stood absolutely still while Gina measured distances between three different bones.

Gina said, "Show bone structure," and Shania's skeleton appeared surrounding the lungs. Gina made three measurements and compared them to the values just taken from Shania.

"Shrink projection five percent." The change took place instantaneously. After Gina completed the measurements from the bones to the cancerous tissue, the two women began their return to the isolation ward.

The doctors discussed the procedure as they walked back to the medical building. As Gina explained her thoughts, the Martian doctor gained great respect for her fellow physician. Shania was strongly in favor of what Gina wanted to do. This was going to be a grand experiment, but if successful, it was going to remain secret until the right conditions prevailed.

Shania was prone on the operating table when Gina gave her an injection of sarcophacaine to eliminate any possible pain from the needle penetration of her chest wall to obtain a small sample of cancerous tissue. The sample was taken to the dual-binocular microscope and examined by both physicians. The cancer cells were obvious.

The next step was to procure a small sample of blood from Licon or Miranda. A ten-microliter sample was all that was necessary. Licon said he would like to give a sample of red water for Shania's experiment.

"I'm going to poke your finger with this needle, Licon. It's very sharp and shouldn't hurt much. Your mother is right here."

"Okay. I won't let it hurt." He began clucking to Miranda and Gina poked his finger for a tiny drop of blood. "That didn't hurt, Gina Burke."

"Good. I thought you were very brave."

"Yes, I am brave."

Miranda looked at Licon's finger and frowned. "Can I do that, too?"

"We'll see. We might need more of the red water. You can donate some if we need it."

"Okay." Miranda smiled. Her excitement and willingness to give blood surprised all four women, but they gradually realized she was competing with Licon. She wanted to take part in the experiment, too.

Gina transferred Licon's blood specimen to a ten-microliter pipet and carefully added the fluid to the cancerous growth on the microscope slide.

"Oh, my God!" Shania gasped. "Did you see that?" She looked at Gina in disbelief and grabbed Gina's arm.

"Amazing! I've never seen cancerous tissue just disappear like that. The normal cells weren't even affected. I think the cancer cells were broken into component molecules and were dissolved in the saline solution."

Shania squeezed Gina's hands and said, "Do you realize what this means?"

"I sure do. We have to keep this a secret, or these little people will be confined to a laboratory and their blood will be periodically harvested, or they will be murdered so the pharmaceutical companies and physicians can continue to get rich from the oncology trade."

"What are we going to do right now?"

"We don't know whether the antibodies from Licon are being metabolized or what their half-life is. I think we should give you 100 microliters and observe the change in your tumor, then we'll know what the next step is. I'll infuse it in your arm and we'll monitor the tumor hourly. What do you think?"

"Shall we use Miranda's blood this time?"

"Might as well. She's eager to join in the experiment. They will both be happy to contribute. I'll ask her mother first. Let's see what Triel says."

The proposed treatment/experiment for Shania was explained to Triel. She held both hands of Miranda as the little girl stood in front of her sitting mother.

"You're sure you want to let Gina take some of your red water to try to help Doctor Shania?"

"Yes. That will be okay. I won't let it hurt me."

Triel looked up at Gina, smiled, and nodded. "She said it would be all right, Gina."

The first x-ray, an hour after Shania's infusion, showed nearly all the cancer was gone. Following the second x-ray, Gina checked Shania's blood, and could find no trace of cancer. A urine specimen indicated a trace of blood, but on microscopic examination, the blood was from Miranda, not Shania. Shania appeared to be cancer free.

There was a general celebratory mood under the dome and the forty-three members of the colony met to celebrate. Gina, Triel, and Monel were invited to a dinner, but only Gina attended. The mothers and children remained in the isolation ward. Gina didn't stay at the party for long, but she got reacquainted with the members of the beta group she hadn't seen in over a year. They asked her many questions, but she deferred the answers to a later date. As she left the gathering, she walked by the refreshments table and picked a handful of napkins and a frosted cake that had only one piece missing. One of the members of the beta group, Jim Frieland, accompanied her back to the isolation ward. Jim was about the same size as Sunul, wore glasses, and had short blond hair. He wasn't particularly good looking. Gina couldn't remember him from the time in New Mexico, but she had only been interested in Sunul.

"Word is that you have two children with you."

"Yes. I wish I could introduce them, but they're in quarantine. This cake is for them and their mothers. The kids have never had cake before."

"They're too little to know about cake. They'd probably just smear it all over their faces."

Gina realized Jim didn't know about Miranda and Licon, or perhaps he was on a fishing expedition. She wasn't going to divulge anything.

"Yeah, but they'll get a taste anyway. Their moms will enjoy it."

"Who are their mothers? I should remember them from the training mission."

"Triel and Monel."

"Oh, yes, I remember them. Tell them hello for me."

"I'll do that. Thanks for the escort. We'll probably see you again."

"I don't think so, you'll be returning to Earth very soon. Enjoy the trip. Goodbye."

"Really? I haven't heard anything."

Without another word, Jim turned and walked away.

Gina entered the hospital and followed Bert to the isolation ward. Bert smiled and opened the isolation chamber entrance, bending the flexible door back to allow her easy passage with the cake.

"I have something for everyone!"

"Gina Burke, what is it?" Licon and Miranda ran to see what she had up close.

"It's something to eat. It's called a cake. You get to try a piece."

Monel and Triel used a scalpel and sliced small wedges for the kids and larger pieces for themselves. The kids were holding their cake, wondering how to eat it.

Gina said, "Like this." She took a big bite from her wedge and began chewing. "Umm, good!"

The children mimicked Gina and watched their mothers as they ate. They acted like they had been starved for many days.

Licon was the first to react. "More?"

Miranda wiped her lips and moved toward the cake, holding her little hands out for another piece. She wiggled her fingers as if she were playing a clarinet or flute.

Monel said, "Let's take it back to the ship and give a little bit to everyone. Okay?"

Gina stepped out and talked with Bert. "Could you please take us back to our ship? I think we are finished here, and I don't want to stay in isolation any longer."

"I don't know. Let me contact the base commander."

Bert turned, stepped back a few paces, kept his back to the guests and spoke into a microphone on his collar in a whisper. About ten seconds elapsed. He spun around and said, "Yes. It's all right for you to go. Corey isn't available right now. I'll drive you to your ship."

The crawler was filled with chatter from the kids about the cake. It was a new experience they would probably never forget, especially since it was a highlight of their trip to the surface of Mars. Gina was having a difficult time keeping quiet about her interaction with Jim, the guy she couldn't remember being at the New Mexico training facility. She wanted to ask Monel and Triel if they remembered him, but if he was a snoop of some kind, she didn't want Bert to know of her suspicions. She would mention her misgivings at a group meeting as soon as they were back in the ship. She wondered if Jar'l could sweep the ship for listening devices that might have been planted before they ever occupied the complex on 5K23m.

Maybe she was just worrying about shadows, but she couldn't seem to shake the strange feeling about Jim. Is he an intelligence operative of some sort, and why would he be on Mars?

Back in the ship, Gina asked Jar'l to mask any and all conversations in the ship with white noise. She talked with Sunul before sharing her experience with the crew. He couldn't remember anyone fitting Jim's description either, but he had to admit he was mostly checking out the women, one woman in particular. Sunul called a crew meeting and Gina took over. Neither Monel nor Triel had any recollection of Jim, nor did any of the others. He must have lied about remembering them, unless he had seen their pictures in the astronauts' files. But why would he lie about remembering them from training in New Mexico?

When Gina finished updating the crew about Licon's and Miranda's tiny amounts of blood killing all the cancer cells in Shania's lungs, she brought to their attention the value of such treatment. They grasped the significance immediately.

Hugh suggested, "From what our friend, Jim, said, there must be a ship from Earth on the way to pick us up. Someone must have contacted Earth about the cancer cure. I believe we're going to have trouble."

Monel spoke up, "Is there any legal way they can take the children from us? I'll fight to keep Licon, no matter what they do."

Leanne answered quickly, "We have no power. The agency will do anything they want to, with no consequences. Look how they've already lied to us, putting us out on the edge of the solar system to fend for ourselves. If Sunul hadn't saved those engines, we'd still be out there."

"I feel like finding a cave and hiding." Triel was holding Miranda on her lap. "I'll be damned if anyone is going to take Miranda from me."

"I think that's a great idea, Triel." Jar'l seemed enthusiastic about something. It was like a light had suddenly come on.

"What idea, Jar'l?"

"Hiding in a cave. We could do that. There are plenty of old mineshafts in the mountain west of the United States. There are probably some natural caves as well. There are forests out there that have never been fully explored. If we're careful, we could hide there for years, until the kids are grown and can make their own decisions." Jar'l leaned back surveying the faces looking at him.

Sunul said, "I don't like running, Jar'l. Let's think this through. Maybe there's a better way."

Gina and Leanne had their heads together talking quietly as they fed their babies. Gina raised her hand to talk. Sunul called on her.

"That would be twelve of us hiding away and for how long, five years, ten years, maybe longer. Too many things could go wrong in that period of time. Half of us would stand a better chance of remaining hidden."

Leanne said, "I agree with Gina, but we could help the others surreptitiously. It wouldn't be like we weren't working together. Jar'l and

Monel could devise some method of communication. We could even visit periodically, on ski trips, while mountain climbing, or when hiking mountain trails. I'll bet we could have some fun planning and carrying out meetings in out-of-the-way places. We could assemble where there's tree cover so satellites couldn't detect us."

Monel was thinking far ahead. "If we are corralled as a group and sequestered, how do we get away? I mean Jar'l, Licon, and me and the Patels? How would we travel, together?"

Sunul commented, "Let's wait and see what's in store for us. As soon as we become aware of our future and that of the children; I mean all the children, we can set up a plan. Perhaps our future will not be as bad as we are imagining."

Monel said, "You're being too optimistic, Sunul. Aren't you suspicious of the agency?"

CHAPTER 34
MARS TO EARTH

A voice boomed over the intercom. It was Corey, the red-headed taxi driver. "I'm sorry to have to tell you this, but you'll have to remain in your ship until tomorrow noon. That will be eighteen hours and thirteen minutes from now. If you were wondering, Mars' rotational period is only thirty-seven minutes longer than earth's. At that time, a driver will take you to the spaceport so you can begin your trip back to Earth. I am really sorry you can't stay here longer, but it will be another month before the next supply and passenger ship arrives. We don't want to keep any of you in quarantine for that length of time. It is imperative that we adhere to a strict schedule on Mars."

Sunul surveyed all the faces and said, "Let's have a big dinner and get some rest. We want to be alert for anything that is thrown our way. Make sure you have everything you want to take packed, including your valuables." He laughed and continued, "Talk to Rob if you need adjustments made to size or shape of any valuable material."

It had been more than a year since the entire alpha group had slept, or tried to sleep, for an eight hour period. Sunul and Jar'l had gotten up at dawn and had been theorizing what might be taking place under the dome and back at the agency on Earth. As the others arose and began moving around the ship, the two men decided their best option was to wait and see; they had been successfully solving problems since their arrival on 5K23m.

An hour before they were to be taken to the space port, a crawler was attached to the main hatch. Gina was sitting with baby Miles on her lap when she heard pounding on the hatch.

She smiled and said, "Come in." The rest of the crew laughed. Hugh turned on the intercom to receive communications.

"This is your driver speaking. Please be ready for travel to the spaceport in thirteen minutes. You will not need any EVA equipment. The taxi is equipped with portable breathing units, but there is little probability you will need them." There was a pause and then the voice said, "It is thirty minutes to the space port. We must be on time. I will ask you to open the hatch in eleven minutes. Please be ready to go."

The crew hustled to their quarters and changed to their normal travel clothing: shirts, pants, and non-magnetic shoes. There was little time for any discussion. The men had at least one duffel bag, but each mother had two.

"Open the hatch."

"I know that voice! At first, I couldn't place it but now I recognize who it is. It's Jim Frieland." Gina looked around at everybody and said, "I'm sure it's him."

When the hatch was opened Jim Frieland was standing at the opening in a uniform. She gave everyone a thumbs up. At first, Gina thought it was the official attire of a spaceport worker, but then she noticed a gun. He had a holster integrated into his trousers.

"Hello, Jim. You're driving us today?"

"Yes, doctor." He hardly looked at Gina, he was glancing at the various bags the crew was carrying. "Those will have to be searched. No flammables are allowed on the ship to Earth."

"We don't have any flammable material, except for a few ounces of alcohol on the medical lab."

"We still have to investigate all luggage going to Earth. We'll search you and your luggage as you climb aboard the ship."

The spaceport was out of sight from the dome in a shallow depression between two hills. Looking down from the surrounding hill between the dome and the spaceport, Sunul thought the area looked as if it had been a floodplain ages ago and perhaps it was true that Mars once had oceans, or at least lakes and rivers. Gina had mentioned that Dr. Kaiser had bones he thought were from a sea creature, but he was not a zoologist.

The launching pad was strangely shaped compared to what existed on Earth; it was a great circle containing three metal tracks, encompassed by the walls of the flood plain. Several large odd-looking shuttlecraft were parked in line near the periphery. The ships resembled the shuttles used by NASA in the late twentieth century, but these craft had larger, much broader, wings. Sunul wondered if they were only used for transiting the Martian atmosphere.

The crawler tipped and began moving downhill, passed under the circular structure and approached the front of the first ship. The cabin of the crawler began rising, lifting its occupants to the door of the sleek silver excursion vehicle.

"Please remain seated until the airlock is sealed. You will hear three tones when you may board the transit craft." A woman's voice had made the announcement. Sunul wondered if Jim was going to search their luggage, but a woman, dressed in a blue uniform with a security badge on her belt, took position next to the exit door. She possessed one of those faces easily forgotten. Only her uniform would be remembered.

Monel, Jar'l, and Licon were first in line, followed by the Griswalts. Jar'l's bag was searched first. The anonymous agent, pulled neatly folded articles of clothing from Jar'l's oversized duffel bag, piled the items in the nearest seat, and seemed to be almost complete with the search when she held up a fist-sized rock and asked, "What is this?"

"That is a sample from the asteroid where we refueled. We all have a sample, a memento from our trip." That was Jar'l's first lie as an astronaut.

She tossed the rock back in the bag, repacked the clothing, and said, "You may be seated, sir."

Each of the crew and the offspring were treated respectfully, as Jar'l had been, and when all twelve were seated in the craft, the door was sealed, and the cabin was pressurized to one Earth atmosphere.

A woman's voice announced, "This is your captain. We will be accelerating around the circular track you passed under when arriving at the spaceport. At the end of the third revolution the ship will be catapulted into the air, the rockets will fire, and in less than five minutes, we will begin docking with the interplanetary spacecraft, IS-05. Enjoy the ride." There was a pause and she continued, "Don't be alarmed at the noises and bumping, the sounds are normal. The trip to Earth will take slightly over thirty hours. Don't hesitate to make requests. Regular meals will be served. Restrooms are at the rear of the ship."

IS-05 was a large craft, much like the ship that had taken the alpha group to 5K23m, but twice as big. The passenger compartment was very comfortable, cushioned reclining seats, and screens for entertainment. Sunul opened a compartment, marked MSA, below his chair, and found magnetic shoe attachments that allowed walking upright in zero-g environments.

There were two attendants, Sunul guessed thirtyish, one male and one female, both dressed in blue uniforms. Name patches sewn above the left breast pocket of their Nehru-like jackets displayed Erin Bohne and Eric Bohne, probably a married couple, but possibly siblings.

Sunul asked Erin how to pronounce her last name.

She replied, "Like bone as in funny bone," and smiled. She stood beside her coworker and listened to his message.

"We will be accelerating for about thirty minutes; please stay seated with your belts fastened securely. The children may be held, the force will be gradual. When the green light flashes, we will be at maximum velocity. Lunch will be served following the green notification. You may choose from the menu on your travel screen, just ask for the lunch menu."

The 5K23m crew was surprised by the taste of the lunch; it was just like being home in the US. Multiple conversations were in progress after eating, but Sunul began to notice members of the crew were falling asleep, apparently while they were talking. Hugh had been talking to his wife when he fell asleep, Triel looked at Sunul, gave him a puzzled look, leaned back, and fell asleep. Miranda was sleeping with Licon in an adjacent seat. Sunul had no time to react, except to press the stop time button on his grandfather's old watch; his eyes closed.

When Sunul awoke, he could hear conversations among the crew. He glanced at his watch and compared the time with the digital time on his entertainment screen.

Four hours twenty-one minutes had elapsed since he had stopped time registration on his watch.

"How long did you sleep. Gina?"

"A little over four hours. Everyone woke up about the same time."

"Isn't that a little strange?"

"Now that I think about it, yes. That is a bit strange."

"I think we were drugged. They put something in our food to knock us out. Notice any strange reactions?"

"Licon and Miranda both said their arms hurt, but not bad."

Sunul pulled up his sleeves and checked his arms. There was a small puncture wound above a large vein in his right arm.

"Someone took a blood sample, Gina. Check your arms."

Gina gave Miles to Sunul, stood, and rolled up both sleeves. "Yep, someone poked me, too. I'll check our crew." Gina asked, "Have you all got puncture marks on your arms?"

Everyone stopped what they were doing and verified they had been subjected to a needle poke without their knowledge, or permission.

Sunul spoke into his screen, "Erin, we would like to discuss something with you."

A full five minutes later, Eric entered the passenger cabin. He looked as if he had just gotten out of bed, his uniform was wrinkled, and he rubbed his eyes with his right fore-finger knuckle.

"Sorry about the delay, Erin doesn't feel well. How can I help you?"

"Why did you take blood specimens from us without asking?"

"We were following standard procedures for off-world visitors. We can't afford any alien viruses to invade Earth. Two of your party have alien viruses, the two larger children. They will not be allowed to leave the isolation laboratory in Florida until a complete battery of tests has been conducted and the virus eliminated or shown to be non-threatening. Euthanasia is not out of consideration."

Gina was incensed. "What? Who conducted these so-called tests? Those children do not possess any viruses!"

"Our tests show the older children carry unknown viruses. If you want to contest our findings, you will have to wait for arrival on Earth. I will contact the medical team at the agency and let them know you are disputing our findings."

"Good! You do that!"

CHAPTER 35
BACK ON EARTH

The ambulance ride from the landing pad to the medical center was funeral-like, the darkened sky adding to the gloominess, although the adult crew was ready to assault the first individuals wearing security uniforms that wanted to separate Licon and Miranda from their parents. The alpha group was determined to stick together, no matter the consequences.

Sunul and Jar'l had begun to form an escape plan. As the bus passed by the meal preparation building, Sunul noticed a worker carrying some empty boxes to the recycling dumpster. The boxes were marked LIVE CHICKENS. He tapped Gina's arm and pointed at the boxes. Jar'l had also noticed the containers and said, "Great idea, Sunul." Gina frowned at first, wondering what the men were contemplating, and then smiled. She too, had suddenly realized what her husband and Jar'l were thinking.

Gina whispered to Sunul, "We're going to need two cars, with big trunks."

Sunul grinned, "How about a truck; all of us in one vehicle, or better yet, a bus."

Jar'l was listening. "I'm for the bus, luggage and boxes in the back. All of us can ride in seats."

"Good idea, Jar'l." Sunul had at least two of the crew thinking along with him. "Gina, talk with Triel and Monel to give them a heads up. They're probably very concerned about Licon and Miranda. Tell them we're working on a plan of escape with the kids."

A medical team, two women and two men, dressed in green fatigues, met the bus and escorted the alpha crew to a medium sized waiting room, much like a patient would encounter when visiting a doctor's office. A slightly overweight gentleman, bald and wearing wire-rimmed glasses, came through a metal door and announced, "I'm Dr. Glen Forsythe. I'll be conducting interviews and verifying your medical data. Dr. Virginia Burke, please come with me. You may bring your baby."

The examination room looked very sterile. A single base cabinet containing a small, oval metal sink, a table, and two chairs furnished the white ten-foot-square room. With Gina seated, the doctor began the interview.

"I've found nothing of concern in your medical history or that of your child. I was told you have a concern about the two older children in your group."

"Yes, doctor. They do not have viruses and I don't see any medical reason to keep them in isolation."

Forsythe flipped through a small stack of papers on his clipboard and folded back about half the pages. Using his pencil as a pointer, he read the blood analysis. "This is the evaluation of the youngster, Licon, son of Mr. and Mrs. Mason. He possesses a virus that is unknown to Earth's medical community."

"Let me inquire, doctor, how old is the subject?"

Forsythe said, "Estimated to be three to four years of age."

"Do you know how long the Masons were off Earth?"

The doctor flipped back a page and said, "Hmm. It says thirteen months."

"Was Mrs. Mason pregnant when she left Earth?"

"No. She was not."

"Don't you find Licon's age to be a little peculiar?"

"Well, yes, he should be about four months old. That is a bit strange."

"Have you checked his DNA?"

Forsythe checked Licon's records. "No, DNA analysis has not been conducted."

"Well, if you would do an analysis, you would find that Licon and Miranda have twenty-five pairs of chromosomes and do not suffer any abnormalities. What you have attributed to a virus is undoubtedly due to the extra chromosomes. You needn't worry about them spreading their DNA throughout the world. They will not reach sexual maturity for at least five or more years. By the way, their IQs are off the charts."

"Let me level with you, Dr. Burke. We suspect the two children have a natural immunity to cancer. A member of our security team on Mars informed us of this unique trait. That is the reason the agency wants to keep them in isolation. We do not want drug companies to prohibit development of a 100% effective cancer drug. A drug of this type would save the world billions of dollars each year, and countless lives. You know of this possible outcome, of course, or at least have surmised what would happen if this information got out."

"Yes, our group knows all about it. We have discussed the problem from many aspects. Thank you for leveling with me, doctor. Do you still want to see the others?"

"No, that's not necessary. I believe you'll want to leave the base to find a place for the night. The two older children must stay here in foster care. We have a very nice facility for children. Many of the astronauts place their youngsters here while off-world. I understand the kids like it very much."

"Okay. Where is the children's care office? We'd like to go with the kids to make sure they understand we will come back to see them tomorrow."

"It's in the building adjacent to the food prep structure, which is building 401. The children's unit is in building 402. We like it there so we can cater to any immediate food requirements of the children. You know, allergies and such, occasional birthdays. Oh, yes, you'll be accompanied by a couple of security people. They have to register the children."

Two male security agents climbed on the bus with the alpha group and the kids. They sat in elevated chairs on both sides of the driver, allowing them to view all the passengers. Gina wanted to talk to the alpha group about her discussion with Dr. Forsythe, but the presence of security made it inadvisable. She felt like she was on her way to prison.

As they had climbed aboard the bus, however, Sunul and Gina whispered to as many of the group as they could to be on high alert and memorize landmarks of the base. Unfortunately, the base lighting was only adequate near the major buildings. Structures 401 and 402, being smaller buildings, were not well lit at night, except for the main entrances. They would have to use that fact to their advantage.

A debriefing took place at 0800 the next morning. Each crew member was questioned about the voyage, starting with landing on 5K23m. Except for bathroom breaks and feeding the babies, the interrogation extended for nearly four hours. When they broke for lunch, they were taken to a base mess hall. It was nowhere near building 402. None of the crew could recognize their location with reference to what they had seen the night before.

On his way to the men's room right after eating lunch, Hugh made a wrong turn down a hallway and noticed a map of the base indicating firetruck routes. He studied the map for at least a minute before moving on. When he rejoined the group, he drew what he could remember of the map on a paper napkin and stuck it in his pocket. He had concentrated on the power grid, buildings 401 and 402, and the road to the nearest base exit.

At 1330 the debriefings concluded. While the rest of the crew waited, Monel and Triel visited with Licon and Miranda at the children's center. A base bus driver returned the crew to their temporary lodging, a travel park, Space Station Lodges 99, where they had rented rooms for the week.

They assembled under some palm trees in one of the two parks adjacent to the rentals. Two picnic tables were moved together for the meeting. As planned the night before, Triel had coaxed the kids into mimicking the sounds of chickens. Triel played a recording from a chicken farm and the kids acted like the birds, even with strutting and scratching. She admitted the noises from the kids were almost indistinguishable from the real thing.

Rob had some bad news. "I noticed the vehicles are weighed when passing through the entrance gate. It's a fast procedure; I didn't notice it the first time through the entry point. We need to know the kids' weight so we can carry in some rocks. When we get the kids in the bus, we toss the rocks in the recycle bins."

Jar'l stated, "I don't know what Licon weighs, but I'll bet it's close to thirty pounds, and due to Miranda's slightly smaller size, I'm guessing twenty-five to twenty-seven pounds for her."

Sunul was mulling something over and said, "Can we hack into the medical computer system?"

"Jesus, Sunul, that will take some time, maybe days, and undoubtedly someone would be alerted. The security system is similar to the one on the 5K23m computer."

"Okay, Jar'l, that's out. Any ideas, anyone?"

Gina sighed, "I think we'll have to wait another day before we get the kids. We've got to work out a better plan or get more details before we act, otherwise we're gonna get caught."

Monel commented, "The code for entrance into the kid's area in building 402 is 1-5-9. I saw the security agent enter the code. I hope they don't change it very often."

Rob said, "I'll rent a bus from that place down the street. They rent everything; hovercraft, cars, vans, you-name-it. We'll drive it to the base tonight when we see the kids. The guards will be familiar with it when we show up again tomorrow. Maybe they won't look too closely and see the rocks." Rob wasn't convinced using the rocks was a good concept. The others could tell by the sound of his voice he wasn't fond of the idea. He suddenly grinned, "I think I've got a better idea. I'll attach some lead weights under the back seats; they won't be seen during a search."

Hugh stood up and said, "Come on, Rob, let's rent a bus. We'll attach weights approximately equal to the weights of the kids. We can make some adjustments, if necessary, after we know the real weights. The weighing system at the gates is probably only accurate to ten pounds for something as heavy as a bus."

Sunul had been quiet, thinking about the plan. "That's not going to work. We've got to take some live chickens in boxes into the base. We have to take some boxes because they will be checked going in and coming out. Let's put four live chickens in two boxes big enough for the kids to hide in. We'll leave the chickens and some weights and bring out the kids."

Rob asked, "How much does a live chicken weigh?" He started to laugh and so did everyone else. Nobody knew the answer.

"Does anyone have some sleeping pills?"

"So, you want to put the chickens to sleep?" Rob was still laughing.

"Shut up, Rob. This isn't funny." Gina was contemplating how to anesthetize the workers at the juvenile facility. She didn't want to rely on the males to knock anyone out physically. She knew Sunul could do it with one punch.

Leanne answered Rob's question, "A hen weighs about eight pounds. I just looked it up."

"Okay. Tonight, we'll go in normally. Tomorrow we'll take four chickens and some weights in cardboard boxes. We'll leave the weights and the live chickens and exit with our two chicks in the boxes."

CHAPTER 36
EXTRACTION

"Have you got the pliers, Rob?" Sunul was the last to get on the bus for their trial run to the base and he was checking for equipment he thought they might need. If the live chicken boxes had staples in them, he wanted to be able to fold up the boxes. He would have to pull the staples.

It was 1930 hours when they left for the base, Hugh was driving. All eight adults were on the bus, and in addition, the two babies were in safety seats secured beside their mothers. As they entered the base, Hugh leaned out the window and asked, "How accurate is your scale, officer?"

"It's within five pounds. We recently upgraded to prevent smuggling. How long will your group be here tonight?"

"About ninety minutes, maybe a bit longer. No later than 2130, the kids will be asleep then."

The young security officer smiled and waved the bus through the entry point. Hugh saluted back and said, "Thanks."

"Christ, five pounds! Wouldn't you know?" Now Sunul was worried about the weight of the two boxes they wanted to pick up from the recycle receptacles.

As they pulled into the parking area between buildings 401 and 402, Jar'l saw something. "Hey guys, there's a security camera on that flagpole on the right. It's pointing right at us."

Rob stated, "It might be motion activated. Let's sit here a minute and see if it starts scanning." They watched the camera, hoping it would begin to swing back toward the other side of the parking lot.

"You're right, Rob. It is motion activated. When we get ready to leave, get in the bus and swing it around and pick us up at the door. I'll walk behind the bus and grab the boxes from the next door dumpsters. Drive as close to the buildings as possible. Make sure you stop to give me enough time."

Jar'l said, "Don't worry, Sunul. When Hugh stops, I'll get out and check the tires on the camera side. You'll have plenty of time. I'll slap the side of the bus when we're ready to move on. We can't stop for very long or someone will show up to see if there's a problem."

As the alpha group entered building 402 and passed by the registration desk, Gina stopped to talk to the attendant, "Why don't we have to sign in?"

"Oh, our cameras record everyone's face. We have a facial recognition system that identifies each person that enters the building and records when they leave."

"Thanks, Angie. I was wondering about security for the building."

Angie laughed and replied, "We've never lost a child."

Gina thought to herself, "There's going to be a first time, Angie."

When everyone was in the children's activity room, Monel came up to Gina and whispered, "The code hasn't changed." Miranda and Licon came running into the room and tried to jump, but their little legs were not strong enough and they stumbled. Their dads gathered them off the floor and decide to sit on the floor with them.

Miranda began to cry and Licon wanted to, but he was able to hold back his tears.

"What's wrong, sweetie?" Triel brushed Miranda's bangs back from her face and could see the tears gushing from her red eyes.

"I want to go with you. I don't like it here. They take our red water; they call it blood. Is that what it is called on Earth? A man hurt Licon."

"Monel, Miranda says a man hurt Licon. Check him over to see if there are any marks."

Monel put her hands on Licon's cheeks and asked, "Where did the man hurt you?"

Tears began to flow down Licon's cheeks onto Monel's fingers. He pointed to the quicks of his fingers. Needle marks were beneath the fingernails of each digit of his left hand. "I'm sorry, mama. I don't want water to come from my eyes."

Monel stood up and stomped her feet. "Son of a bitch! Can we get them out of here tonight?"

Gina crouched beside Licon and asked, "Do you know what room the man comes from?"

"I show you."

Licon grabbed Gina's hand and pulled her down the hallway to an office marked Dr. Kilmer. She tried the door, but it was locked, as she had expected. "Damn! I can't get in!"

Licon said, "3-2-1."

Gina pressed the code pads, the door swung open, and the lights came on. The drug cabinet behind the desk was locked! There was no digital keypad; she needed a key. A quick search of the desk drawers was fruitless, except a pair of scissors was as good as a key. She wrapped her hand with a towel, grabbed the scissors, and hit the glass door of the drug cabinet, making a fist-sized hole next to the lock mechanism. Gina reached in and slid the lock open.   "Dr. Burke, you aren't allowed in there, I'm going to sound the alarm if you don't get out of that office right now."

"All right, Angie. I had to get a Q-tip and some anesthetic to clean Licon's ear. He says it hurts. I'm leaving right now." Her stalling gave her the time she needed to grab a one-milliliter plastic syringe and a vial of an anesthetic agent she knew well. She hurried back to the activity room with Licon trying to run ahead of her. He was able to keep from falling by bumping the wall. Gina tried to grab Licon, but he was moving too fast.

Sunul, with baby Miles, met Gina and said, "What can I do?"

"Stand still, right where you are." Looking over Sunul's shoulder, Gina could see Angie entering the room with a security guard. She jammed the needle into the vial, injected a syringe full of air, and withdrew a syringe loaded with anesthetic. Gina spoke into Sunul's ear, "Have Jar'l help you take out the guard. Give Miles to Monel." As Angie and the guard approached Gina said, "Monel, could you please hold Miles?"

Monel reacted quickly and accepted Miles from Sunul. Sunul motioned to Jar'l to join him as he moved away from Gina. Angie and the guard approached Gina.

"What did you take from Dr. Kilmer's medicine cabinet?"

"A vial of medicine." She held it up so Angie could see, but her fingers covered the label.

"Let me see."

Angie stepped closer and Gina gave her the vial. As Angie raised the little bottle to read the print, Gina stuck the syringe into Angie's arm and injected the drug.

"What did you do?" Angie sighed as she collapsed to the floor.

The guard was surprised and as he stepped forward toward Gina, Sunul and Jar'l pinned his arms to his side. Gina quickly loaded another syringe and as the guard struggled to move away, she plunged the needle into his deltoid. He opened his mouth to speak, but nothing was uttered. The men let him sag to the floor beside Angie. Gina tossed the empty syringes in the waste basket and said, "Let's go!"

Sunul started toward the door, realizing they didn't know the exit code. They were stuck inside the entertainment room; the metal door could not be jimmied! "The damn door! Does anyone know the code?" Sunul scanned the faces, but all the heads were moving from side to side.

Rob said, "Try to kick it open, Sunul!"

A voice, almost a whisper, was heard, "9-5-1." It was Miranda. Somehow, she had learned the exit code.

Rob pressed the numerical panels, and everyone heard a metallic click. "Good girl, Miranda!" The door was still swinging open when the last member of the alpha crew was in the hallway running toward the exit. The bus filled quickly, Hugh started the engine, and they were off toward the western base exit point. The bus was not slowing for anyone or anything. The big vehicle hit the side exit gate with full force and blasted through, heading for the vehicle rental agency.

Ten minutes later, the bus owner was surveying the damage.

"Look, Mr. Bacon, we're in a hurry. Here's something that will pay you for the damage. Take it to an assayer, you'll get several thousand credits for it." Hugh gave the owner his one pound chunk of asteroid but didn't tell Bacon its origin.

"We need to borrow two SUVs. What do you have?"

"Umm. Are they gonna be returned damaged?"

Sunul answered, "I don't think so, but here's another valuable rock, just in case. We've got to get out of here, one of our kids is sick. Will you give us the cars?"

Bacon was holding one piece of asteroid in each hand, realizing they were heavy, and his only thought was they could contain gold. "Okay, the blue one and the gray one, over there next to the fence. I'll get the keys. There's a digital code on the keys; if you don't want the keys, or lose them, make sure you write down the code." He started toward the office, turned and said, "Or memorize it."

Five minutes later, each SUV containing two families, was speeding away from the medical center area. They could barely hear sirens sounding far behind them. Alpha group decided to split up, the Burkes and the Patels began driving north, and the Masons and the Griswalts headed toward Florida's west coast. The Mason group would travel by sea to Texas and then drive north through the mountains of northern New Mexico into Colorado. The Burke group would drive overland to Colorado. The four families were scheduled to meet in Jacob's Cliff, near Poncha Springs, in four weeks.

Jacob's Cliff wasn't a cliff at all, but a site of a former religious leader's son's tomb hollowed out of a rocky prominence. Few people, including locals, knew of the historic place in the mountains. Rob was the only member of the crew who had ever heard of the place. He had been there once with his grandfather when they gave the ashes of his father to the wind and soil of the high elevations of Colorado. It was a three-mile hike west from the nearest road, state highway 17. Rob gave everyone the GPS coordinates and told them not to write them down but commit them to memory.

The Burke-Patel families drove north about 100 miles, disposed of the blue SUV, and hitched rides for over 200 miles. Staying off the main roads was easy but finding a source of credits was their biggest problem. During the days, they split up and met in parks or camping sites for the nights. Gina was their chief source of credits. She had a fifty state medical license and worked several days at shelters and hospitals. After three days she caught up with the others at a prearranged meeting place. After nearly three weeks the Burke-Patels were in Missouri with only nine days left to reach Jacob's Cliff. Disguises had become necessary; astronaut photos had been spread throughout the country. They were wanted for kidnapping.

The Mason group left their SUV at an intersection before reaching the Florida coast. The two families separated and set out for Gulf View, a small coastal community along highway 19. It was Rob's theory that he could find work repairing boat engines and perhaps get passage to Galveston as payment. Jar'l had similar ideas. He could work on computers or repair communications equipment for a boat ride to Texas. The women thought the probability of Jar'l and Rob finding work for immediate expenses was minuscule.

The woman had discussed the problem before the families split up. Neither of the men knew what the women had planned. They needed credits for food and diapers, and they didn't want to beg. As they hitched rides, Monel and Leanne picked up plastic bottles and aluminum cans as they walked on the shoulders of the roads. Licon had a keen eye for items they could redeem. He had fun retrieving bottles and cans. His little legs were getting much stronger with exercise.

When the two families rendezvoused in Gulf View, the ladies took their loot to a recycling center next door to a supermarket. After feeding their accumulation into a machine, the printout showed five credits; one credit had been received for three items. Before Monel pressed the print pad, she said, "Licon, can you get the machine to print ten times this number?" She held him up so he could read the screen showing the credit number.

"Sure, Mom. I can do that." He ran his hands over the numeric keys, but didn't press them, just paused over several of the keypads. He repeated the procedure two more times and said, "Put me down, Mom. I fixed it." Monel did what Licon asked and pressed the print credits pad. Monel and Leanne watched as the credits issued totaled fifty. They looked at each other, laughed, and bumped fists. The two women and the children bought groceries and diapers, enough for at least three days. Leanne wrote down the name and address of the market so they could reimburse the owner for the loss when they had enough in an account to pay back the stolen credits. She grinned as she said to Monel, "We have short-term dishonesty."

The men were surprised when the ladies showed up with boxes of groceries and diapers. Jar'l asked, "How did you get so much for the bottles and cans?"

Before they could reply, Rob said, "We'd better not ask, Jar'l, but tomorrow we'd better find jobs."

CHAPTER 37
DESTINATION COLORADO

In the morning, after having slept on the warm, sandy beach, Rob heard pounding. While the others were stirring, he followed the sounds to a small dry dock where two men, about Rob's age, were hunched over an engine they had apparently removed from a boat sitting on a portable dry dock. The boat, only a few yards from the water, was supported by hull pads on the remote controlled apparatus. The moveable dock looked like the bottom of a Martian crawler with adjustable cushions elevated by hydraulic cylinders.

"I don't know, Ed. I think we need a professional. This looks too complicated for our meager talents."

"Well, this time I hate to admit it, but think you're right." Ed threw an oily rag on the sand and whistled as he exhaled. "I'll call that repair shop on the highway. It's not far from here, maybe they'll send someone down."

Rob stepped closer and said, "I can fix that for you. It'll take me about an hour." He stuck out his hand and said, "I'm Joe Brandt, mechanic extraordinaire."

Ed and Del Briskowe stepped forward and introduced themselves. They had purchased the forty-four foot boat at auction on a whim. They had sold their forty percent share of a physical fitness and sports therapy clinic for professional athletes and wanted to tour the Caribbean for a couple of years with their wives. The reasonably good looking ruddy complexioned brothers were slightly over six-feet tall and could be mistaken for professional athletes. Slightly sunburned, their skin hadn't been saved from the Florida sun by wearing cowboy hats. Rob had accidently hit a gold mine, the twin brothers were from Houston, Texas. From Houston, the trip to Colorado would be a snap.

Del said, "Can you help us? There's something wrong with this motor, the other one's fine."

"Press the starter." Rob had to know what to look for by listening to the sounds emanating from the stricken engine. All he heard was ka-thunk. The shaft of the engine vibrated but wouldn't rotate. He took the cover off the magnetic drive unit and discovered the wire that controlled the electromagnetic lock to the drive shaft was defective.

"No wonder." He looked at Ed and Del and said, "See that wire? There's an open circuit; the wire is broken. It looks like it was cut on purpose to kill the motor. I'll have to replace the entire wire; it can't be soldered."

Ed asked, "What can we get for you?"

"Do you have some tools in the boat? Let me look through them, it will save you some credits if I can use what you have."

Ed said, "Don't worry about the credits, but it might save time. Tools are in a yellow box in the engine room."

The men climbed aboard and moved to the engine room. Rob found the tools he needed, and they returned to the disabled engine.

"What else do you need?" asked Del.

"Twelve gauge marine wire, about four feet, and a cartridge of silicone seal; a small tube will do."

"Okay, I'll be back in fifteen minutes." Del held up his hand and Ed tossed him the key to their jeep, a used piece of junk they must have found parked next to a recycle bin.

Rob told Ed, "I'm going to talk to my family and get something to eat, I'll be back when Del returns."

"Do you know anyone that can fix a GPS unit? Our navigation system needs some help."

"I sure do. I'll bring him back with me."

Rob returned in twenty minutes, a little late, but Del hadn't returned with the materials yet. Jar'l had accompanied Rob and was introduced to Ed as Roy Walker. They shook hands and Roy went aboard to the bridge on the second level above the main deck.

"Roy isn't much of a talker, is he?"

"Not really, but he's one of the smartest guys I know. He's got a young son that is surprising. By the way, when do you plan on taking the trip back to Texas?"

"As soon as she's seaworthy." He motioned toward the boat. "While she's out of the water, we thought we'd paint the hull. We told our wives we'd be back in three weeks. That was eight days ago. Why do you ask?"

"We'd like a ride, if you'll agree to take us to Texas, we'd certainly appreciate it. We're scheduled to meet some friends in St Louis in ten days. Roy and I don't want to hitch rides all that way with our wives and kids. It wouldn't be so bad if it was just him and me. We'd like passage instead of credits for payment for our work."

"How many people are we talking about?"

"Six, total. Our wives can help with painting the hull. They're both good workers, smart and strong."

"It's all right with me. Del won't care, but I'll ask him, just to be sure. I don't want any family arguments." He grinned.

Jar'l called out from above, "It's gonna take all afternoon to get the navigation system running. I have to replace one of the highly integrated printed circuits. Someone blew it with a high voltage spike. Looks like sabotage to me."

Ed shook his head and said, "Just as Del and I suspected, the boat was probably seized by the government during a drug raid. Someone aboard disabled it to allow the state authorities to arrest the crew and the boat was confiscated."

"Joe?" Rob recognized Leanne's voice and turned to motion her and the baby to come closer. Monel and Licon were right behind her.

"We want to see what you're working on."

Rob introduced the wives and kids to Ed. Del pulled up in the jeep and hopped to the ground carrying the wire and silicone sealant in his right hand. Rob continued with the introductions.

Ed said, "Instead of payments by credits, they'd like to sail with us to Texas. It's okay by me, what do you think?"

"Yeah, the more the merrier. I hope the women can cook, we sure can't."

Rob replied, "They can do a pretty good job. Do you have a microwave on board?"

Everyone laughed.

"Where's Roy?" Monel was looking around but hadn't seen Jar'l.

Rob pointed up at the bridge. "He's up there trying to repair the navigation system. Somebody applied a high voltage to one of the integrated circuit boards. Say, I told Ed you ladies could help paint the hull. Want to help?"

Leanne handed Juni to Monel, rubbed her hands together, and said, "Where's the paint?"

Del lifted a five-gallon container from the back of the jeep and handed it down to Ed, who carried it to the boat. He climbed on board, disappeared for a few seconds, returned to the gunnel, and tossed two rollers with extension handles to the sand below.

"There you are ladies. I'll get you some rags and an eight-foot ladder. Don't worry about stirring the paint, I just picked it up a short time ago. It was thoroughly mixed at the marine supply store."

The women painted in thirty-minute shifts. While one painted, the other took care of the children. They took a half-hour break for lunch, but with Del's assistance, they covered the entire hull in time for dinner. As Leanne and Monel applied the turquoise-blue paint, Rob and Jar'l completed the repairs and successfully tested the engine and the navigation system. The twins invited the two families to stay for dinner.

During the meal, the four astronauts kept the conversation centered on the Texans. To avoid having to construct too many lies about their past and being on the run from the authorities, Rob and Monel did most of the talking for the two couples. They attempted to give short, uncomplicated answers to Ed's and Del's questions, but Rob blundered once and mentioned the ship they had been on. He caught his mistake and changed ship to boat in the next sentence. The Texans didn't seem to notice.

When there was a lull in the conversation, Monel said, "It's getting late. I've got to put our son to bed. May we sleep on the boat tonight?"

Del stood up and replied, "Sure. Y'all can stay here tonight. Del and I have a room at the Beach Front B&B just up the street. We'll see ya about eight in the mornin'." He took off his hat, rubbed his forehead and said, "We'll get the boat in the water and have the marine rental place come an' get their dry dock."

Ed added to his brother's comments. "The city sheriff will be here about noon to renew our temporary marine license, but if we're gone, we'll save another hundred credits. This beach rental area is costly."

Jar'l had no desire to meet a sheriff who had undoubtedly been notified of a kidnapping on the other side of the state. "We won't slow you down. We'll be waiting. We'd like to be on our way, too."

The old jeep showed up just before eight o'clock. Ed and Del didn't appear to be very enthusiastic about leaving for Texas, although the boat was in great shape. Jar'l and Rob walked to the jeep to say good morning while Monel and Leanne sorted through all four of their bags on deck to check on the food they had available for a two day trip on the gulf.

From the charts in the bridge, they had estimated the distance to be about 740 miles, the speed of the boat at twenty miles per hour, so at least thirty-seven hours on the water. But they didn't know if the motors could run at night, the solar collectors wouldn't be operating. Rob thought the batteries could only be used for a few hours without recharging. Gasoline engines had been outlawed twenty years earlier. Too many oil spills on the ocean finally caused the world to react and enact laws with severe penalties for the use of petroleum based engines. Solar cells for electric motors and wind-filled sails were the only sources of power for propelling small boats. Large cruise ships and supertankers had nuclear powered turbines for ocean travel.

The twins climbed from the jeep, stood side-by-side facing Rob and Jar'l. Del said, "We saw a police announcement on TV last night. Are you some of those kidnappers?"

The question was not unexpected. Jar'l responded, "Yes, but we're not kidnappers. The children with us are ours. Have you talked with the police yet?"

The twins shook their heads. Ed responded, "Nope, we figured we should let you guys tell us your story first."

Monel yelled, "Coffee's ready!"

"Come on, boys, we've got a story to tell you while we have our morning coffee." Rob pointed up to the deck of the boat.

Two cups of coffee later, Ed asked, "So you two are astronauts?"

Jar'l nodded and said, "All four of us are astronauts. We just got back to Earth after being inside a moon in the Kuiper belt." Jar'l had anticipated the next question.

"Kuiper belt? Where's that?" Del swung his head toward Jar'l.

"It's beyond Pluto at the outer edge of the solar system."

"Jesus, Del. We've got a lot to learn about the stars and planets."

"Uh-huh, but we'd better get the boat in the water so we can get these people on their way to Texas."

Rob's frown turned to a smile. "You're not turning us in?"

"Hell, no. You haven't done anything wrong. The government's at fault. Call that rental place, Del. We've got to get out of here ASAP."

A half-hour later, the boat, christened Houston Star, was moving away from the beach, her two electric motors humming as the Star picked up speed carrying eight people to the west.

Ed and Del had taken a seafarer's navigation class but were relying on the boat's GPS system to find their way across the gulf. Fortunately, they knew to find land, they just had to head north.

Jar'l and Monel had lots of smiles at the naivety of the brothers, but they never butted in. They just kept an eye on the chart and their position. As the sun dropped near the horizon that first day, they shut down the motors and used sails to keep them moving throughout the night.

CHAPTER 38
COLORADO

Sunul, Gina, and little Miles entered an assay office in St. Louis. If Jar'l had seen them, he would have had trouble recognizing the couple. Sunul's beard, unkempt hair, rumpled clothing, and somewhat sunken eyes, made him look twenty years older, approaching fifty. Gina had dyed her hair black and it hadn't been washed in more than two weeks, nor had it been combed or brushed. Her blouse had been taken from a backyard clothesline late at night and was several sizes too large. Miles, however, looked well taken care of and was content.

Gina and Miles waited on a bench along a wall perpendicular to the front windows while Sunul approached the counter to submit his ore sample. Sunul took a pen, filled out a sample submission form, and handed it to the clerk.

"That'll be twenty-five credits for the analysis, sir."

"I don't have any credits. Could you run it on a promise to pay? I'm pretty sure it's valuable."

"Sorry, sir. We'd go broke doing that. We get a lot of fool's gold."

"There's no fool's gold in it. It's rich in platinum. My sister told me so."

"Oh. Should I know your sister?" The clerk smiled and then frowned. "Well, show me your sample."

Sunul pulled his sample from his pocket and dropped it on the counter. The thud could be heard by everyone in the room. There were three men apparently waiting for analyses.

"Where'd you get this?" The clerk was squinting as he turned the sample end for end.

"It's from South Africa, part of a meteorite."

A tall, well dressed, man of about forty, one of the other men waiting, stepped up next to Sunul and asked, "May I see that specimen?"

Sunul dropped the chunk of rock from the asteroid in the stranger's hand. He turned it over and over, scrutinizing the sample from all orientations.

"Been cut with a laser, hasn't it?"

"Hell, I don't know. I just took it out of a box my sister sent me. We need some credits, so I figured to get something for it. It doesn't mean nothin' to us."

"I'm Sidney Knotts. I'll pay for the analysis if you give me first chance to buy it from you."

Sunul shook hands vigorously and said, "I'm Frank Becket. It's a deal."

Sunul pushed the sample across the counter to the clerk and said, "Elemental analysis, please."

Mr. Knotts handed one of his credit cards to the clerk who processed the fee and returned the card to Knotts. The amount processed glowed on the card for five seconds and faded from view.

The two men talked at the counter for about a minute. When the clerk returned, he gave Sunul the sample and said, "The isotope ratios are all wrong. Where did you say you got the sample?"

"My sister said it's from a meteorite that was discovered in South Africa."

"Well, it's not from the earth, that's for damn sure. The isotopic abundances are all off. It's about one quarter platinum. That makes it worth about 9,000 credits."

"Wow! I didn't expect it to be that much. I hoped for a couple thousand."

Mr. Knotts said, "I'll give you 4,500 credits for it, right now. You won't have to look around for a buyer."

"Geez, that's only fifty percent." Sunul looked Knotts in the eyes.

"Okay, 5,000. That's my best offer. I have to get it processed."

"Sold!" Sunul didn't want to risk losing the 5,000 credits.

"Let's go to my bank, it's down the street on the corner."

Gina and the baby waited in the assay office while Sunul accompanied Mr. Knotts to the bank. When Sunul returned, he waved the card, smiled and said, "Let's meet with the Patels and find a rental car. We have six days to get to Jacob's Cliff to meet with the others. It should be easy now."

"Whose name is on the credit card?" Gina hoped Sunul hadn't forgotten and accidently used his real name.

"Nobody's. It's a possession card."

"Oh, that's good! Any of us can use it."

Sunul looked askance at Gina, smiled, and shoved the card into his pocket.

Jar'l, in Houston, had carried out a similar approach to Sunul's, but he had gotten 6,000 credits for his sample. The twins had helped him sell the meteorite sample he had obtained from "a Canadian friend, a miner from the Yukon." The Masons and Griswalts had spent three days in

Houston before getting back on the road in a ten-year-old SUV that set them back 2,300 credits.

Two days later, they were in Santa Fe where they stopped to visit the open market on the downtown sidewalks. Jar'l and Rob wanted to buy their wives some silver and turquoise jewelry, but they had to ignore the wanting looks of the women. They would come back some other time. Credits were going to be in short supply after they purchased camping supplies in Colorado.

The alpha group would have to be careful when redeeming any more of their asteroid samples. They were afraid if they left a trail of breadcrumbs, the authorities would trace them in the direction of Colorado. A manhunt would follow, and they would have to be ready to move through the mountains to a new location and start building a new home or experiencing the worst case scenario; they would be caught and the special children would be lost. However, they decided the next redemption would have to take place in either Idaho or Washington. The authorities would hopefully be led away from Colorado to British Columbia or perhaps Alaska. They had talked about this problem before and made plans to avoid permanency when constructing their mountain residences. The alpha group was going to be forced to become minimalists.

Twenty-eight days after breaking Miranda and Licon out of the juvenile detention facility, the two halves of the alpha group were close to reuniting at Jacob's Cliff, both groups driving old clunkers. They had changed vehicles again in small towns where little chance of surveillance would occur. Both halves of the alpha group had gotten rid of their plastic and aluminum four wheeled hulks the same way; they found narrow roads with densely-forested steep inclines and pushed the empty cars to their deaths in the valley below. The two groups had no idea they were less than a half-mile from each other when they ditched their grave-ready vehicles.

Sunul's group had been hiking for a half-hour when Miranda said, "I hear somebody!"

She had stopped and turned her head northward. Everyone stopped and listened.

Triel said, "I hear it, too."

Suddenly a deer crashed through a copse of young trees, leaped over Miranda's head, and vanished into a five-foot high cluster of shrubs.

"How wonderful! How beautiful!" She exclaimed as she smiled and began to laugh.

"Hello over there! Who are you?"

At first Sunul thought the voice might be from a game warden or forest ranger, but he had heard that voice before. He recognized Rob's voice.

"Sunul and party!" Everyone listened for a reply. Sunul announced to his group, "It's Rob!"

Hugh yelled, "Hey, Rob. Join us. We've been wondering when we'd see you again."

"Sunul, stay where you are. We'll be there in a few minutes. These trees are blocking our way. Did you happen to see a deer?"

Triel yelled back, "It just jumped over our heads. We thought it might be you guys, but we knew you couldn't jump that high unless you were on the moon."

"Very funny Triel!"

Handshakes and hugs took several minutes to complete. Tears were plentiful as they celebrated the reuniting. When the activity settled down to general conversations as everyone found a place to sit down on boulders, fallen trees, and the pine-needle-covered ground, Jar'l announced, "We have to move on and find a place to camp for the night. In spite of the season, the temperature will drop significantly when the sun goes down. It will be cold tonight and we can afford only very small fires. No one knows we're here and we don't want to announce our presence."

Sunul added, "We'll build larger fires for heating and cooking when we can construct proper containers to block light and absorb smoke. Let's try to get to Jacob's Cliff before we lose light. We can't attempt to traverse the forest at night."

Rob took the lead and the single file wound its way up the hill and rested at the top for a few minutes. Licon and Miranda had been holding hands, trying to keep from stumbling, as they trudged along between Monel and Triel.

As the group proceeded into a shallow valley, Rob picked his way from tree to tree using the pines and firs to prevent slipping and headlong tumbling toward the valley floor. At the bottom of the hill, they crossed a narrow valley, only thirty yards wide, forded a narrow stream and started up another hill, not quite as taxing as the one just negotiated.

Licon announced, "Legs tired." He began jabbering with Miranda in their own language which Hugh had called Kuiper Tongue.

Rob, still leading the pack, said, "We're almost there, Licon. It's over the next hill."

"Don't like hills." Everyone laughed, even Miranda, Licon's confidant.

Rob was correct, there was a marker made of cement and rocks with a metal plate announcing the site as Jacob's Cliff, 1837. There was no explanation. The tomb was rather inconspicuous, a small concrete block structure almost hidden in a rock wall, nearly overgrown with vines and wildflowers. It appeared as if no one had cared for the site in many years.

While dinner was being prepared, Rob and Sunul set out to find a place to camp for the night. Fifteen minutes of hiking brought them to a stand of mature evergreens seeming to be standing watch over a stream of crystal clear water. They backtracked to Jacob's Cliff and ate dinner with the others. It was a quick meal, biscuits and honey, and protein bars. The ladies promised a real dinner would be available the following evening after they established a semi-permanent camp site. After their statement, the group set off for the spot where water was cascading through the big trees.

Dry brush and pine needles were used for a fire, so smoke was not a problem. The canopy and tree trunks prevented light from escaping into the night sky. They ate and talked for about an hour before sleeping through the night.

Everyone was slow to rise in the morning. It was cool and it would be several hours before the sun was high enough in the sky to be seen and provide direct warming rays. After eating, each of the couples set out to look for a more permanent place to camp, staying as far as possible from roads. They were to meet at a GPS location Hugh and Triel had selected because of its position where water was thought to be present. The satellite views of the mountains were almost useless due to the dense tree cover. They had to depend on topography maps for most of their information.

Rob and Leanne were working their way through some underbrush at the foot of a rocky incline when Leanne decided to take a short rest to catch her breath. They had been moving up a slight incline for about ten minutes. As Leanne checked Juni in her chest carrier, she noticed an opening in the rocks at eye level.

She sat on a boulder and pointed, "Rob, what's that?"

Rob moved closer, stumbled, but didn't fall, and kicked at what had caught his foot. He reached down and picked up the remains of a board that had saw marks on two sides.

"Hey, this is building material." He looked around and noticed another piece of wood projecting a few inches from the cavity Leanne had noticed. He pulled on it and a two-foot piece of lumber came from the hole. He flipped it over and saw UA 1863 scratched in the cracked hunk of wood. "That was during the Civil War, Leanne. What does U-A mean?"

Leanne thought for a moment and suggested, "Union Army?"

"I think you're right. This must be an old silver mine."

They busily cleared away the rocks and shrubbery to reveal the opening to a cave. Rob cut a small branch from a neighboring tree and used it to remove spider webs from inside the opening. Illumination from his LED flashlight revealed a cavern about twenty-feet in diameter and a ceiling high enough for him to stand. They entered the cave and noticed two tunnels that extended into the side of the hill.

"It's warm in here, Rob. This might make a great place to stay. I almost feel like it's the size of the command center of the ship we left on Mars."

"Yeah. It's a little tight for all of us, but with winter coming on, I think it'll do 'til next spring."

CHAPTER 39

THE NOTE

It wasn't long before the spelunkers became cave dwellers. Once the eight-member alpha team put their talents to work, the old silver mine was converted into a 1,000 square foot home with running water and a small bathroom at the end of one of the tunnels. The other tunnel had been dug to allow fresh air to come through the underground mine. The underground passage gradually sloped uphill for about twenty yards. Air currents seemed to filter through the rock ceiling. The end of the tunnel was hollowed out so it could be used for cooking; smoke was trapped in the rocks and not able to escape to the atmosphere.

Rob and Jar'l constructed a water wheel generator, mostly made from junked car parts. It was installed in the bathroom, used to recharge batteries and run the cave's LED lights; it ran continuously. They had found a coil of rope in the cave which they used to lower themselves to the cars they had disposed of in the valley a few miles away. Sunul constructed a map of the surroundings to a radius of three miles so no one could get lost. He gave each adult a whistle that contained a compass, another step to prevent loss in the forests. When Sunul was constructing the maps, he discovered a small town, Divide Park, population 131, five miles from their camp. Miners, hunters, and mountain rescue personnel lived there.

Although they had a twenty-two caliber rifle, four bows were made from tree limbs for hunting bear and deer. Two smaller bows were made for Miranda and Licon so they could learn basic hunting techniques. Competitions were held so steady improvement at killing game occurred.

Winter arrived with a ten-inch snowfall, which never seemed to melt. The depth of snow kept increasing day-by-day, week-by-week. Before the snow was two feet deep, Jar'l and Sunul visited Divide Park to buy some necessary supplies. They entered the minimart on the highway through the center of town and bought items from a list the women had given them.

"You men stocking up for the winter?" the overweight, red-bearded clerk asked with some suspicion. "Never seen you around here before."

Sunul replied, "That's right. We're just passing through. We're going to meet a winter-war-games team north of here at higher altitude."

"Is that right?"

"Look mister, do you want to sell some supplies, or do you want to talk? We've got things to do. What do we owe you?" Jar'l was showing signs of irritation.

"That comes to 285 credits. Anything else?"

Sunul replied, "That's all we need for now. We might be back in a couple of weeks, maybe a month or so." He handed the credit card to the clerk and began stowing the items into his backpack.

The clerk made the transaction and gave the card to Sunul.

"I didn't catch your names."

"We didn't give you our names. I'm Captain Anonymous and this is Captain Blank, Special Forces."

The clerk frowned and watched Sunul and Jar'l leave the market, each man carrying two packs stuffed with their purchases. They moved up the road until they were out of sight of anyone from town and then cut across a field to the trees, attached their snowshoes, and headed back to the cave. It had started snowing as they left the road. Their tracks would soon be concealed by fresh snow.

It snowed a foot during the night, but the cave dwellers were snug in their lair. During the next few months, they started a school for Miranda and Licon, teaching handwriting and English. Sunul had started teaching math but soon found out his students were only challenged with high school algebra and geometry. Their mathematical abilities were astonishing. The two babies, Juni and Miles, had not begun to talk except for something resembling one word, 'mama.'

Just prior to the first Christmas in Colorado, Sunul and Gina left the cave on an expedition to the closest metropolitan area to get a variety of medicines, primarily for the babies. The greatest need was for vaccines for measles, diphtheria, mumps, and whooping cough. Antibiotics, tetanus, and rabies were some of their other concerns. Even though the group was isolated from contact with other people, they knew prevention was of utmost importance. Eventually, they hoped to return to the more civilized areas of the country, or in the extreme, immigrate to Canada. Exposure to the general population would heighten the risk of preventable diseases. While Gina collected medical supplies, primarily from the underground, Sunul went to southern Idaho to redeem another pound of the asteroid. The couple returned home after three weeks of life in cities.

They were welcomed with a performance by Licon and Miranda entitled The Changelings. The Burkes were totally surprised. The children had even provided props.

Licon and Miranda were going on a picnic in the forest. Licon went behind a tree, made from a branch, and called to Miranda. She went behind the tree and when they reappeared, Miranda was black, possessing the same color skin as Licon. She said, "I always wondered what it would be like to be dark skinned."

Licon said, "That is the way I have always been." Then they disappeared, returning as white skinned. Licon announced, "I always wondered what it would be like to be white."

The two performers clasped hands and returned to their normal color as the crew applauded the skit.

Gina was flabbergasted. She gasped and said, "How...how did you do that?" She knelt before the children and said, "When did you discover you could do that?"

Miranda answered, "I had a dream about being dark skinned like Licon, so we figured out how to change our skin color. It isn't hard to do, but it doesn't last very long. Then we change back."

Monel commented, "They tried it on us before saying anything. I reacted the same way you did."

Sunul carried a bag over his shoulder as if he were Santa Claus. "We brought presents for everyone. Ho, Ho, Ho!" Sunul and Gina handed out gifts; things that were easy to pack and carry over long hikes. They were able to buy three com units that were untraceable and unlicensed. Now they could keep track of the proceedings of the rest of the world and use the units for teaching without the worry of discovery by signal tracking.

When the second Christmas arrived, announcements of new babies were the talk of the alpha group and by the third Christmas, the group numbered sixteen. The crew decided it was time to move on after some close calls with hunters and forest rangers. People in Divide Park were getting suspicious, the original story given by Sunul and Jar'l was leaking like a sieve.

By June of 2084, the four families had relocated in the White River National Forest, more than fifty miles northwest of their original campsite. They found a stream for fresh water, fish, deer, and a lower elevation than before, having to contend with less winter snow. After some discussion, a decision was made to construct cabins; everyone had tired of cave life. The women had complained of cave dwelling being too much like living in a basement; it wasn't too bad for a short time.

A month later, there were four cabins at the points of a compass, sheltered under tall pines and less than twenty yards from a stream abundant with trout. A fire pit was placed at the center of the four cabins. Once a month during the summer, the group would go for excursions in the woods to gather plants, animals for pets, and other items that they liked.

Licon and Miranda were nearly adults in stature; Licon was a five-ten young man and Miranda was a striking, five-seven young woman. Mentally, they were college graduates, but they lacked social skills; the experience with other people was minimal, but the adults were constantly surprised at the rate Licon and Miranda learned new skills. Social awareness would be conquered in short order.

During the second day of one of these outings on the second anniversary of their new location, the young children were growing tired. It had rained most of the night and everyone was wet and in a poor mood. The kids wanted to return home early, so the team packed up and headed back. Before the families had gone more than a few hundred yards through the forest, Licon and Miranda asked if they could run ahead. The Masons and Patels agreed and the youngsters disappeared amongst the trees.

After trudging through the damp underbrush for nearly two hours, the alpha group arrived within sight of the cabins. The six-year-olds, Miles and Juni, scampered to their cabins looking for their older 'cousins.' They returned to tell the adults they couldn't find Licon and Miranda. Triel and Monel rushed to their cabins and when the rest of the group arrived in the clearing around the fire pit, the two mothers came from their cabins, each clutching a sheet of paper, tears pouring down from their tired eyes.

Jar'l called to his wife, "What is it, Monel? What's wrong?"

Hugh said, "What's the problem, Triel?"

Monel, her entire body shaking, held out the sheet of notebook paper to Jar'l. "They've gone away!"

Without a sound, Triel gave her note to Hugh. He read the note and called to Sunul, "Licon and Miranda have left us—for good." He crumpled the paper, stuck it in his pocket and said, "I'm going after them!"

Sunul asked, "Let me see the note, Hugh."

Hugh gave the wadded up note to Sunul, who smoothed the paper out and studied the writing.

Sunul quickly scanned the writing:

"Thank you for introducing us to your world. You have educated us and allowed us to grow to adulthood in loving, devoted families. We know you have sacrificed greatly for us and now we must leave you to seek our own way. Without us, you can return to your normal way of living and give our younger brothers, sisters, and cousins a proper life.

Please don't try to follow us, you will be unsuccessful and will be wasting your time. We will be observing you occasionally to make sure you are all healthy, but we will not contact you.

We must seek our own way now and have taken new names: Adam and Eve, as in one of your great books. With love, goodbye."

BOOKS BY THE AUTHOR INCLUDE:

Glacier Fires and Ornaments of Value

Missing Notes, Hidden Talents, and Other Stories

Wolves' Hollow Murders

Detour in Oregon

An Iceberg's Gift

The Lighthouse Library

The Lighthouse Fire

The Distant Lighthouse

The Niffits

The Kuiper Belt Deception

The Antarctic Deception

A Professor's Affair

The Kidnapping of Megan Isaacs

The Bitterroot Diamonds

The Bitterroot Fire

The Twig Lady and A Crystal for Charity

ACKNOWLEDGMENTS:

Thanks to Bob Griswold and Barbara Schroeder for their proof reading and to Alain Douchinsky for her great assistance in editing.

www.ingramcontent.com/pod-product-compliance
Lightning Source LLC
Chambersburg PA
CBHW021307190726
48288CB00003B/727